ROUGH CUT

ROUGH CUT

BRIAN PINKERTON

BAD MOON BOOKS

ANAHEIM - CALIFORNIA

FIRST EDITION

Cover Design, Interior Design & Typesetting
by César Puch

Copy Editing
by David Marty & Steve Souza

Bad Moon Books Logo Created by Matthew JLD Rice

ISBN-10: 0-9832211-9-7
ISBN-13: 978-0-9832211-9-7

BAD MOON BOOKS
1854 W. Chateau Ave.
Anaheim CA 92804
USA

www.badmoonbooks.com

Dedicated to my parents for encouraging my creativity
...even when it got weird.

Acknowledgments

This book was inspired by my childhood affection for monster movies—the good, bad and ridiculous. In particular, I am indebted to *Famous Monsters of Filmland*, the movies of Ed Wood, *Kolchak: The Night Stalker* and WGN's *"Creature Features."*

ROUGH CUT

Surfer Psycho is a wipeout. The surfing is spare, the psycho is listless, and the movie just drags pointlessly from scene to scene, as if the script got buried in the sand. Occasionally a supporting cast member is introduced in a Speedo or bikini and then dispatched with a splash of dime-store gore. Too bad the filmmakers couldn't be the killer's first target. *Surfer Psycho* deserves to be lost in the endless march of low-budget, high-concept, empty-headed horror movies that are regularly flushed into discount DVD bins across the country. Don't catch this wave.

—Robert Murphy
Los Angeles Daily News

Harry Tuttle surpasses the cheerful ineptitude of *Surfer Psycho* with another bucket of celluloid slop, *Soul Snatchers*. The pseudo-thespians on display here appear to be random citizens grabbed from the local supermarket and asked to recite lines without emoting. The movie aims low, hoping to find an audience with college stoners looking to discover the latest camp classic, but fails to produce any legitimate thrills, chills, or coy self-awareness. Tuttle's career has been in steady decline for more than a decade, and his earliest movies—*Valley of the Zombies*, *Slash*, and the sublime *Grip of Terror*—remain his strongest work, backed by confident budgets and a certain filmmaking finesse.

■ **Don Bis, *Fangoria***

I must confess that I cannot write an honest review of Harry Tuttle's Ghost House III because during the course of this direct-to-DVD monster mush I (a) dozed off from boredom, (b) made myself a sandwich, (c) read the morning paper and completed the Junior Jumble, and (d) eagerly accepted calls from telemarketers. If anyone has ever sat through this snoozer from start to finish, perhaps they should claim some kind of prize. Like a cyanide pill.

Mark Estdale
Videoscope

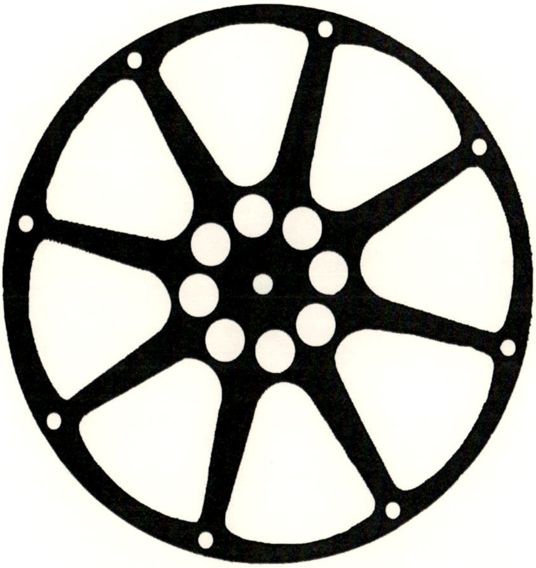

REEL ONE

1

Please God, don't let him wake up.

Nora Hurley peeled back a corner of the down comforter, virtually soundless, a small ripple of movement in the dark.

Lenny didn't move.

Her husband slept soundly, a mountain of flesh at her side. He faced her, eyes shut, mouth open, producing a gurgling snore. Claw-like tattoos snaked up his thick neck. His hand lay near her, huge, hairy, and balled into a fist. Why did he make fists in his sleep?

He was tense. Always tense. Regularly on the verge of some kind of eruption.

The next time he erupted—whether it was screaming, breaking things, or pounding someone—she would be long gone.

Nora peeled back the second layer, the blanket. Only a thin sheet remained, touching her legs and chilling as it met the air.

Lenny didn't move. Nora strained to look at the clock.

One-forty-five a.m. Unusually late for her, but she wasn't tired. How could she be? She trembled from the excitement of escape night. The three cups of coffee during her waitressing shift at Dottie's Diner didn't hurt, either.

When Lenny stumbled home earlier that night, shortly after twelve, sloppy drunk—nothing new—she had already retired to bed. She faked sleep, drawing on her acting skills for a good performance. He banged around for a while, ate something, probably made a mess in the kitchen, and then crashed into the bed beside her.

The only thing he said to her was "Jesus Christ your feet are cold." She rolled away from him, wordlessly. He hacked loudly, cleared his throat and scratched below the waist. He smelled like gin and cigarettes. The stench clung to his beard. Inside of ten minutes, he was still.

She waited. She kept waiting. She wanted his sleep to be deep. No restlessness. No awareness of the room. She wanted his senses shut down.

I hate you Lenny.

Nora peeled back the final layer, the bedsheet. She was now completely uncovered. She remained on her back in her flannel pajamas. She already felt liberated, simply by lifting the thin blue linen.

Her cell was open. It was time to leave the jail.

Nora moved one leg off the side of the mattress. For a moment, she held the fear of Lenny's big hand snatching her shoulder and his voice booming, awake and alert, "*Going somewhere?*"

But it didn't happen.

She began moving her other leg off the bed.

Both feet touched the floor. She began to rise, transitioning her 125 pounds from the bed to the ground.

The floorboards creaked.

She froze. She didn't even breathe.

Absolute silence.

Nora made short, cautious steps around the bed. She left the room. Her pace quickened in the corridor. It was dark, but she knew the small house well; and her instincts guided her into the kitchen, where an outdoor streetlamp provided a splash of illumination through the window.

Nora opened the cabinet under the sink, where the cleaning supplies were kept. Since Lenny had never used a single cleaning supply in the course of their three-year marriage, there was no danger of him finding what she had stashed inside a plastic bag in the back: getaway clothes.

Nora undressed, letting the flannel pajamas pool on the floor. She pulled on jeans, two sweatshirts—it was freezing outside—socks and gym shoes. Her yellow winter coat, with scarf and gloves shoved in the pockets, hung on a chair in the living room.

She brought the coat into the kitchen and pulled it on in super slo-mo.

Lenny typically slept soundly—especially when soaked in booze—but she couldn't risk a small noise waking him up.

If caught, there would be a beating. The face was fair game. And he would never take his eyes off her again.

Nora posted her farewell note on the refrigerator, under a Philadelphia Flyers magnet.

The note simply said, *Don't come after me. This is forever.*

Nora left the house.

Lenny's pride and joy, his 1988 Gulf Stream Sunstream RV, crowded the dirt-and-gravel driveway. For a big man, it was a big vehicle, stretching thirty feet. The interior needed a lot of work, but he had picked it up at a good price from a co-worker at Berger's Auto Body. Lenny had promised Nora long, scenic vacations to the Grand Canyon and Niagara Falls, but instead filled the vehicle with his buddies and their beer coolers for weekend camping and hunting trips.

Nora opened the RV door and retrieved two suitcases from where she had stashed them in the dinette booth. The suitcases were heavy, consisting of everything that would accompany her to her new life: mostly clothes and toiletries, plus a few treasured mementos, such as a photo album with faded pictures of her dad and grandma. She'd also packed a book, *Actors on Acting*, checked out from the public library and not going back.

Nora shoved the suitcases into the backseat of the blue Mercury parked curbside. She closed the door without a slam. It didn't hook correctly, but she could fix that a few blocks away. It was dead silent outdoors and any noise would be amplified.

Nora gave a final look to the square brick house that had held nothing but pain and misery since the day she got married and moved in. It was truly a haunted house. Lenny could have it all to himself now. He could guzzle malt liquor, punch holes in the walls, and scream her name 24 hours a day. She didn't care.

She wouldn't hear it. She wouldn't see it. She was going to erase him from her memory. *Delete Lenny.*

Nora looked at their bedroom window, drapes closed, nothing but darkness behind them.

This is forever.

Nora turned the key and started the engine. It hummed in the cold. She had to give it a moment, however brief, to warm up.

My God, this car is loud, she realized as it shook and rattled in the winter air. It needed a new muffler. She had never noticed before. Lenny usually drove. She hardly ever—

The bedroom window lit up. Nora gasped.

Immediately she threw the car out of park. She jammed it into drive.

With a roar, the Mercury plunged down the street. Nora cried. She could feel the heat from Lenny's explosions taking place behind her. He was erupting. He was storming through the house calling her name. His footsteps were pounding the floor. There would be no response, just her note.

Forever.

* * *

Snow began drifting across the windshield as she reached US-422, the highway that would whisk her from Pottstown to Philadelphia. Although daybreak was still hours away, tomorrow had arrived. It was February 16, a date that would live in infamy.

Weeks of preparation and anticipation had led to this jailbreak. Lenny had been left behind in the cold and dark. She would never see him again. She would never see snow again. A warmer climate awaited. A brighter hope.

Lenny would be sorry, eventually. The sad, remorseful little boy beneath the hot-tempered ogre would make one of his rare appearances; but it would be too late. She would never deal with him again. He would eventually realize one thing in that dense head of his: he had messed up a really good thing.

That's because Nora was destined for greatness.

Few people knew it. She didn't discuss her destiny openly, because most of the people around her would be dismissive. They wouldn't see it. And that was understandable, given the circumstances.

In her hometown, Pottstown, and many of the other surrounding middle-class suburbs, the crumbling economy had wiped optimism off most everyone's plate. Pennsylvanians were buckling under years of heavy job losses in manufacturing. Steel mills, tire companies and garment factories had shut down, leaving thousands of blue-collar workers, including Nora's friends and relatives, unemployed. Many of the jobs that remained were shipped overseas. A feeling of powerlessness hung heavy in the air. The small towns around Philadelphia were depressed in every sense of the word.

One day, sharing a break with Pedro, her gay friend at Dottie's Diner, Nora revealed her dream, a secret aspiration she had never mentioned to Lenny. He would have laughed, hard and mean.

"I want to be an actress."

Pedro's eyes grew big. He smiled, "Well then go for it."

"Yeah, right."

"Don't get all 'yeah, right' on me. Sweetheart, you want it, it's yours. What's stopping you?"

"Lenny."

"No, he's not."

She gave him a long, weary stare, "You don't know Lenny."

"The only person in your way is you. Think about it."

And she did.

At Owen Roberts High School, she had performed in some musicals—*West Side Story*, *Oklahoma*, *Annie*. Her drama teacher, a veteran of community theater, said she was one of the best in the class. "You act from the heart," he told her. "When you do that, it reaches the back row. Don't ever let that go."

She knew that stardom was possible for a girl like her because it had happened before. One of Nora's friends, Crissy Cryer, knew someone who knew someone who had a neighbor who was friends with Lesley Banks. Lesley had started out as a small-town Pennsylvania girl, cute and scrawny but not stunning, acting in a few local shows and television commercials. One day she headed west with a cousin and wound up landing a small part on a short-lived sitcom, *What a Shame*. Two years later, she reappeared in a bigger role in a more successful sitcom about zookeepers. Feature film roles followed. The local papers touted their hometown success story. The men in the neighborhood ogled Lesley's magazine pictures, and the women marveled over her newfound fame and fortune.

Lesley's rise to stardom fascinated, then inspired, Nora. She fantasized about ditching Lenny and following Lesley's footsteps to Hollywood. The more she thought about it, the more vivid it became. She could see the flashing bulbs of the paparazzi, hear the autograph seekers calling her name, and feel the red carpet beneath her feet. As Nora served patrons in Dottie's Diner, she imagined telling them, *One day you'll see me on TV and you'll say, "That's the girl who used to serve me hash browns."*

Between servings, Nora plotted her escape. She scheduled the date: two days after Valentine's Day. The only person in the world who knew about Nora's plans was Pedro. She told him on her final night at the diner.

He hugged her.

"Seize your destiny!" he told her, so loudly that she shushed him.

She didn't tell her boss, Mr. Murray, that she wasn't coming back. She told him, "See you tomorrow," waved, and laughed inside.

Pedro chased her out the door.

"If you get really, really famous..." he said to her in the parking lot, "...don't forget the little people."

"You can visit anytime," she promised. "You can swim in my pool and ride in my limo."

"Will you introduce me to Brad Pitt?"

She laughed and walked the four blocks home, barely feeling the bitter wind cutting through her clothes.

* * *

The 40-mile drive into Philadelphia was quick and gloriously uneventful. Nora found herself glancing in the rear-view mirror a lot, fearful of a single image: Lenny in the RV speeding to catch up with her.

But it was not to be.

The big lug had no idea where she was headed. He was probably frantically calling her sister or her mother, but they didn't have a clue. Only Pedro knew, and Nora didn't think Lenny was even aware Pedro existed. Good thing, too. Lenny hated gays.

Nora pulled the Mercury into the Stuckey's parking lot. It was still dark out, but more drivers were sprouting up on the roads, and a lot of trucks.

She pulled the two suitcases out of the backseat and placed them on the ground. She slipped the car keys under a floor mat and shut the door. Lenny could come get the car. She wasn't going to steal it.

Nora dragged the two suitcases inside Stuckey's and called a cab.

The cab arrived and transported her deeper into Philadelphia, to the curbside of the Greyhound bus terminal. She paid the driver from a thick wad of bills that caused his eyebrows to rise.

She didn't have a lot of money, but what she did have was in cash. She had scraped together funds by accumulating small amounts over a long stretch of time, not wanting to arouse Lenny's suspicion. She had also drained her secret savings account, money left when her father died, before she married Lenny.

In the bus terminal, Nora bought a one-way ticket to Los Angeles and patiently waited for departure. She dozed a little bit on a bench, but then became afraid of missing her bus. She forced herself on her feet and headed over to the newsstand.

Happy, fresh faces greeted her from magazine covers. They had glorious suntans, white smiles, shapely bodies, perfect hair and dazzling clothes and jewelry. Celebrities.

One day that will be me. The ticket to Los Angeles was her winning lottery ticket. Her golden pass.

Nora bought *People*, *Us*, *Star*, *The National Enquirer*, and *Entertainment Weekly*. It was an impulsive splurge that made her feel great.

When the bus began boarding, she was the first person in line. The baggage handler loaded her suitcases into a space beneath the bus. She grabbed a window seat, but didn't intend to spend much time looking outside.

The bus rolled out of the terminal. The scenery was familiar, gray and bleak: peeling billboards, webs of electrical lines, dirty curbside snow, slumped road lamps, and miles and miles of industrial wasteland. She focused instead on her stack of magazines and tabloids. She consumed them cover to cover, absorbing the details, often returning to material she had already read. She placed herself inside the dreamlands depicted on the color pages. Sprawling mansions. Expensive clothes. Steamy lovers. Extravagant shopping. Parties and awards. Hanging out with the rich and famous.

Maybe she'd look up Lesley Banks. That would be a good place to start. Someone who had made the same journey and could share some pointers. Surely Lesley would help a fellow Pennsylvanian break into the big time.

Nora shut her eyes, leaned back, and imagined cameras capturing her peaceful slumber. She imagined opening credits for the scene. NORA HURLEY starring in NORA'S NEW LIFE. Best Picture, for sure.

It would be another two-and-a-half days until she reached her destination, but Nora was patient. She could savor the transition. Every mile was progress and made her happy.

She squeezed *People* magazine. All of a sudden, she wanted to shout out loud to release the excitement swirling inside. She wanted to stand on her seat, unleash a whoop, and thrust a fist in the air—imagining a Golden Globe, Emmy or Oscar in her grasp.

Wild applause. The whole world watching. Ugly clouds parting. Lenny and the rest of the doubters slack jawed, whipped into a brand new reality. She was something *special.*

Hooray for Hollywood!

2

H-O-L-L-Y-W-O-O-D.

As Harry Tuttle drove his silver Audi up Beachwood Drive, the majestic sign in the hills hovered like a caption. Palm trees lined both sides of the street; the open sunroof warmed his bald spot, and today was going to be a very good day.

The investors were going to see a rough cut of Harry's new film, and he felt confident—no, absolutely certain—that they were going to be blown right out of their seats. This was his best work in years.

It would be the beginning of Harry Tuttle's comeback. At one time or another, every director hits a bad streak, he told himself. Even the greatest sports athletes can have a down year. Harry's down year just happened to stretch over a decade.

But today he would be reborn. To start the morning, Harry had meditated in his Eagle Rock bungalow, thinking only positive thoughts, cleaning out the clutter. Now, as he drove, his mind was fresh, the toxins rinsed away. The sky had opened up as bright and blue as it could get in L.A. The Carpenters' "Top of the World" played on his car stereo.

The screening of his new movie wouldn't take place for another two hours, allowing Harry to follow his regular morning routine. This included a stop at his favorite hangout, the Village Coffee Shop. Located at the foot of the Hollywood Hills in Beachwood Canyon, six miles from his house, the spot offered an opportunity to kick back with *Daily Variety* or *The Hollywood Reporter,* and enjoy a raisin bagel and frothy strawberry frappuccino. He usually ran into film and TV people he knew—or wanted to meet.

Harry parked, pulled off his wraparound sunglasses and stuffed them in a shirt pocket. He waited for a pokey car of tourists to pass, crossed the road, and entered the coffee shop.

Inside, the good smells gave him an instant buzz. His eyes scanned the room for familiar faces. Other eyes scanned him. He realized he was hoping to be recognized.

Nobody in this town wants anonymity, he thought.

"Harry, good to see you man."

It was Kim Choi, a local musician who had scored several of Harry's films. Choi had a home studio in Glendale with an amazing assembly of computerized keyboards that could emulate an orchestra. He was a wizard and always delivered, on time and cheap.

As Harry waited in line, he chatted with Kim, who was fishing for work. He had just finished scoring a documentary about windmills for a cable channel and was eager for another feature.

"I'm putting the finishing touches on a new script," said Harry. "You know we'll keep you in mind. We always do. Love your work. You're the man."

After Harry got his coffee and bagel, he secured a table and started flipping through the Production Listings in *Variety.* After a few minutes, a young man with disheveled hair approached, cautiously, clutching a bound screenplay.

"I couldn't help but overhear, um, you make movies."

Harry looked up, smiled politely, and already had a sense of where this was going. "Yes...?"

"I've got a script."

Of course, thought Harry. You and everybody else in this town. "You're a writer?"

"Yes." And the young man's pitch rolled out, accelerated, with an urgency to release as much information as possible before getting cut off.

"It's a drama about an ice-skating competition, the up-and-comer against the veteran. There's action, a love story, and a dilemma—the main character, Ginny, has a little brother in a wheelchair who needs an operation; and she needs to win the competition to pay for his operation. Along the way, she falls in love with her rival's boyfriend, and it leads to a big finish that's like *Rocky* on ice."

Harry nodded. "Very dramatic, I love it, really do, but," he said, "it's not the kind of movie I make. It's the wrong genre. I'm sorry."

The young man's shoulders slumped from the news. "What kind of movies do you make?"

Harry grinned and put down his paper. It was time to do a little bragging. "Well, you've probably heard of *Slash*?"

The young man thought hard. "I don't know... Maybe..."

"*Schizo Sisters?*"

"I don't know. Who's in it?"

"Chandra Palermo. Ferguson Slatts."

The young man shrugged. "Sorry."

"You must have heard of *Ghost House*?"

"No."

"*Ghost House II?*"

"Um, no."

"*Valley of the Zombies?*"

"Yes!" exclaimed the young man. "I think I saw part of that once on cable. It's old, right?"

Harry winced. "One of my earlier films, yes."

"Cool. You did *Valley of the Zombies*." The young man mulled this over for a moment, and then said, "Well, I gotta go."

"Good luck with your screenplay," said Harry, and the young man moved into the coffee house crowd, gripping his rolled-up script.

Harry watched him leave. He really did wish the young man luck. For every motion picture released there were thousands of unproduced screenplays, and not all of them were written by amateurs. Every year, the hopefuls streamed to Hollywood, young men and women with a common bond: a passion for movies. Many of them were very skilled and creative, but the number of opportunities never came close to matching the availability of talent.

Don't get down, Harry wanted to call after the young writer. *I've been in your shoes. Just keep at it. Never give up.*

Harry had embraced movies for as long as he could remember. He grew up in an inconspicuous middle-class town in Massachusetts, without brothers, sisters, or a deep stock of friends. Movies became his companionship. His family lived close enough to walk to the local, single-screen cinema; and Harry attended as many movies as possible. First he loved watching films, then he wanted to make them. He wanted to merge with the magical world that came to life on the silver screen.

Harry's father bought him a Bell & Howell Super 8 camera for his 13th birthday, which excited Harry more than a ten-speed bike. He made silent, ultra-low-budget one-reelers. The earliest efforts were crude attempts at stop-motion animation, using household objects. His first mini-epic featured an army of toy soldiers being consumed by a rolling blob of clay. When the animation became too tedious and time-consuming, he focused on live action. He crafted short movies about monsters and superheroes, delirious juvenilia featuring anybody he could rope in from the neighborhood. One of his frequent cohorts was Tim Keneally, a 14-year-old from down the block who also had ample imagination and few friends. Tim was a pyromaniac and designed stunts and explosions, dipping into his older brother's stash of smoke bombs and M-80s.

Harry developed a soft spot for horror films. He liked being scared within the safe confines of celluloid. His exposure to horror pictures began at a young age, when his parents would take Saturday night excursions into the city for symphony concerts and stage plays. Harry's babysitter minimized her responsibilities by turning on the TV the instant Harry's parents backed out of the driveway. She discovered that she could effectively bolt Harry to the couch with "Creature Features," a weekly monster movie showcase out of Boston, hosted by Ghoularie, a pasty-faced beatnik-vampire-zombie concoction who emerged from a coffin and made cornball quips. Harry was later disappointed to discover that Ghoularie, out of makeup, was Jerry Simmons, the weatherman on morning newscasts.

Through Creature Features, Harry discovered the classics: Boris Karloff's Frankenstein, Bela Lugosi's Dracula, and Lon Chaney Jr.'s Wolfman. When Creature Features' weekly broadcasts left him hungry for more, Harry scanned the TV listings for any horror movie airings, no matter how good or bad. He subscribed to *Famous Monsters of Filmland*. He wrote short stories about attacks from outer space and vengeful mummies.

After high school, Harry studied film at Boston University, creating short, experimental films accompanied by music from his Tangerine Dream and Pink Floyd LPs. His final student film—a surreal, 16mm black-and-white effort about a haunted bed that provoked nightmares—impressed his professor enough to earn him an internship at an L.A. production company after graduation.

Fresh out of BU, Harry stuffed everything he owned into his Volkswagen Bug and drove to Los Angeles with a head full of dreams. When he first encountered the Hollywood sign, he made an attempt to scramble up to the letters to touch them. He parked his car and hiked the trails of Griffith Park. However, the seemingly accessible sign proved unreachable. It was a tease.

The internship was a whirlwind of changing duties and hands-on experience, helping out a production company that specialized in network television specials. It was a low-level Production Assistant's job—assisting crew, fetching coffee, answering phones, helping to schedule meetings, and running errands on a moment's notice. Occasionally, he wrote coverage for scripts in the slush pile; and the readings offered lessons in formatting and pacing, a valuable reference for his own future screenplays.

Unfortunately, when the internship was over, it was over. There was no offer of a full-time gig, and Harry was left without a job and very little money. He accepted low-paying, menial jobs that disgraced his college degree.

Then one day he was saved by a strange old man named Max Argas.

Argas was a grizzled hack or Hollywood legend, depending on whom you asked. But there was general consensus that he was the granddaddy of the B film. Since the early '60s, he had been cranking out exploitation pictures of every shape and size: biker films, martial arts imports, LSD documentaries, slapdash teenage comedies, blaxploitation, women's prison melodramas, soft-core porn, and horror. Lots of horror.

In the 1980s, horror became Argas's bread and butter. In the wake of enormous successes like *Halloween*, *Friday the 13th*, and *Nightmare on Elm Street*—and all of their profitable sequels—Argas was efficiently pumping out his own "slasher" flicks at bargain basement cost. The audiences kept coming. Kids looking for an adrenaline fix filled the theaters and drive-ins, while the home video boom delivered a new source of cash flow. Argas, accustomed to a skeleton crew of cronies, found that he needed more manpower to keep supply up with demand.

Instead of placing trade ads, he simply nabbed the eager young people who crossed his path. Harry served Argas soup one day at a restaurant in Burbank. Four days later, he was a second assistant director on *Hell's Hookers*, yelling "Quiet on the set!" Harry always felt that his film degree from Boston University made no difference to Argas.

In fact, Harry learned far more working under Argas's wings than he ever did in school.

Argas was not a warm man. He barked orders and had little patience. But he did shift tremendous responsibility and opportunity to rookies who were eager to learn. He launched dozens of careers.

After his first few pictures with Argas, Harry graduated to first A.D., becoming more involved with the crew and organizing the elements of each day's shoot. He also began offering script input, and impressed Argas enough to become his unofficial script doctor.

Finally, Argas said, "Why don't you just write one of these things?"

So Harry wrote *Screamers*, a thriller about deadly aliens that grew in size and strength by feeding off the screams of their victims.

Screamers did good business and even received begrudging positive reviews, the three-star kind, from critics willing to accept a fun, hokey B film.

Argas was impressed. He was also dying of cancer. A lifetime of chain smoking, bundled with workaholic stress, had taken its toll.

Max Argas's final two films, *The Christmas Killer* and *Demonic Possession*, featured Argas's name as director in the credits; but Harry did most of the work. On *Demonic Possession*, Harry took over on the second day of shooting, after conducting extensive rewrites on the script. The film became a critical and commercial smash, while Argas remained bedridden, deteriorating and frustrated. Harry accepted the lack of credit, given the circumstances. He tended to Argas, provided production updates, screened rushes for him, and remained near his bedside through the final days of his life when the old man turned gray and withered, like something inhuman out of one of his films.

"You're going places," croaked Argas to Harry the day before he died.

"Thank you, sir," said Harry. "I want to do you proud."

Later, as the afternoon light dimmed, and he dipped in and out of consciousness, Argas said, "I'm being pulled to the other side. I can see it. They're expecting me."

"In heaven?" said Harry.

Argas chuckled dryly. "My dear boy, you know the content of my films. Why would I be going to heaven?"

Harry felt the hairs stand up on the back of his neck.

"I'm not afraid," said Argas. "My films probably win Oscars where I'm going..."

* * *

After Argas died, Harry discovered he was in demand. Perhaps his years of quality work on Argas's pictures had not gone unnoticed, or more likely, he was simply experienced in a profitable genre. Nevertheless, in short order Harry acquired a well-connected agent and a two-picture deal with Universal. The budgets weren't big, but there was a promise of creative freedom and wide distribution.

"We need more scary shit for the teenagers," a pot-bellied studio executive told him outright. "And we need it today. I don't know how much longer this horror fad is going to last."

Harry's first film for Universal, *Grip of Terror*, about a babysitter-stalking maniac, was a modest success, bringing in healthy box office receipts and good reviews. One national critic even called it, "one of the best scarefests of the year." Another reviewer enthused, "Tuttle is a talent to watch."

Harry was on cloud nine. *Grip of Terror* also marked a momentous occasion in his personal life: he met and married Julie Kramer, the beautiful young brunette with long eyelashes who portrayed the babysitter killer's first victim. They had dinner one night after her character was decapitated, and Harry fell head over heels in love.

After they married, her career took off. She landed a plum role on a popular TV series about a San Diego private investigator. She kept busy in the off-season with made-for-television movies. Meanwhile, Harry's second picture, *The Thing in the*

Attic, performed okay; but two opposing factors troubled his bosses at Universal: the film's budget was bigger and the box office was smaller. Most of the critics were kind to the picture, but even the good reviews opened with lines like "If you're in the mood for something mindless..."

Soon, the horror movie craze came to an end. Harry's final horror film for Universal, *Gouge*, was a huge flop. By then, his biggest champion at the studio had gone elsewhere, so Harry was unceremoniously cut loose.

That was the beginning of Harry's dark period. He wrote and directed an independently produced horror film that also flopped. He wrote a few movie and TV scripts that never emerged from development hell. Then, in short order, he lost his agent and his wife.

Julie's departure particularly devastated him because it seemed to be in direct correlation with the downfall of his career.

"I thought we were together through thick and thin," he said.

"It's not about your career," she responded. But then she revealed she had been cheating on him with a hotshot British director, and had accepted a role in the director's next film.

Harry argued pointlessly to keep the marriage together, but she had turned it off, like a light switch.

"We have reached a fork in the road of life," she said. "This is where we go our separate ways. I'll always treasure the love we shared. But now we must free ourselves to find our true destiny."

When he recognized it was dialogue she had lifted from one of her TV movies, he knew it was the end.

Harry spent money on therapy, attended self-help groups, and tried to regain his self-esteem. He taught screenwriting for a while at a community college. He wondered if he would ever write or direct again.

Then one April morning he received a call from Paul Jacobs.

"I apologize for calling you direct," spoke the smooth and youthful voice on the other end. "I wanted to contact your agent, but I have been unable to get your agency from the Guild."

"I'm between agents," said Harry.

"Then it's okay if we deal direct?"

"I would prefer it."

Paul talked and Harry listened to a long, organized and very slick pitch.

Jacobs held an MBA from Stanford and had spent several years at a downtown brokerage firm selling variable annuities and mutual funds. He was great at it, but found the job boring. He wanted to get involved in the movie business. "I don't want to sell annuities anymore. I want to sell fun."

Jacobs express-mailed Harry a detailed proposal to create an independent film production company, funded by private investors, which would produce low-budget feature films for international home video and cable television. Theatrical release would be a bonus, but not the focus.

Harry read the proposal and agreed to meet Paul for lunch at a French restaurant in Brentwood.

At lunch, Paul impressed Harry. He was a bundle of fresh energy, barely able to sit still, dressed in a dark suit like a banker. He resembled Harry from 20 years ago: a full head of hair, straight posture, and trim. He continued his pitch, "Especially in foreign markets, there is a thirst for Hollywood product that can't be quenched. Consumer video sales are going through the roof. New cable channels are popping up all the time. Who is going to feed this monster? We are. We could be a great team. You have the moviemaking skills I'm looking for. You write; you direct; you know indie filmmaking. I know you can work magic with small budgets. I have seen your films, dating back to the Argas stuff. You are my first choice. If you don't want to jump at this opportunity, I understand. You might have bigger and better things in the pipeline. If you say no, I go to number two, then three, all the way down. But this production company is going to happen. I have the start-up funds. I can take us global. I am very tenacious. I know how to rally investors. I know how to raise money and make money from money. I know what I want to do with my life and this is it. What do you say?"

Harry thought about it for about a nanosecond.

Then he asked, "Where do I sign?"

* * *

PJ Productions established an office in Westwood on Wilshire Boulevard, opened for business, and never looked back. While everything was on a much smaller scale than Harry was used to, the operation was a well-oiled machine; and he was making movies again. The titles rolled out in a steady stream: *Valley of the Zombies*, *Slash*, *Schizo Sisters*, *Surfer Psycho*, *Soul Snatchers*, the *Ghost House* series, and more.

Paul trusted Harry with the scripts and direction. They established a network of reliable, cheap talent to hire on a per-film basis. The budgets were limited, the shooting schedules tight, and the final products never as polished as Harry would have liked. But he had artistic control. Paul never hovered over the filmmaking process. He rarely set foot on the sets. He remained in the office, on the phone, arranging lunches and meetings, maximizing the money flow.

Paul made them both a lot of income. Harry paid back all of his debts from his "black period," and even had money left-over each month to help out his parents, who lived in Anaheim and were scraping to get by on his father's skimpy pension.

Everything was back on stable ground except for one thing.

Critics hated the pictures.

Paul told Harry not to agonize over the reviews, but Harry couldn't help it. His new career was a mixed blessing. Sure, he wanted to make movies. Sure, he wanted to make money. But he also craved respect and admiration. Once, long ago, for a short time the reviews had been good; and people had said nice things about Harry Tuttle. And now...

"Another dismal offering from Harry Tuttle," read one review.

"Tuttle's monster dreck just gets worse and worse," read another. "He's not the bottom of the barrel, he's *beneath* it."

Even magazines devoted to horror movies and "psychotronic" films joined in the public thrashing.

"The new Harry Tuttle movie is poor and sloppy, don't waste your time," reported *Monster Fan*, a crude, stapled fanzine riddled with typos.

All of the venom and cruelty merely provoked Harry to work even harder at delivering a comeback film. He knew he had it in him. He could work around the skimpy budgets—good writing and directing would always win out in the end. He could hide the shortcuts and compromises.

Harry poured his heart and soul into his newest film, *The Beastly*.

He labored over the script, a terror tale about a teenage mutant whose puberty unleashes homicidal impulses. He obsessed over the direction. *The Beastly* had unexpected twists, scares, and pathos. It had a contemporary edge. Harry was certain it was the best work of his career.

And now, in less than an hour, *The Beastly* would be unveiled to Paul's investors.

Harry was hopeful the investors would applaud his efforts, deliver praise, and the buzz would begin. His comeback underway, Harry would return to form. He was long overdue.

Harry finished his last sip of frappuccino. He checked his watch. It was time to leave the Village Coffee Shop and head to the offices of PJ Productions. He needed to meet up with Paul and get ready for the screening.

As Harry returned to his car on Beachwood Drive, he couldn't help taking one more glance at the Hollywood sign. It recharged his batteries. It reminded him of his reason to live. It renewed his vigor and enthusiasm.

"Look out, Hollywood," he said. "Harry Tuttle is back, and he's better than ever."

3

"What a piece of crap!"

Cal Stillwall's outburst shattered the long silence that greeted the end of *The Beastly*.

Following the conclusion of the credits, Paul Jacobs had snapped on the lights in the small screening room. The brightness jarred 76-year-old Ellie Kirby from her slumber, and she caught herself in mid-drool. The other investors, filling three rows of folding chairs, appeared in various degrees of disinterest and displeasure.

Stillwall's eruption opened the gates for the others. Sara Connelly, a red-haired real estate attorney from Bel Air, exclaimed, "Nobody in their right mind is going to see this picture." Alan Fisch, a periodontist from Pasadena, grumbled, "You promised a major star."

Paul stood with confidence before the group, chest pumped out, wearing his blue Armani suit. He beamed to deflect the scowls. "A major star you wanted and a major star you got. Didn't you see Corey Summers?"

"Who?" said Jimmy Nancarrow, who owned a string of car dealerships.

"Corey Summers, the great child actor from the long-running television sitcom *Oh Brother.* He played the second victim. Remember the power drill scene?"

"You mean that 40-year-old guy?"

"Sure, he's older now," said Paul. "His show's been off the air awhile, but he's been waiting for the right vehicle..."

"I thought Corey Summers was dead from sniffing paint thinner," said Sara Connelly.

"You're thinking of Corey Singer," suggested Mel Orr, who owned a chain of pet stores. "That little freckled kid from *Hijinx.*"

"You could see the boom mike in a couple of scenes," spoke up Fisch.

"How come in that one scene you could see the dead guy scratch his stomach?" said Nancarrow.

Paul dismissed them with a chuckle. "We'll fix it in post."

"I don't see how this movie is going to make any money," said Fisch. "It's just plain bad."

In the back of the room, Harry Tuttle sank deeper into his chair. He felt like a pincushion being pierced by needles.

Dick the Greek came to his rescue. Dick was a large, stubbly man who lived in Las Vegas. He rarely attended Paul's screenings but remained one of the key investors in PJ Productions since fueling the company's start-up.

"Ladies and gentlemen, don't kid yourselves, this is not about art," said Dick in his low, gravelly monotone. "This is about commerce. Once you get past that, I can testify to the profitability of these films. I do not defend their aesthetics. This is not even the type of film I like. I like westerns and musicals. But I also like money. These pictures make good money. Paul has never let me down, and I have invested in seven of his productions."

"Thank you, Dick," said Paul. "A perfect segue." He clasped his hands together and addressed the group. "I'd like to take this opportunity to reiterate our business plan. Some of you in this room have invested in our projects in the past, and some of you are obviously newcomers. It is for those newcomers that I would like to restate our *modus operandi.*"

Paul paced along a wall decorated with lurid promotional posters for previous PJ Productions: *Hillbilly Cannibals, Ghost House IV, Swamp Monster.*

"First and foremost, we are not Paramount or Disney or MGM. We do not make big-budget theatrical films. We do not hire big stars. We are an independent film production company that is not financed by any studio. We rely on private investors who are attracted to our track record and would like a taste of Hollywood. We shoot exploitation movies on the low-end of the budget spectrum, essentially for the video market and cable television. Our films are tightly scripted, quickly shot, with as much in-house post-production as possible. We put most of our muscle into marketing and distribution. We are an international company."

Paul stopped at a French movie poster, *Soeurs Schizophrenes,* featuring two buxom women in lingerie, back-to-back, wielding axes dripping with blood.

"Including the United States and Canada, there are more than 65 countries hungry for Hollywood product. That means 65 sources of revenue from home video, pay TV, and cable TV rights. You may not see our films making a big splash, but they do generate ripples around the globe. Our movies make money in Germany...Italy...Spain...the UK...Japan...France. They all want some of that Hollywood magic."

Paul pointed across the room to a poster for *Soul Snatchers.*

"That video there, sold 37,000 units in South Korea alone. And because we're not paying Tom Cruise's salary, or spending tens of millions of dollars on extravagant special effects, the rate of return to our pockets is significant."

Paul picked up a dog-eared copy of the PJ Productions prospectus from the snack table. He waved the document.

"I hope all of you took the time to read the fine print. Everything we do is SEC compliant. We have outlined all the risk factors. Everything is on the books. There is no mystery behind our agenda. It's really quite simple."

Paul tossed the prospectus to Alan Fisch while still addressing the group. "A few years ago, our company entered a new phase. We went totally digital. It has created an immediate impact on the bottom line. This is the 21st Century. Theaters are using digital projectors and testing satellite projection. Thirty-five millimeter is dying, and we are ahead of the curve. We have eliminated the expense of buying film stock, paying lab processing fees, and making prints. Today's digital equipment can replicate the look of film at a fraction of the cost. It costs less to buy and own high-end digital video cameras than to rent 35 millimeter cameras."

Paul gestured to the blank projection screen at the front of the room. "The movie you saw today. Looked like film stock, no? Well, it wasn't. *The Beastly* was shot entirely on Digital Betacam, using as much natural light as possible. We captured the footage into a state-of-the-art Apple workstation and stored it on massive hard drives. We used the latest nonlinear editing software to prepare a high-resolution master that can be burned to DVD. Most of our post is conducted in our own facilities: titles, transitions, sound mix, color corrections, effects. This company may be small, but make no mistake, we are cutting edge."

Paul returned to the snack table and picked up a DVD from a stack of complimentary screeners of recent releases. He displayed the clamshell artwork to the group.

"This is *I'll Skin You Alive!*, one of our recent horror pictures. It never realized a theatrical release and it was very profitable. We shot on video, we released on video. Even with major studio product, you are seeing less time between a theatrical release and the direct-to-consumer DVD. We just close that gap entirely. The direct-to-video business is not just kiddie programs and exercise videos. Instead of going to the movies, people are bringing the movies home. They have home theater set-ups. They rent and buy movies in huge numbers. And the cost of duplicating DVDs...it's so cheap it should be illegal. We can do the duplication in-house. We churn them out while we sleep. We can sell up to 18,000 copies of one of our titles to Walmart alone. We sell thousands more direct to customers on our web site. And that's just DVD sales. I haven't even touched upon the global television markets: cable TV, premium channels, local and national networks from here to Singapore. In-room pay-per-view movies at hotel chains. We're even exploring download-on-demand movies online. The opportunities are endless. Fortunately, we have a strong relationship with a distributor who knows the markets, builds relationships, and likes to travel. Our sales agent is one of the best in the business. He is more valuable to us than any flash-in-the-pan movie star."

Paul paused to take a potato chip out of one of the snack bowls. He bit into it with a crunch. "Finally," he said, and he extended an arm to the back of the room, "we have the great fortune of an exclusive relationship with one of the best creative minds in the business, Harry Tuttle. I like to refer to him as 'Scary Harry'."

As faces turned to look at him, Harry made a small, reluctant wave.

Paul said, "Harry writes, directs, and produces our films. He has already completed the script to our next feature, *The Vampire of Sunset Strip*. I consider Harry the fastest, most efficient moviemaker in Hollywood. He can shoot a movie in 21 days, and everything he's touched for us has turned a profit. Harry works with a network of hard-working, cost-efficient, free-lance talent. He knows the cinematographers, editors, production designers, gaffers, soundtrack composers—you name it. The man knows how to assemble a crew and manufacture a movie like nobody else. He's done it so many times, he could do it in his sleep. And because we own most of our equipment—the cameras and sound gear, the lights, and so on—we just need to hire the talent. We don't lease the supplies. It gives us further cost control. And there's one other way we save costs...Sometimes, when casting, we look to one of our own."

Paul stood beside Ellie Kirby, an elderly, very rich widow from Beverly Hills. Ellie smiled shyly.

"I hope all of you noticed Ellie's fabulous cameo as the lunchroom lady. Did you enjoy seeing yourself up there, Ellie?"

Ellie continued smiling and patted Paul's hand. "Oh yes. Thank you Paul."

"We should call her the 'world-famous Ellie Kirby'," said Paul, "because they're going to be watching her stellar performance in Portugal...in Taiwan...in Venezuela...you name it. And where else can any of you get that opportunity? Sure, you could invest in stocks and bonds...ho hum...or real estate... yawn...but that doesn't offer you *immortality*. Long after Ellie leaves this earth, bless her, future generations will still be watching her performance. Mel—they'll see you as bystander number four in the crowd scene. Alan—for years to come, they'll see your name in the credits as one of the executive producers."

Paul's voice grew quiet. Almost a whisper. "Movies are magic. All of you are now part of that magic. And you're going to make some money off that magic. So hold tight; be patient. If you don't believe me, just ask for a refund, because I have a waiting list of other investors who would like to be a part of this special partnership. Anyone here can be replaced, if they so choose."

Paul finally stopped talking. A long silence ensued.

When no one spoke up, Paul said, "Thank you for coming to our world premiere. Are we ready to break out the champagne?"

* * *

"They hated it, Paul."

Harry Tuttle remained anchored in the back row of the small projection room. The investors had left. Harry hadn't moved.

Paul paced around him, energized. "Hated it? No. Some of them—a few of them—just don't understand. You'd think they would read the prospectus and recognize that we aren't making *Twilight* or *Avatar* here. It's a different business model."

"Cal Stillwall looked like he was going to overheat his pacemaker."

"Hey, nobody pulled their investment. Most of them are on board for the next one. They keep coming back, don't they?" Paul nibbled on some of the leftover popcorn.

Harry felt a stone in the pit of his stomach. "I used to make big films. Movies that played for weeks all over the country.

Sometimes they even got good reviews. Now I just churn out garbage. My name is becoming synonymous with crap. Harry the Hack. Maybe I should take my name off the picture and use a pseudonym. Alan Smithee or John Doe."

"No Doe," said Paul. "Get serious. You are the one and only 'Scary Harry,' the best in the biz. You have a loyal following. They keep coming back for more. Look at the numbers. Revenues are up, earnings are up."

"But the reviews..."

"You get good reviews," said Paul. He pointed to the poster for *Ghost House IV: The Final Chapter.* He read out loud the blurb above the title, "'An instant classic. One of the best horror films of all time...*The Movie Review Gazette.*'"

Harry gave him a long look. "You know and I know that *The Movie Review Gazette* is your cousin's web site. He only reviews our movies, and he only writes good reviews."

"But nobody knows that. I thought we were talking about public perception."

Harry sighed. "You don't understand."

"You're dragging me down, Harry. I'm trying to be positive. There's no reason to believe this movie can fail. What's wrong with you today?"

Harry shrugged. All the build-up to the screening...and then a massive letdown. It felt too familiar. He just felt lousy. The meditation wasn't helping lighten his load. Maybe more therapy?

"Maybe I'm having my mid-life crisis," said Harry.

"Then rejoice," responded Paul. "You're 46. If you're having your midlife crisis now, that means you'll live to be 92. Do the math."

"That doesn't cheer me up."

"Listen to me," said Paul. "You are the best writer-director in the horror field today, bar none."

"Because I'm the cheapest. I can work with puny budgets and no-name talent, and turn a profit."

"And those profits guarantee that you can make more movies. Do you know how many directors struggle for work after a couple of big-budget failures? Your filmography is going to be a block long."

"It's about quality, not quantity," said Harry. "Sometimes I get thinking about my legacy. After I'm gone and only the movies remain, what will people say about me, if anything? You know, my best movie I didn't even get credit for."

"What are you talking about? I always give you credit."

"No. This was before PJ Productions. My best movie, *Demonic Possession*. I took over the directing for Max Argas after he got sick with cancer. But we kept his name on it. He was dying. It wouldn't have been right."

"You're a noble man, Harry."

"The *Denver Post* called *Demonic Possession* one of the best horror films of the 1980s, and a new standard. They called Max brilliant."

"Your turn will come."

"Not with direct-to-video."

Paul sighed. "What can I do to cheer you up, my friend? What is it you want?"

Harry thought hard. "I'm tired of the minor leagues. I'd sell my soul for some respect in this town. I want to be part of the big time, Paul."

* * *

Two days later, Paul phoned Harry at his Eagle Rock bungalow, interrupting his morning meditation.

"Remember, you told me you wanted to be part of the big time?"

"Yeah."

"Your wish has been granted. I have been invited to a big-time party, and I want you to come with me."

"A party?" Harry's tone fell flat.

"Richard Metherell, industry legend. He's been a top dog at Warner Brothers and New Line. He's won Oscars and launched a thousand careers. He's turning 70, and there is a mega-bash at his mansion in Brentwood. Everybody who matters is going to be there. I have an 'in', and now I'm going to be your 'in'."

"I don't know..." said Harry.

"Knock it off, sad sack! This is a place to be seen. You gotta check out the house, it's in the hills, it's bigger than a country club."

"With my luck, I'll run into my ex-wife," said Harry. "She'll probably be there with Nigel, her new and improved husband. He's got an Academy Award."

"It's a British Academy Award," said Paul. "Doesn't count. So, are you going to the party or not? Otherwise, I'll invite one of our investors. I'll bet Jimmy Nancarrow would love to go stalk a few starlets."

"I'll go," said Harry.

"Attaboy."

"But you can't force me to have a good time."

"Harry," sighed Paul. "Lighten up. I think our next horror movie should be about you. The Mope from Hell."

Harry said nothing. Paul was right. He was in a miserable

funk. He needed something—anything—to get his career back on track.

He was starved for a hit, and it was killing him.

4

Harry tried not to get lost as he traveled the meandering streets around and over the foothills of the Santa Monica Mountains. Large, plentiful trees and lush planting established an almost rural feeling for the rich and famous who lived here.

Metherell's Mediterranean-style mansion was situated behind gates on a sprawling property decorated with exotic gardens that must have required a full-time landscaper. Harry joined the line of vehicles filling a long, winding driveway. A valet showed up at his window and asked for the keys.

Yes, thought Harry, this is the big time.

As Harry entered the home's two-story foyer, he immediately felt self-conscious. He didn't belong. He stepped through several rooms, recognizing a jarring mix of celebrities. Sitcom stars mingled with rock musicians. Famous athletes interacted with movie icons.

Metherell's mansion was tastefully luxurious at every turn, with grand-scale rooms, crown moldings and limestone floors. Under the high ceilings, Harry felt shrunken. He heard classical music—a Strauss waltz—and went looking for the entertainment system. He found a string quartet.

Who am I going to talk to? Where's Paul?

Paul was probably trolling for investors. Surely he smelled the green.

Harry wandered, got a bit lost, and wound up in the maid's quarters, which at least more accurately reflected the dimensions of his own home.

He finally found Paul in an elaborate media room equipped with recessed, built-in projection equipment.

Paul's back was turned to him. As Harry approached, he heard Paul's loud and proud voice rising above the rest of the chatter.

"I'll tell you what sells, it's the poster art and DVD cover. Everything else is secondary. We call it disposable entertainment. You put something gross on the cover, a title that's a grabber, a high concept that anybody can describe in one sentence, and you're good to go. Most of our sales come from abroad. They eat them up over there, doesn't matter what's inside the packaging. Our strategy is to sell the sizzle, not the steak."

Harry stopped advancing on Paul. He backed up.

He felt stingers in his heart. He had always assumed that this was Paul's true sentiment, but somehow it was much more painful to hear it aloud...in a gathering of Hollywood's heavy-hitters.

Screw PJ Productions, I'm going to quit, thought Harry.

He drank some wine to build up his courage and began approaching strangers. He mingled. He networked. He sniffed for new opportunities.

He introduced himself as a writer-director and name-dropped some of his earlier, successful pictures. Unfortunately, even those accomplishments failed to register with most of the people. Occasionally someone had heard of Max Argas, "that B picture guy."

Harry was willing to get his foot in the door anywhere. He talked to a few TV network people, and then several indie producers with modest budgets that still represented a step up from PJ Productions. Some of them feigned interest, but he could see their eyes roam the room for more compelling connections. Every conversation seemed to end with "I'll give you a call," but he doubted any of them would ever pick up the phone. In particular, there was the woman from Disney who accepted his business card with nods and smiles. Two minutes later, Harry saw her deposit the card on a passing tray of drinks.

He couldn't blame her. When she asked for the names of his latest pictures, he felt embarrassed to even speak them aloud. Titles like *I'll Skin You Alive* were never his idea—it was Paul's marketing strategy. Harry's working title for *I'll Skin You Alive* had been *Night of Fog*, which Paul found "too understated for the target market."

Harry's conversation with an executive from Sony proved to be the shortest one yet—just under three minutes—before the executive broke it off with "Pardon me! I just saw my old friend Joe from CBS!"

Harry then watched the Sony executive get a slice of birthday cake, and stand alone in another corner of the room.

Just when it looked like it couldn't get worse, it did.

Julie, Harry's ex-wife, appeared at the party with Nigel, her second husband. Julie looked great, Nigel looked great, and Harry was gone from the room.

He pushed a few people aside and earned dirty looks, but this was an emergency. He stepped through narrow doors that took him to a terrace. The terrace offered a stunning ocean and canyon view. He could be alone here with his glass of wine, and that was good.

Not too far below, party guests circled a large swimming pool. Shimmering blue, the pool consisted of different connected sections, with a waterfall tumbling on one end. Nearby, he could see an illuminated tennis court and workout facility.

I'm finishing this glass of wine, and then I am out of here.

That's when he noticed he wasn't alone.

She was in a corner of the terrace, under shadows. A stunning young woman with straight blonde hair and a simple, thin white dress. She held a glass of wine.

She looked at him.

"Hi," she said.

"Hello," said Harry.

"Pretty out here."

"It is."

The conversation ended there. Harry wanted to keep it going, but didn't know what to say. Her focus returned to the view, while his attention remained on her face.

She had soft, open features, like a child. She had a certain delicate, porcelain look to her. She also looked somehow familiar. He tried to dismiss it, but the curiosity grew. He knew her. It started to gnaw at him.

Harry kept staring and then blurted, "You're the whore."

Startled, she looked at him. "Pardon?"

"I'm sorry—you were on *Crime Busters* last week. Am I right? You played the girlfriend of the pimp—you wore the big fur, spiked boots, all that makeup—but that was you, wasn't it? Or am I out of my mind?"

She broke out in a shy grin. "You're right, that was me. I'm flattered. I can't believe you remember that. It was such a small part."

"I guess you made an impression."

"Because I was so bad?" She laughed with self-deprecation.

"Not at all."

"Nobody watches that show. I think it gets beat in the ratings by the Home Shopping Network."

He moved closer and she did the same, stepping out of the shadows.

Her eyes were a striking shade of blue. She was altogether beautiful in a common way for L.A. Yet she would stop traffic in Cleveland.

"You do a lot of TV?" Harry asked.

"I'm just getting started. I just got a small part in a miniseries about Hollywood scandals in the 1920s. But I don't have any lines; I'm doing background. *Crime Busters* was my first role with any dialogue."

"You were outstanding. I really thought so."

"I had two lines. 'Hit 'im, Bruce!' 'Bruce get up!'"

"Well, you stole the scene. Really." Harry realized he was fawning and told himself to rein it in.

"Thank you," she said. "Are you an actor?"

"Actor? No. I'm a director." Harry chose his words carefully. "I write and direct...suspense films."

"I love mysteries."

"Well, these are more like horror." Harry couldn't help a self-conscious cringe.

"That sounds cool. Anything I would have heard of?"

Harry ran some possible titles through his mind and finally said, "*The Beastly* is my new one. In fact, we just held the premiere. It went over...pretty good."

"How exciting. I'll look for it." Then she glanced at the ground, looked back up at him, and half-smiled. "I know you must hear this all the time, but...if you're looking for an up-and-coming actress, I know of someone I can recommend. Fresh out of UCLA. Got her SAG card. Can play a great whore."

Harry reacted quickly. "Great, I'm always looking for actresses. We make a lot of movies. I just finished the script for my next one, and we've started casting. It's a vampire picture."

"I can do vampires, I can do horror. I've got a good set of pipes. I can scream, I can shriek, squeal, whatever you need. Let me give you my number."

She reached into her purse and pulled out a business card. He gave her one of his PJ Productions cards, and she promised to send a headshot and full list of credits.

Harry told her, "I just have to let you know...the budgets aren't real big. It's independent. So the pay is modest."

"The money's not important. The exposure is. I'm open to low-budget."

Harry swallowed, then admitted, "When I say low-budget, I mean really low-budget. Under one million dollars for the whole picture."

She nodded. He saw her interest sag slightly. "Well," she said, "why don't you send me the script and a couple of your films, so I can see what you're all about."

"It's a deal."

She examined his card. "Harry Tuttle." She looked up and shook his hand. "Thanks, Harry. I'm Rachel. Let's keep in touch."

He promised he would, and she left the terrace to return inside the house. He watched her disappear into a sea of people and called out, quietly enough that she couldn't hear him but loud enough to get it off his chest, "If you're interested, I'm single."

5

George Grubbis sat in his Toyota Camry, parked curbside on Del Marino, watching the ramshackle ranch house across the street. A few minutes ago, two young men he had never seen before had answered the door. They told him that Marcus had gone out to grab lunch. He should be back soon.

Then the tall one with the red beard and deep voice asked, "Who are you?"

Grubbis didn't answer. He merely said good day, returned to his car, sat and waited.

He wanted Marcus.

Looking at the ranch house, Grubbis felt sick about how unsightly it had become. Like many others in the neighborhood, it was a simple, single-floor home, long and narrow, sitting low to the ground on a concrete slab, dominated by a big picture window.

But it had become decidedly unkempt, with shingles missing, chipped paint, and a front lawn of brown grass, weeds, and garbage. An old sofa, lamp, and other furniture had been dumped in a heap at the foot of the sidewalk. Several of the sofa cushions had strayed across the yard.

Two Asian kids on bicycles approached the discarded furniture. They stopped for a moment to poke through the clutter, but found nothing of interest and left.

Five minutes later, a Latino couple examined the sofa. The woman shook her head no, and they moved on.

San Gabriel was a city of ethnic diversity and integration, even as many of its citizens surrounded their homes with gates and chain-link fences. Grubbis figured that fewer than half of his renters these days were whites. And the whites typically gave him the most trouble. People like Marcus Stegman who knew nothing about responsibility and obligation. Everything was an entitlement.

Grubbis flexed his fingers. His hands were stiff and arthritic. His back was sore from a herniated disc that sometimes caused him to sleep on the hardwood floor.

He was 68 years old and felt every bit his age. His bones ached. Sitting in this car all day wasn't helping...

...but God damn it, he wanted his money.

After 15 minutes, Marcus Stegman arrived home. He pulled his rusted white van into the driveway and stopped short of the carport, which overflowed with junk.

Grubbis opened his car door and stepped into the street.

Stegman didn't see him. He carried two white bags of fast food and headed for the house. He was dressed in jeans, gym shoes, and a black T-shirt with "Godzilla, King of the Monsters" on the front.

"*Marcus!*"

Grubbis stepped into Stegman's path before he reached the front door. Stegman had a french fry hanging out of his mouth.

"You know why I'm here," said Grubbis.

Stegman finished the french fry, nodding.

"I don't like chasing you down like this every month," said Grubbis. "It's childish."

"I lost track of the calendar. Am I late?"

Grubbis looked into Stegman's face. He could see black bags under his eyes. He looked like he hadn't slept in weeks. His hair was long and oily. His goatee was more poorly manicured than his front lawn.

"Come on," said Grubbis. "I don't need this. If you can't pay your rent, go live someplace else. It's as simple as that. The only reason I've been patient this long is out of respect for your mother. She was a good woman, and she wanted you to stay in this house; and I appreciated that. But it can't go on like this."

For eleven years, Audrey Stegman lived in the Del Marino house without giving him any problems. She worked six days a week as a cashier at a grocery store, always paid her rent on time, and still found the time to keep the property in good shape. Marcus was a shameless freeloader, a kid getting older but not more mature, sponging off his mother, avoiding any real work and spending all his time watching videos in his bedroom.

A succession of strokes, each more crippling than the last, finished off Audrey Stegman. One of the last times Grubbis saw her, she told him, speech slurred by paralysis, "Take care of my son. He means well."

For the past year, Grubbis had tried hard to remain patient about the delinquent rent payments. But the house wasn't going to go for free. Grubbis had limits.

Stegman said, "I'll get the money to you next week. How about Monday? You want a french fry?"

"No and no," said Grubbis.

Stegman sighed and made nervous noises with his lips. His

eyes roamed. He clearly wanted to squirm back into the house, but Grubbis had positioned himself by the door.

"What's all this crap on the lawn?" asked Grubbis.

"I cleaned out the den. I need the space. It's for my editing equipment."

"I see. You have plenty of money for editing equipment, but not rent."

"It was my inheritance money from my mother. It's an investment."

"Investment? In what?"

Stegman said firmly, "My movie. I've been working night and day on this thing. I've been incredibly busy. But it's all going to pay off. I'm almost done, and then I'm going to go out and get a deal; and everything is going to be a lot different. I'll be able to buy this house."

Grubbis frowned, both saddened and angered by this young man's delusions. "I think you pissed away your mother's inheritance, and pretty soon you and your editing equipment are going to be out on the street. Is that what you want?"

Stegman said, "I can get you some money on Monday."

"I've heard this before, Marcus..."

"I mean it. On Monday, I'll be getting my deposit back on some camera equipment. Call the rental company if you don't believe me."

"I will not subsidize your movie."

"You aren't. You'll get paid. I have to juggle a lot of things right now. I'm just getting started..."

"Marcus, I've known you for a long time. I don't like this anymore than you do, but it's time to wake up and smell the coffee." Then he muttered, "I wish you could have learned something from your mother."

"I did," responded Stegman. "She died without having ever fulfilled any of her dreams. I don't want that to happen to me."

Grubbis sighed through his nostrils. His hands hurt. He noticed two sloppy young men looking at him through the windowpane in the door. It was the tall redhead, joined by a dark-skinned young man with an earring.

"How many people you got living in there anyway?" asked Grubbis.

"Garon and Terrance. They're helping me with the movie."

"How about if they help you with the rent."

"Listen, we're starved. We just want to eat lunch and get back to work on the film."

Grubbis finally relented. He stepped out of the way and said, "You might want to rethink your priorities."

"Nothing's more important than making movies," said Stegman, taking the door handle.

"Yeah. Well I don't care if you're Steven friggin' Spielberg. You pay up or move out. I have evicted actors, actresses, directors, screenwriters...I don't care. You Hollywood wannabes are a dime a dozen."

Stegman entered the house.

Grubbis got a glance inside. It was a pit, an absolute hellhole of trash: movie equipment, tripods and cables, pizza boxes, soda bottles, and precarious stacks of boxes and plastic bucket containers.

Dear God, I can't stomach this...

"Did you get my Thai Taco?" asked the deep-voiced roommate.

"So who is that creepy old dude?" said the other.

The door shut.

Grubbis returned to his car. He was not optimistic about

getting his money on Monday—not even a portion of it. But for now, the kid was getting another chance. Somewhere, Audrey Stegman was smiling at him, but next time...Well, that would be another story.

As Grubbis drove from the property, he slumped in his seat, soured by the sinking feeling of inevitability. He was going to evict this kid one day.

Movie boy would have to face up to reality.

6

Harry snapped on the light and faced three walls of movies. The complete works of PJ Productions surrounded him, stored neatly on long shelves in deep quantities. The archive room collected his movies in every conceivable medium: digital and analog videotape formatted for consumer and broadcast use, PAL and NTSC DVDs, as well as film cans of the earliest 16mm pictures, and even some reels of 35mm prints.

All of the hard work—from drafting script treatments to final sound mixing—ultimately led here, to the end product. Every time he stepped inside this room, he felt a lift of pride. These were his babies.

Harry Tuttle's *Soul Snatchers*. Harry Tuttle's *Hillbilly Cannibals*. Harry Tuttle's *Ghost House* and its three sequels. And so many others. His legacy.

His *oeuvre*.

Now the struggle began.

Rachel, the beautiful and warm young actress he had met at Richard Metherell's party, had asked to see a few of his films. She was unfamiliar with Scary Harry. Harry was eager to respond.

But which movies? It was a tough decision...best made through a process of elimination.

He ruled out the more violent pictures. The gore might turn her off.

Next, he decided against choosing any of the more recent, super-low-budget ones. The quality might disappoint her.

Finally, he rejected sending any of the old pictures. She would consider him a has-been.

That eliminated almost everything.

Harry started over. He decided to mix up the styles, a Tuttle sampler.

First, an all-out monster movie...*Valley of the Zombies.* Some critics liked that one. A reviewer in a Rockford, Illinois newspaper had said, "A competent chiller with decent effects."

Second, one of his more suspenseful, Hitchcockian efforts, *Frightened Whispers.* It had good acting, fancy camerawork, sharp plot twists, and an interesting mystery at its core. Only a few people got skewered in it. Many of the scares were suggested or subliminal, rather than in-your-face. It was one of his artier works.

Third, *Slash.* A traditional serial killer-on-the-loose thriller featuring a hard-as-nails female FBI agent. A trustworthy premise. Lurid, sure, but *Silence of the Lambs* won a bunch of Oscars, so how trashy could it be? Instead of Anthony Hopkins and Jody Foster, he had a couple of no-names in the lead roles, including the girlfriend of one of his investors, but she was actually damn good; and you could barely notice her reading off the teleprompter.

Three movies, each a little different.

He brought the DVDs into his office and placed them inside a box with bubble wrap. He added the screenplay for *The*

Vampire of Sunset Strip. He handwrote a label from the address she had given him at the party. Then he penned a short note on official PJ Productions stationery, "It was great meeting you..."

His game plan was to pursue Rachel from two angles: for his next movie and for a date. After giving her a few days to review the script and DVDs, he would follow up with a phone call, asking her out to dinner.

Harry's imagination projected the storyline in his head: a perfect dinner would ignite a long-lasting and loving partnership. She would become his leading lady in movies and real life.

He pictured Rachel giving a passionate performance on the set of one of his films, delivering lines he had written with breathtaking precision and soul. He wouldn't even need to direct her; she would know him so well she would read his mind and deliver the performance as he felt it. After a long day of filming, they would go back to his house and unwind in the hot tub. He would rub those marvelous shoulders, lift the tangles of golden hair and gently kiss the back of her neck—

"Harry!" Paul Jacobs entered the room, clapping his hands together.

Harry nearly dropped the box of DVDs.

"I am ready to roll," said Paul. "This is it. You're on your own for the next four weeks. I'll have my BlackBerry and my cell phone. You run the show, big guy."

Paul slapped a piece of paper in front of Harry. "Itinerary."

It listed Paul's travels for the coming weeks. First, Paul was headed to London for an independent film festival. He was sitting on a producer's panel, networking with distributors, and holding digital screenings for his latest movies, including *The Beastly*.

Next, he was headed to Milan for the annual international

film and TV markets conference, essentially a massive tradeshow for the entertainment industry. Distributors and buyers from around the globe would gather to strike deals for theatrical, broadcast and home video rights. Filmmakers would showcase their product. Paul would be joined by Sam Kaplan, his aggressive and well-connected sales agent. They would operate an exhibit stall, meet with foreign rights people, and personally secure licensing on a territory-by-territory basis—far more profitable than leaving it up to a corporate distributor's network and getting ripped off blind.

After the Milan conference, Paul was staying in Italy to be joined by his latest girlfriend, Krystal, for an extended vacation. Paul and Krystal planned to roam the country: Rome, Venice, Florence.

"Krystal says I work too hard and don't spend enough time with her, and she's right. So, after the Milan conference, I'm not going to think about PJ Productions for two whole weeks."

"Hah," responded Harry. "Do you really think you can do it?"

"Of course," said Paul, "because I am leaving the company in your good hands."

"I promise not to burn it to the ground."

"You'll be better off without me. You have everything you need for the vampire picture. The money's in the account. And I want you to know that I upped your budget 25 percent."

Harry looked at Paul, startled. This was unusual. Paul had been systematically tightening the budget for three years. It had been a major bone of contention between them.

"You mean it?"

"The money's all there. Go crazy. Treat yourself to some special effects, some stunts, a car chase, I don't know, maybe get some name talent. Your call. You've never let me down, so this is my thank you. Here's the catch: I want you to deliver a home run."

"I'll do my best."

"Good enough." Paul checked his watch. "The limo is going to be here in five minutes. Have I forgotten anything? I shipped eight boxes ahead of me. Press kits, posters, screeners, continuity scripts for foreign language dubbing..."

"Whatever you forget, I can send to you."

"I wish you were coming along, partner. We are going to wheel and deal like nobody's business. Sam is pumped. Say, did I ever tell you how big you are in Sweden?"

"Sweden?" Harry always took Paul's grandiose claims with a grain of salt. While he could never really determine the extent of his name recognition overseas, he knew one thing for sure: in Los Angeles, where it mattered, he was small potatoes. That's why his wife had left him for a well-known, brand-name director of action epics.

Harry's career had left her unfulfilled.

Paul's eyes caught the label on Harry's box of DVDs. "Rachel Stoller?"

Harry said, "She's an actress I met at Richard Metherell's party. I want her in my next movie."

"Is she cute?"

"Very."

"Ask her if she'll do a topless scene."

"Knock it off."

"You know it would help shift units." Paul walked over to the window and surveyed the traffic on Wilshire Boulevard. "The limo better not be late. It's going to take forever to get through international."

Harry finished sealing the box that held the script and DVDs. He stared at Rachel's name on the label.

He wondered which movie she would watch first. Which one she would like best. He imagined her in his next horror movie. He wondered if she had a good scream...

7

Harry buried himself in preproduction details for *The Vampire of Sunset Strip*. He drafted a 21-day shooting schedule, worked on the script breakdowns, secured the proper location agreements and filming permits, arranged equipment rental, and assembled a cast and crew from his file cabinet of resumes and headshots. Many of his first choices were available, and if not, he had a deep stock of trusted alternatives. His favorite affordable director of photography was available, and his second-favorite sound guy. It was a mix and match of talent he had worked with before. A smooth operation oiled by familiarity.

Ultimately, only one position remained unfilled: the role of Moon, the sexy and vibrant girlfriend of Ronos the vampire hunter. Harry had reserved that role for Rachel. By now, she would have received the script, along with the DVDs of choice prior works. In a few days, he would follow up with an offer. He couldn't wait to put the lens on her.

With Paul traveling, Harry worked alone, putting in long hours at the PJ Productions offices. Paul called nearly every day to report his progress in the international marketplace. To begin one call he declared, "You're a god in Malaysia!"

Harry shrugged off the hyperbole. Perhaps they had dumped a lot of product there, but he had yet to run across Harry Tuttle fan clubs anywhere on the globe.

The first day of principal photography for *The Vampire of Sunset Strip* was scheduled for the following Thursday. Harry had rented a cheap soundstage in the worst part of East L.A., and started storyboards for the death scene of a medical lab technician. In the scene, the handsome young technician discovers evidence of a vampirism virus transmitted by sexual contact, which is rapidly spreading throughout the Hollywood youth culture. Before the technician can go public with his discovery, two vampires confront and kill him in his lab, slashing his throat with a broken test tube and dining on his blood.

Harry liked the scene and hoped to create an AIDS allegory with the vampirism virus: intimacy can lead to becoming a member of the walking dead. He prepared the call sheet and shot list, noting props, and putting together a list of ASAP tasks for his PAs. He was feeling good and organized about things when the phone rang.

Not the outside ring, but the intercom buzz. It was Kelly. PJ Productions shared a receptionist on the fourth floor with an entertainment attorney and a literary agent. Kelly sat behind a barren desk near the elevators and spent much of her time reading paranormal romance novels.

"A Mr. Stegman to see you," said Kelly.

"I don't know a Mr. Stegman," said Harry.

Harry heard a male voice in the background, "Tell him it's important."

"He says it's important," said Kelly.

"Fine. Let him through."

Harry grunted and stood up from his desk, immediately greeted by aches, and a head rush from sitting all day. He advanced down a skinny corridor that connected his office, Paul's office, the screening room, a conference room, two storage areas, and a small kitchenette. He followed the path to a sitting area just inside the company entrance. The entrance itself created the impression of grandeur: two heavy glass doors, adorned with the company logo in silver, with brass fittings. Harry often wondered if the doors cost more than some of his movies.

A tall, pasty young man stood behind the glass. To Harry, he appeared indistinguishable from a lot of other young Hollywood males working hard to look hip: ponytail, goatee, black turtleneck. Upon closer inspection, Harry could see evidence that this youngster was weathered beyond his years. The hair looked greasy and dark bags hung under his eyes. He looked undernourished.

His hands clutched a manila envelope.

Harry tugged open the heavy door and the young man seemed to gasp.

"Harry Tuttle," he said.

"Afraid so," said Harry.

"It's an honor to meet you. I hope I'm not disturbing anything."

"Not really."

The young man stuck out his hand and exclaimed, "I'm Marcus Stegman."

Harry shook it. "Hello, Marcus."

After a silent moment, the young man said, "You don't recognize the name?"

Harry thought for a minute. Maybe they had worked together on a project? But the name and face did not register. "No. I'm sorry..."

"I've written you several times. I'm a filmmaker. I wrote to you about my movie, *Deadly Desires*."

Harry still couldn't make a connection. "We get a lot of unsolicited pitches, I really can't remember..." In reality, most of the unsolicited pitches got pitched.

Marcus Stegman looked anxious, and his entire body seemed to fidget. "Are you free for just a few minutes? I promise I won't take long."

Harry suppressed a big sigh. "Sure. I guess. A few minutes." He really didn't like this type of thing: someone he didn't know showing up unannounced to sell himself. As entry into the industry got more competitive, people were getting more aggressive. Once, a screenwriter wannabe waited for him in his driveway and wouldn't take no for an answer until Harry threatened to call the police.

Harry led Stegman into the PJ Productions conference room, flipping on the lights. "I've only got a few minutes," he warned. "I'm in preproduction."

Stegman marveled over the posters on the walls. "Wow. *Schizo Sisters... Swamp Monster... Hillbilly Cannibals*."

Has he really seen them, or is he bullshitting me? Harry wondered.

"I loved the pitchfork-in-the-eye scene in *Hillbilly Cannibals*," said Stegman, and Harry smiled. At least this guy had done his homework.

"Thank you, Marcus. Have a seat."

They sat.

Stegman began the conversation with a declaration, "Mr. Tuttle, I am the world's biggest horror movie buff. I know that sounds exaggerated, but it's true. I've been a fan of your work since the beginning. I really admire what you do."

"Thank you," said Harry. "I appreciate that." He found his spirits lifted and realized that it had been a long time since someone had spoken highly of his work—not counting Paul, who was a professional bullshitter.

"You and me, I like to think we're kind of similar," said Stegman. "You see, I'm also a filmmaker. My focus is horror films. I'm just getting started, but I'm very good. Right now, I'm just trying to break into the business. I don't know if you're looking for writers or directors..."

Stop right there. Harry didn't want the young man to get his hopes up. "Frankly, we're a very small company," he said. "I do all the writing and directing."

Stegman persisted. "I think I could be a real asset to your company. I could help build your success. Let me give you some context. I have studied the horror genre all my life, from top to bottom, across the history of cinema. The silents, the Universal classics of the thirties, the Hammer pictures, Roger Corman, George Romero, Wes Craven, and on and on. You should see my collection of memorabilia. I have old posters and soundtracks. I used to have a dog named Kolchak, after the TV series. I just love horror. I know horror. And now I have a horror movie of my own." He placed the manila envelope on the table. "Please, I know your time is valuable, but I'd like you to look at it."

Harry chose his words carefully. "I'd be willing to look at your script, but I'm really busy with my next picture, so it might not be for..."

"No, no. It's not a script, it's a *movie,*" said Stegman.

Harry blinked. "You already filmed it?"

Stegman took the envelope and shook out a DVD case. He passed it across the table to Harry. "I shot it on digital video, did all the editing on an iMac, burned it to disc. The movie is done. I need your help and advice on how to sell this and get it out."

"Congratulations," said Harry. He opened the plastic case, finding a shiny DVD-R with *Deadly Desires* handwritten on the surface. "This is no small feat. I know how hard it is."

"My God, you don't know the half of it," said Stegman. "I have worked twenty-hour days, seven days a week, for months. I have maxed out a half dozen credit cards and taken out loans. I have dodged the unions, called out favors, begged, borrowed and stolen to make this movie. But you know what: all that stress and penny pinching, I think it actually helped. I don't like horror films that are really slick and expensive, because you can see all the filmmaking on the screen. They use famous stars, elaborate special effects and steadicams—you just know it's all a production, so you never get scared. You can see the machinery. That's why I like your stuff—it's direct, it's in-your-face. So is mine. Mr. Tuttle, I have a horror movie that delivers real scares."

Harry Tuttle smiled and stood up.

"Well then, I look forward to checking it out. Again, it may not be soon. I'm up to my eyeballs in my next picture, but I promise I'll take a look. Your contact information is on here?"

Stegman nodded. "On the case." He appeared startled that Harry was moving to end the meeting. Harry felt guilty because this guy wanted to chat, but he simply didn't have an hour or two to spare, to discuss this kid's project and the history of horror films.

Harry moved to the door, and Stegman had no choice but to rise from the table and follow.

"What's your next picture about?" asked Stegman.

"Vampires," said Harry, continuing to the front entrance.

"My favorite vampire movie is the original Nosferatu," said Stegman, trailing behind him. "Max Schreck. Do you think Schreck really was a vampire?"

"There's not a lot of history on him. He was a bit of an enigma, so it's easy to speculate."

"Wouldn't it be awesome if he really was a vampire?"

They reached the glass doors.

Harry stuck out his hand. "Nice meeting you, Marcus. Best of luck to you."

As they shook hands, Harry felt something drop on his wrist. He looked down. It was a red spot of blood.

He pulled back his hand.

"Shit, sorry," said Stegman.

Harry looked at him, startled.

Stegman had a bloody nose.

"I get these all the time," said Stegman, tipping his head back, feeling in a pocket. "Ever since I was little. I have a deviated septum, born with it. I hope I didn't freak you out. Here..." Stegman produced a tissue and offered it to Harry.

Harry wiped the spot of blood off his wrist. Stegman took another tissue and held it to his nostril. "Such a nuisance," he said. "Great timing, huh?"

"Don't worry about it," said Harry. He couldn't wait to wash his hands with lots of soap.

They exchanged farewells.

Stegman departed for the elevators, head still tilted, tissue pressed against his nose.

Harry quickly went to the kitchenette to clean his hands, disturbed. *Yuck. What if I had an open cut? Who knows what I could catch from him?*

After thoroughly scrubbing his hands with soap and water, he retrieved the DVD from the conference room.

"*Deadly Desires*," he mumbled to himself. He slipped the plastic DVD case back into the manila envelope.

Harry walked down the corridor and took a left into one of the storage rooms. He flipped a light switch and said hello to the monster known as Mount Slushmore.

Mount Slushmore was the name he and Paul had given to the big pile of unsolicited screenplays, treatments, query letters, tapes and DVDs they received from Hollywood hopefuls. Everyday, the mail delivery brought more. It was staggering and heartbreaking to see dreams pour into the office and unceremoniously get dumped into the slush pile. Harry always had good intentions of reviewing some of the submissions, maybe even responding to a few with constructive criticism; but it was a bottomless pit and there was never enough time. Also, it was sadly unrewarding. Many of the scripts were in the wrong format, the wrong length, or simply horribly written. Too many of them were blatant rip-offs of existing movies. People even sent in scripts featuring characters or adapting books they didn't even have the rights to. And most of the tapes and DVDs were simply unwatchable.

It was no secret how the submissions found them. The mailing address of PJ Productions had wound up on web sites and in directories catering to the legions of wannabe moviemakers. So every day Mount Slushmore grew bigger and bigger, out of control, the potential subject for its own horror film perhaps. Every six months, Harry and Paul sent the stacks off for recycling. The following day, a new pile was born.

Harry placed Marcus Stegman's envelope on the top of

the pile. In a couple of days, it would be buried beneath more scripts and pitches, disappearing from view. It made Harry sad for a moment.

He stepped out of the storage room and turned off the lights. The door closed, and Mount Slushmore went dark.

8

Rachel Stoller stepped into her apartment and almost got kicked in the head. Her roommate Maria was rehearsing dance moves for a music video for the hip hop group Dog Bowl, scheduled for taping the following morning on an outdoor basketball court in South Central LA. A compact stereo pounded out beats from a prerelease CDR, and she did not hear Rachel enter the room.

After the near miss, they both broke up laughing. "Join me, girl," said Maria, and Rachel dumped her purse and portfolio, and started to bump and grind alongside Maria, trying to mimic her moves. They were hopelessly out of sync, and then Rachel banged into a coffee table and swallowed her gum.

Maria turned off the stereo, laughing again. "I think you should audition for the Comedy Channel."

"Great, a bruise," said Rachel, clutching her shin. "Good thing I don't have any modeling gigs coming up."

"You could do an ad for Band-Aid," said Maria.

Rachel wobbled over to the couch and fell into a seated position. She put her feet on the coffee table. "I'm wiped."

"How was the audition for the pilot?"

"A cattle call. The whole town was there."

"So were you any good?"

"It was just a cold read, no sides. I didn't stink, but I didn't blow anybody away, either."

"Maybe my dance instructor could get you in some music videos."

"I'm not a dancer," said Rachel. "I want to act."

"Sometimes you have to take what you can get so you can get some exposure."

"Been there, done that," said Rachel. She had performed in her share of commercials for cell phones, slim wear pantyhose, and yogurt. Because of her youthful face, she had been cast in cornball PSAs for teen runaways and teen alcoholism. She had appeared as an extra in crowd scenes and accepted nonspeaking roles as "customer number 3" or "girl reporter number 2."

"I want a big, meaty role with range," she told her roommate. "Something dramatic I can really sink my teeth into."

"Sure thing, honey," said Maria. "You and about a million other girls."

Rachel threw a sofa pillow at her. She was used to Maria's tough talk. They had been close for more than a year, first meeting through a "roommate wanted" classified in the *L.A. Weekly.* Maria was a Hispanic model from Texas, a former cheerleader. She marketed her good looks and had no interest in acting. "I don't feel comfortable speaking other people's words," she once said.

Rachel, on the other hand, was a native Californian with family roots in the entertainment industry and a strong passion for acting. Rachel's father was a production designer, and her mother had worked many years in wardrobe and now owned a boutique on La Cienega Boulevard. They began whisking

Rachel to auditions before she was old enough to speak. Rachel the infant appeared on television and in print ads for everything from diapers to baby food. During high school, she was among the youngest students to take classes at the famed Creative Actor's Workshop and study under Grant Pole, a method guru.

After high school, she attended UCLA for two years, an inevitable drama major. She performed in local stage productions at the Footlights Playhouse and specialized in Children's Theater. On the side, she auditioned for TV roles, sometimes landing small parts, but more frequently losing plum opportunities by a millimeter. She seemed to be everybody's favorite second choice.

After leaving UCLA, Rachel moved to West Hollywood, a wonderful madhouse of 40,000 people packed into less than two square miles. Her first roommate, Margaret, another fledgling actress, went broke after six months and retreated to Seattle to teach grammar school. Soon after, Rachel moved in with Maria; and they hit it off right away.

Maria had a fierce and contagious energy. She showed Rachel how to market herself, finding her a better talent agency, encouraging her to create a personal web site, and helping her to spice up her bland resume.

Maria also shared her boyfriend's subscription copies of *Backstage* with Rachel, circling promising opportunities with a red marker.

"We gotta help each other," said Maria, "because no one else will. It's dog-eat-dog, cat-eat-cat out there."

As Rachel sat on the couch, feeling the pain from her shin subside, she noticed a small box on the coffee table and asked about it.

"Special delivery to Rachel Stoller," said Maria, picking it up and handing it to her. "It came this morning."

Rachel looked at the return address. "Harry Tuttle, PJ Productions. Hey, this is the director I met at that party last weekend. He said he was going to send me a script and some of his movies."

"Awesome," said Maria. "Open up, let's see."

Rachel found a pair of scissors and used the blade to slice the packing tape. She opened the flaps on the box. Maria watched over her shoulder.

A shrieking, bloody face greeted them.

Maria wrinkled her nose. "What the heck is that?"

Rachel took out three DVDs packaged in bright, lurid slipcase art.

Maria read the titles out loud: "*Valley of the Zombies... Frightened Whispers...Slash.*"

"Horror movies," said Rachel.

"So he wants to paint you up like a zombie or something?"

Rachel laughed. "I don't know." She reached into the box again and took out a screenplay, roughly one-hundred pages bound by two brass brads.

"*The Vampire of Sunset Strip!*" said Maria, and she broke out laughing. "Oh well, I guess there's an audience for everything."

Rachel took the *Valley of the Zombies* DVD case and opened it. "Let's check this out."

She turned on the television and inserted the disc into the player. Then she joined Maria on the couch, and they watched the first ten minutes of the movie.

The silence was broken when Maria said, "This is really bad."

Rachel shrugged. "It is what it is. He makes monster movies."

"Is this how you want to launch your career?" asked Maria. "As some kind of low-budget scream queen?"

She sighed. "Probably not."

"I mean, do these things ever get shown anywhere? I've never heard of these titles. He probably makes them in the basement with his allowance money."

They both erupted into laughter.

Maria opened the screenplay to *The Vampire of Sunset Strip* to a random page and began reciting some of the dialogue aloud, in a cartoony voice. Rachel giggled.

"This is bad," said Maria.

"How do you know? Maybe your reading is bad," teased Rachel. "You're the one who says you're not an actress."

"Fine, you read it." Maria flipped the script into Rachel's lap.

She scanned a few pages. She read through part of a scene, then said, "It's not so bad. Believe me, I've seen worse. It's a horror movie, it's not supposed to be *Othello*."

Maria said, "Sure, it could be a great movie, but if nobody sees it, what's the point? Have you ever heard of this guy before?"

"I don't follow these types of movies."

"Who does? I'll tell you who: creeps and wackos who like to watch blood and guts. This guy's probably a pervert."

Rachel said, "You're not being fair. I met him. He's actually a very nice guy."

"That's what they say about all serial killers."

Rachel moved the script off her lap. "Maria, you crack me up."

"I'm not half as funny as these movies. So, what are you doing tonight?"

"Tonight?"

"One of the choreographers for the video gave me tickets to see Shellshock at the Roxy. I think it's sold out."

"Sure," said Rachel. "I'm up for it. Any cute guys in the band?"

"Yes. Just stay away from the bass player," said Maria. "He's mine."

On the television screen, a pair of zombies in tattered clothing staggered across a graveyard, arms outstretched.

Rachel grabbed the remote for the DVD player. She pressed stop.

9

Fatty Arbuckle, wearing silk pajamas and a robe, chugged from a can of Mountain Dew. Harry bumped past Arbuckle on his way across Stage 18 on the Paramount lot, trying to keep up with the pimply production assistant. The soundstage had become a large, disheveled San Francisco hotel suite from the 1920s, the backdrop for a wild, prohibition-era party. A team of set decorators positioned liquor bottles, tipped glasses, scattered clothing, jazz 78s, and a large Victrola. Extras gathered on the sidelines, a parade of show girls with short hair, bare arms and legs, and baggy dresses with plenty of fringe.

"I just saw her here a couple of minutes ago," said the PA, and then his attention was pulled away by an actress looking for her wig, and a gaffer complaining about craft services.

Harry continued forward, alone, into the hotel suite, carefully avoiding cables and lighting equipment, studying faces on the extras. Not her...not her...not her...

Wait, it *is* her.

His eyes bounced back to one of the show girls. It was Rachel, barely recognizable. She wore a short, sleek peroxide-blond wig, a black headband, long eyelashes, and a black feather boa.

She spoke to another costumed extra, gesturing with a 12-inch cigarette holder. The layers of fringe on her black dress swayed with every move. She wore fishnet stockings, legs exposed from the knee down.

She was beautiful in any era.

Harry walked over, waited for a pause in Rachel's conversation, and greeted her.

She looked at him for a moment before remembering his name. "Harry. Harry Tuttle, right? How are you? What brings you here?"

"Well, you know, I do a lot of business on the Paramount lot. It's like my second home," he lied.

In actuality, Harry had gained entry to the set through an old friend, Shawn O'Malley, who happened to be Director of Photography on the project.

"So this is the roaring twenties," said Harry. "I feel like I just stepped off a time machine. Are you having fun?"

"Sure—when the camera's rolling. Otherwise, it's a lot of hurry up and wait. I'm here all day for about two minutes of screen time."

"Do you have any lines?"

"No. I just get drunk on bathtub gin and dance on the bed."

"Even better."

"Yeah, it's my Oscar moment. I'm attending a party thrown by Fatty Arbuckle, a comedian from the silent movie days. He gets accused of raping and murdering a chorus girl."

"Ah, yes. Virginia Rappe. The first Hollywood scandal."

"That's the part I really wanted. Instead, I got flapper number three."

"Pleased to meet you, flapper number three." Harry then

switched his tone to something more businesslike. "Listen, I don't want to take up too much of your time, but I did come here with a purpose. I hope you got the package I sent. I'm in preproduction for my new movie, and I have a role saved just for you. I'd like to make you a formal offer. I can work through your agent, or we can talk direct, whatever you'd like."

Her bland expression immediately sent him warning signals. She struggled for the right words, but he knew what was coming. It created a sinking feeling in his gut.

"Harry..." she said. "I really appreciate your interest. But I have to be honest. I watched the films you sent, and I took a look at the script; and it's just not the right vehicle for me right now, at this time in my career."

"Oh," said Harry. He mustered a smile. "That's fine, that's okay."

"Maybe another time, another project," she offered, but it wasn't very convincing.

Harry found himself rambling, apologizing for the quality of his own work. "I know, the movies aren't very good. You can be honest. I don't like them all that much either. Sometimes they're embarrassing to watch. It's the budgets. They're real small — but they're getting better. We're really restricted —"

"Maybe some other time."

"Sure. Some other time. Absolutely."

An assistant director started barking orders to the crew. People began moving at a faster pace.

"I have to go. They're setting up the next shot," she said.

"Sure," said Harry. "Have a good shoot. Tell Fatty 'Hi' for me. Whatever you do, don't let him take you into the bedroom."

She laughed and said, "Right."

He watched Rachel join the other flappers as they prepared for the next scene. Harry turned to leave and nearly knocked into a tabletop of liquor bottles. He eyed the display, still dazed. *A highball would be nice right now...*

"Sir, please don't touch the props. You'll mess up the continuity. We need you to clear the set."

It was another one of the ubiquitous PAs. Some kid half his age.

"Sure," said Harry. "Sorry. I'm leaving."

He saw Shawn O'Malley huddling with his technician crew, laboring over the framing and lighting. Harry waved goodbye to Shawn, but Shawn did not see him.

Harry left the soundstage and stepped into an alley on the Paramount lot. A small cart honked, angry, and zipped around him. Two hulking medieval warriors in full armor sat in the back. One of them spoke into a cell phone.

Harry drove home to Eagle Rock, a neighborhood in northeastern L.A. His house, nestled in dense foliage, wasn't large by any means, but today it felt oversized. He wandered from room to room, restless.

Aside from the heartbreak of rejection, he now had a big production problem to deal with. He had a hole in his cast.

His new movie would soon enter principal photography. Rachel's part needed to be filled immediately. Who would be available on short notice?

As Harry paced, he brainstormed for possible actresses. Frances Walker was a safe bet. Frances worked part-time for an L.A. insurance broker, acted on the side, and was always game to ditch work to appear in a movie. She had appeared in several of his pictures, willing to do just about anything, including portraying a corpse with a mouthful of live worms.

Harry called Frances. She said yes, but asked if she could bring Tiny, her poodle, to the set.

"Sure," said Harry, even though he had promised his sound guy that he would never allow Tiny near the set again, after some ill-timed barking caused a rash of ruined takes on *Surfer Psycho*.

Harry slid a Budget Gourmet Fettuccini with Chicken and Broccoli into the microwave. He turned on the small kitchen television as he waited for dinner to heat up. After clicking through a variety of channels, he landed on the start of *Flick Picks*, a popular movie review program hosted by Walter Wiggins, a short, tubby critic from the *Los Angeles Star*.

Wiggins always wore outrageously tacky clothing. He spoke with a harsh lisp and sat in the front row of a mock-up movie theater as clips played on the silver screen.

After the bouncy theme song, Wiggins addressed the camera.

"Greetings from the front row. I'm Walter Wiggins and this is *Flick Picks*, your movie guide. To start off this week's show, we're going to look at a growing trend: ultra-cheap movies that never reach the movie theater. Instead, they go direct to video, where they're mass-marketed among legitimate titles to an unsuspecting public."

Harry froze. He moved closer to the television, eyes fixed on the screen.

The microwave dinged. Harry ignored it.

Wiggins showed a clip from Harry Tuttle's *Swamp Monster*. Totally out of context, without the proper establishment of mood and build-up of tension. The monster pursued his victim through a darkened beach house, upsetting wicker furniture in his path with a dramatic "*Urrrgh.*"

Wiggins said, "One such movie is the incredibly bad *Swamp Monster*. Shot on a home-movie budget with bad acting, bad directing, bad editing and—well, bad everything—this DVD is just one of many phony flicks polluting the film industry."

Another clip from *Swamp Monster* played: the creature peeking in a cabin window to watch a well-endowed young woman in bra and panties prepare for bed.

Wiggins continued in voice over, "Look closely and you'll actually see a *zipper* running up the back of the Swamp Monster's costume. It would be funny if it weren't so sad for all those folks who are wasting good money on these losers."

Harry couldn't take it anymore and snapped off the television. He stared into the dead screen. He could see his reflection. He didn't budge. The shattering critique from Wiggins echoed in his head.

First Rachel's rejection. Now Wiggins' public humiliation, syndicated from coast to coast.

It was too much to bear.

Harry shut his eyes. He spoke out loud, uttering the dismal truth, releasing a heartfelt confession, summing up his entire life and career in two simple words that hung in the air like rotten fruit on a dead tree.

"I suck."

10

Harry didn't always suck.

The evidence lived in scrapbooks neatly stacked on a shelf of his bedroom closet. Harry dragged them into the light and sat on the floor, turning the thick pages. The yellowed clippings greeted him like an old friend.

Good reviews. Pleasant critics. Enthusiastic labels like "suspense master," "skillfully scary," and "Hitchcockian."

He read through two scrapbooks and tried to feel better, but it actually made him feel worse. All that potential...down the toilet. Instead of a career that steadily got better, he had gone into a long and painful decline.

The joy of making movies had faded like old film stock. It had been left behind with his youth.

Deeper in the back of his closet, behind the scrapbooks, a shoebox held several reels of Super 8 shorts created during childhood: *Super Pickle*, *The Mummy Strikes Back*, *Return of the Mummy Strikes Back*, and several unauthorized sequels to *Star Wars* on a dime store budget.

He recalled the pure, simple pleasure these films brought to him. He made them with his closest friends, regardless of talent. He held world premieres in his basement, passing out free popcorn and filling folding chairs with classmates and neighbors. The films weren't designed for critical acclaim or mass consumption. They were constructed for his own amusement and satisfaction.

When did my agenda change? Why did he need universal acceptance now to feel decent about himself? Wasn't that the disease that ruled L.A.? It wasn't drugs or booze. It was the applause. Applause junkies. Love me, love me, love me...because I don't love myself.

Harry decided to start the next day fresh, flushing Rachel's rejection and Wiggins' scorn out of his mind.

At 7 a.m., he meditated.

At 8 a.m., he played a new age CD by Kami, master of the soothing, floating synthesizer chords.

At 9 a.m., he sat in his favorite Beachwood coffee shop and read *Daily Variety* while sipping a strawberry frappuccino and nibbling on a raisin bagel.

Finally he was feeling good again...relaxed even...until he read the article about *Army of Steel.*

Budgeted at $110 million, *Army of Steel* was destined to be the next Hollywood blockbuster. The sci-fi action extravaganza had been designed by committee to launch a lucrative franchise. The big studio marketing muscle would crush all other films in its path.

The movie's plotline was simple but effective: in the future, to combat growing terrorism on U.S. soil, Los Angeles introduces a new breed of homeland security, part cop, part soldier, all machine. The prototype is a warrior named Simon Borg (aka Si Borg). Simon performs admirably, but must be retired when he sheds a tear, revealing a fatal flaw: human compassion. For Version 2.0, the aggression level is boosted and the sensitivity element lowered. The new cyborg patrol is activated and hits the street, attacking crime. However, a doomsday fanatic downloads a virus into the machine men and turns them against their own country. Simon Borg comes out of retirement to battle the bad 'bots before they can carry out their orders to set off a string of underground nuclear blasts that will trigger massive earthquakes throughout the West Coast. Millions of lives are at stake. Only Simon can save them.

The movie had already secured various merchandising tie-ins, including action figures, toys, video games, comic books, and a promotional campaign with a major soft drink brand. The studio planned a parade of sequels.

In a few weeks, *Army of Steel* would begin shooting on location throughout Los Angeles. Entire city blocks would be closed down for elaborate action sequences. The media buzzed with manufactured excitement. *Army of Steel* had been presold to the public.

The big studio bombast, relentless marketing machinery, and crass commercialism annoyed Harry, as always, like seeing a bully flaunt his strength. But that was how the game was played. He was resigned to the system and the way it barely allowed breathing room for smaller, independent pictures.

The *Army of Steel* movie by itself did not send Harry's heart sinking into his gut. Rather, the crushing blow was delivered by two names he discovered in the fine print: his ex-wife and her new husband.

Julie and Nigel Howard. *Army of Steel*'s leading lady and celebrated writer-director, recently pronounced one of Hollywood's hottest couples by their publicist.

Harry saw their names amid all the hyperbole, and felt the

wind knocked out of him. He was still fully convinced Julie had left him because he never graduated from his "rinky-dink" low-budget horror pictures.

Now she had found her perfect man.

"She's my leading lady on set and off," read a quote from Nigel. "I am excited by the opportunity to make her a major star in a major movie."

Harry put down the paper.

First, Rachel's personal rejection. Then Wiggins' public ridicule. And now his ex-wife's sudden rise to stardom, portraying the love interest of a cyborg, featured in a "movie classic in the making" by her new husband.

Harry felt tension branch through his body, followed by a blast of self-pity, wrapped in a layer of deep melancholy.

All that meditation down the drain.

He ditched *Variety* and left the Village Coffee Shop. He drove to the offices of PJ Productions. He entered the building and hurried to his office, sat down at his desk, and began making phone calls.

He pounded a stake through the heart of *The Vampire of Sunset Strip*. He contacted the cast, the crew, his locations, and told everybody the same thing: shooting had been canceled. The movie had been shelved.

He apologized. He took full responsibility. He would pay kill fees out of his own pocket.

Harry simply had no motivation left in him to make another movie. All inspiration and confidence had ground to a halt. He couldn't go on.

During Harry's calls, Paul Jacobs left a voicemail, "Hey, Harry, just checking in. How's the new movie going? I know I'm going to love it."

Harry didn't call Paul back. He didn't know what to say to Paul's phony, jabbering enthusiasm. He just couldn't deal with it right now.

By the end of the day, Harry had contacted everyone, including the equipment rental companies. *The Vampire of Sunset Strip* had turned to dust.

The movie no longer existed except as 108 pages of drivel on three-hole punch paper, held together by two brass fasteners. Printed words that would never come to life. He picked up the script from his desk and walked it down the corridor to a storage closet. He opened the door and approached Mount Slushmore.

Harry chucked *The Vampire of Sunset Strip* on the pile. It joined the paper graveyard of dozens of other dead scripts, treatments and pitches.

As Harry prepared to turn out the light and leave, his eye caught a glimpse of the movie Marcus Stegman had given him.

He stopped and looked at it for a moment. The manila envelope rested near the top of the pile, close to falling off the edge.

Harry thought, *Maybe it will cheer me up to see somebody crappier than me.*

He picked up the envelope and brought it with him into the screening room.

Harry opened the plastic slipcase and snapped the disc free, popping it into the DVD player. The machine hummed into action. He shut the door, killed the lights, and plopped himself into a chair.

The opening credits appeared in crude lettering over the backdrop of a deep, moonlit sky.

MARCUS STEGMAN PRESENTS

followed by

DEADLY DESIRES

followed by

**WRITTEN AND DIRECTED
BY MARCUS STEGMAN**

Harry sighed. "Could use some music," he mumbled to himself. After a few more credits, the camera panned several tents, and then reached a faded sign in English and Spanish. *Teotihuacan Camping Grounds.*

Harry sat back, crossed his arms in front of his chest, and watched the movie unfold.

* * *

Ninety-one minutes later, the film concluded and the screen went black.

Harry couldn't move. His heart pounded madly. The back of his shirt stuck to his seat with sweat. Nothing had prepared him for the gut-wrenching tension and onslaught of terror he had just witnessed. He fought to catch his breath as the real world returned, descending around him like a slow curtain.

With relatively few special effects, a small cast, a tight script, handheld cameras, and an intense, direct shooting technique, twenty-something Marcus Stegman had created a stylish and truly frightening horror film worthy of praise and admiration.

Shaken and surrounded by posters for his own work, Harry faced the realization that this talented young man had crafted a better movie in his first try, than anything Harry had accomplished in his entire career.

And he was intensely jealous.

11

Harry telephoned Stegman and said, "Let's do lunch."

They met at an outdoors café on the Venice Beach Boardwalk, next to an art gallery, overlooking the rollerbladers and volleyball games. The beautiful crowd was out, showcasing hard bodies. The colors of the coastline glimmered.

Stegman wore a battered sports coat and yellow, plastic-rimmed sunglasses. He paced nervously before noticing Harry's arrival.

"Marcus!" greeted Harry.

"Hello, Mr. Tuttle."

"Call me Harry."

They took a small table. Harry ordered a portobello club and iced Chai Tea. Stegman chose the avocado chicken melt and a beer. After the waitress departed with the menus, Harry turned to Stegman, clasped his hands, and said, "So. Marcus. I watched your movie..."

Harry let the suspense build for a moment.

"...and it blew me away."

Stegman blinked. Then he broke into a big grin. "Really?"

"Really."

"I am so psyched. That's great. Was it scary?"

"A couple of times, I nearly soaked my pants."

"Way cool. That's the reaction I want. I want to scare the hell out of people. I want them to jump in their seats. I don't want them to see it coming and then *whammo*!"

"Your technique is dead on. I really like what you did with the shaky, handheld cameras to create that anxious, unsettling texture. You leveraged your limitations to feed the suspense, going for a cinema vérité feel. That's very hard to do without appearing amateurish. I know what you're up against. It's tough to make a low-budget film work in your favor."

"I didn't have much money."

"No, but you have style. Some people have it, some people don't. It's a gift from above. Anybody can write a script. Anybody can point and shoot a camera. But not everybody has style. You got it, kid. Congratulations."

Stegman said, "Thanks. Coming from you, this is a big compliment. I mean, you are the standard."

"Thank you. That's very kind. I try."

They continued discussing *Deadly Desires* until the sandwiches arrived. Then, after Stegman had taken the first bite out of his sandwich—and finished most of his first beer—Harry began the negotiations. Harry told himself—be cool, be slick. Imagine that you are Paul Jacobs, Stanford business grad, wheeling and dealing.

Harry said, "When we spoke before, you talked about some of the financial trouble you encountered in making your film—maxing out your credit cards and so on."

Stegman nodded. "Yes, it's very true. Sometimes I let my artistic vision get in the way of common sense. I'm not in a good place right now with my finances. It's catching up with me. It's really expensive to make a movie—even a low-budget movie—and a no-name like me isn't going to attract a lot of investors."

"You have no track record."

"Exactly."

"You don't have any marquee names attached to your project."

"None at all."

"And you are competing with hundreds, if not thousands of other films that have a lot more clout behind them."

"You know it."

"Yes. I certainly do."

Harry felt positive. He was softening the kid up. They were aligned. Now it was time to make the pitch.

"Marcus, I'd like to make you an offer for your movie."

Stegman put down his sandwich. He straightened in his seat. "Really?"

"Yes. This is a unique offer, so I want you to listen carefully. It involves a lot of money. Do you want to hear me out?"

Stegman said, "I'm all ears."

"I love your film. To be blunt, it's everything that my movies aspire to be. Your movie is skillful; it's dramatic; it's contemporary; it's scary. The bottom line is this: You have some talent. I have some financial success. I suggest we make a trade-off that will benefit both of us."

"A trade-off?"

"I'd like to purchase *Deadly Desires* from you for eight hundred thousand dollars."

Stegman's jaw dropped.

"Eight hundred—?"

"Eight hundred thousand dollars, up front and in cash. Some of it is coming out of my own pocket. Some of it is coming out of the budget I've been allocated for my next movie. The catch is this: Once I buy *Deadly Desires*, I assume full credit. The writing, the directing, the whole thing."

A long pause followed. Stegman took off his sunglasses. He placed them on the table. His tired, dark eyes looked straight at Harry. "Let me get this straight. Eight hundred thousand dollars and then you take all the credit?"

"I'm sure we can find a credit for you someplace. A producer. 'Based on a story by.' We'll work something out. But my name would be attached as writer-director. Essentially, I would be the *auteur*."

"I'm a little confused. I appreciate your interest and the compliments. The money is great, but I just don't know..."

"This is Hollywood reality," said Harry. "For better or worse, I have a brand name. You don't have name recognition. My name can cut through the clutter and get this thing out there where it belongs, in front of the public. That's your goal, isn't it?"

"Yes. I want to make horror movies, and I want the movies to be seen by people."

"You want to reach as large an audience as possible, correct?"

"Absolutely."

"This is your first movie. You're going to have to make a few sacrifices. It's not unheard of. My career got started the same way. Did you ever see *Demonic Possession*?"

"Yes. I love that movie. The Max Argas picture."

"Case in point. Everybody calls it a Max Argas picture. Max Argas barely lifted a finger on that movie. His name was all over it, but essentially I wrote it. I was the director. Max was the big name in the credits, the engine that propelled the movie into the public, but he was hardly ever on the set. That bothered me at first, but when the movie was a big success, my career was launched."

"Wow," said Stegman. "I never knew that."

"It's not unusual. It's done all the time in the publishing industry. You've heard of ghostwriters? They're not only used for celebrity autobiographies. A lot of big name novelists use them so they can crank out more product. You've heard of James Peterson, the best-selling author who writes all those mysteries and thrillers? He doesn't really write them himself anymore. He hires a team of ghostwriters. That's why he has a new book every six months. He might construct the outline or something, but the books are written by other people who get paid good money for their willingness to work anonymously. The brand name ensures distribution and success. Marcus, I want you to be my ghostwriter, my ghostdirector, and I will make you rich in the process."

"I've never been a ghost before," mused Stegman.

"Now's your chance. You might like it."

"To be honest, I need to think about this. It's a lot to take in. I just don't know."

Harry said, "The offer is on the table for one week."

Stegman nodded. "OK. Got it. I'll think about it. I'll let you know in a few days."

The waitress returned and they ordered dessert. Harry chose the apple strudel, but barely touched it. He felt angry and discouraged that Stegman had not snapped up the offer. The kid was playing hard to get. It only made Harry more determined than ever to acquire the film.

After dessert, Harry paid the check and thanked Stegman for hearing him out. Standing up from the table, the two men shook hands. Stegman promised to get back to Harry soon with an answer.

"Just to reiterate," said Harry, "the eight hundred thousand will be in cash. There's no reason that Uncle Sam needs to be involved."

Stegman returned the yellow sunglasses to his head. "It's a sweet offer," he said. "Please understand that I'm very flattered. You're like an idol to me. But I don't know if I want to do this."

"I understand," said Harry.

As they walked the boardwalk together, Harry indulged in a shameless creative fantasy. He couldn't help it. It was the filmmaker in him.

He imagined a scene where Stegman died a dramatic death.

The setting, several minutes into the future. The scene, returning to his car, parked on the curb, the director *wunderkind* inadvertently steps into the path of a speeding truck. Or perhaps he trips when given a strategic push in the right direction by his filmmaking rival.

Harry almost chuckled, thinking, *now there's a wild idea for a movie.* An embittered, jealous, washed-up horror film director, kills a hotshot young director and steals his film to bring his own career back to life.

During his drive home, Harry invented a few more tragic death scenarios for Stegman, including a fallen power line that lit up his skeleton like an old cartoon. The imaginary violence released some of his pent-up stress. It was a terrible habit dating back to his adolescence, but no one ever really got harmed. Nobody could read his terrible thoughts.

In fact, people often asked Harry how such a gentle, well-mannered soul could create such brutal and bloody horror films. Harry's response, the two go together, like yin and yang.

"I release tension through my art rather than aggression," he would explain. "It's my pressure valve. It helps soothe my nerves, just like meditation or a salt bath."

Then they would look at him as if he was crazy.

But Harry would continue defending his point. "Think how better off this world would be today if everyone else lived that way. If all the murderers wrote stories or poems about killing, instead of committing the act. If rapists painted their sexual fantasies. If terrorists expressed themselves through songs rather than bombs. If countries went to war with one another in epic films, funded by the government, and blew each other up on celluloid, with special effects, rather than in real life. Everybody would be better off if we all moved our dark side from fact to fiction. Civilization can save itself through art."

"That's a pretty elaborate justification for your shitty little horror films," responded a drunk television network executive, a few years earlier at a party in Culver City.

While tempted, Harry didn't punch him. He simply nodded. He went to work the next day and named a character after the executive, in his next film. He impaled the character through the chest with a four-foot spear...and made him die slowly.

12

The back screen door was unlocked. George Grubbis slapped it open—to hell with knocking, he *owned* the goddamned house—and entered the kitchen.

Half-eaten food and dirty plates filled the countertops. Junk littered the floor. It made his heart sink. This used to be a nice place...

"Marcus!" he shouted. After a long silence, he said, "I know you're in here. Let's not play hide and seek."

Stegman shuffled shoeless into the room, wearing sweatpants and a T-shirt sporting a cartoon of The Incredible Hulk. His unbundled ponytail released a mess of sprawling black hair.

"I was asleep," said Stegman, eyes blurred.

"Good for you. You still owe me half of last month plus all of this month."

Stegman nodded, listening but noncommittal, like a teenager responding to a nagging parent.

"I want to show you something," said Grubbis, producing a document. "Do you know what this is? It's an eviction notice. See that line near the top? That's where your name goes. Take a look. Read the fine print. It requires the renter to leave the property in 30 days."

Stegman rubbed his face.

"You think I'm bluffing?" said Grubbis.

"No," said Stegman. "I don't. I just need more time. The movie's done. I have an offer on the table. I just don't know if it's the right deal."

"You got an offer?" Grubbis did not suppress his surprise. "A real offer? Then stop screwing around. What's the matter with you? I suggest you take it and use the money to start paying your bills. Otherwise you're going to be sleeping on a park bench. Is that what you want? You owe me—"

"I know I owe you!" shouted Stegman. "I owe a lot of people. I've got credit card companies on my ass. I've got a loan shark who says he's going to put me on crutches. I've got money problems, OK? But I'll get it all sorted out soon."

"Soon's not good enough," said Grubbis. "I've been hearing 'soon' for a long time. Soon is a word that doesn't mean shit."

Grubbis glanced at a table littered with empty wine bottles and beer cans. He shook his head sadly. "You need to get straightened out. Your mother, bless her soul, would be a total wreck if she were alive to see this. Nice bar you've got here. Is this your breakfast? What else are you on? Because I don't think it ends here. Either you've always got a cold or you're shoving crap up your nose again. You know what I'm talking about."

"I need to work long hours."

"You're on a path to self-destruction, Marcus," said Grubbis. "Look in the mirror sometime. You're a kid with an old man's face. What do you want to do that to yourself for?"

"I have a passion in life, and I am following my passion; and I will do everything I can to make it happen."

"And ruin your health in the process?"

"I'm not ruining my health."

"What is it you hope to achieve, exactly?"

"I'm going to be the world's greatest horror movie director."

"Why?"

Stegman appeared startled by the question. He had a hard time articulating a response. "Why? Why? Because...it's all I ever wanted."

Grubbis picked up an empty bottle of cheap wine, looked at the label, and put it back down. "Your mother, bless her soul, brought you into this world and raised you to be something, really be something, but I see nothing. A zero. You're a disgrace, Marcus. And I know you've lived your whole life in this house. It's your momma's womb. But sooner or later, you need to leave the womb and face the big, bad world. I'm not here to take care of you. Your mother had the patience of a saint. But I am not your mother. She's *gone*."

And then Marcus Stegman dropped into a chair and began to cry.

Grubbis watched him for a full minute. The sight was pitiful. A grown man reduced to a shuddering, sobbing child, wearing a cartoon T-shirt, surrounded by piles of garbage and booze bottles.

As Stegman cried, reddened mucous flowed from his nostrils. Grubbis pulled paper towels off a roll and handed them over. "Wipe your nose for Christ's sake."

"I'm sorry," said Stegman, choking back the tears.

"You better clean yourself up and take care of business," said Grubbis. "Because if I have to come back, it will be with a court order. Got it?"

Stegman nodded, face in hands.

Grubbis left him.

13

Harry watched Marcus Stegman's movie several more times, hoping it wouldn't be as good as it was the first time.

It wasn't. It was better.

He felt mixed up inside, a sour stew of emotions. There was bitterness about his own disappointing career, admiration for what this young man had accomplished, anger and jealousy because he hadn't acquired the film, shame for trying to buy ownership of someone else's work, confusion over the ugly vanity that drove his actions, insecurity and doubt about his own artistic abilities, hurt over the ongoing public indifference and hostile critical reception toward his work ,and loneliness.

Loneliness was not necessarily connected to the other things, but an ingredient in the mix, nevertheless. With his business partner gone on an extended trip overseas, his next film canceled, and a profound lack of romance in his life, Harry felt more isolated than he had felt in a long time.

He walked the rooms of his Eagle Rock house, restless. His various televisions chattered to displace the silence. Tuned in to different stations, they kept him company, familiar programs showing themselves like old friends.

Then he saw his ex on E!

He happened to be in the den, sorting through piles of old magazines—*DV* and *Film Comment*—when the chirpy host of an entertainment news program began pumping hype into *Army of Steel.*

Harry had a bad feeling in his gut, and a prickly sensation under his skin. He felt sickened yet curious. The sensation mirrored the time he witnessed a gruesome car wreck on Highway 101. A van filled with Hispanic workers had been crushed by a truck. It was a terrible sight he really did not want to see, yet he had slowed down and rubbernecked, straining to catch a view of the twisted carnage.

Instead of leaving the den or shutting off the TV with the handy remote, Harry rubbernecked. He saw his ex-wife Julie, beautiful with big hair and big teeth, hanging on the arm of writer-director-hotshot phenomenon Nigel Howard. They discussed their blockbuster-to-be like proud parents.

"This movie will have some of the biggest, most exciting action sequences ever filmed," boasted Nigel. "We will be shooting all over Los Angeles. You won't be able to miss us. This entire town will become our movie set. The stunts we have planned will set a new standard for the industry."

The interviewer asked Julie about her role in the movie and if it was awkward being directed by her husband.

"Not at all," said Julie. "We get along so great. He wrote the part with me in mind so we wouldn't be apart. It's such a fantastic script, how could I say no? He's the best."

"He's the director on the set, but who's the director at home?" asked the interviewer playfully.

"I am, of course," laughed Julie.

"She is," chimed in Nigel, giving his wife a playful squeeze.

Harry squeezed the remote and the television shut off.

It was all so cute and adorable that he wanted to puke.

Instead, he meditated.

Today's mantra, success.

He imagined that he was pushing bad thoughts out of his pores. He dispelled the negativity into the air, where it lifted away, evaporating into the atmosphere.

Success, success, success...

Is that the phone?

Yes. I forgot to turn off the damned phone.

Let it go. The machine will get it. Don't swear when you're meditating.

"Uh, Mr. Tuttle, Harry, this is Marcus Stegman..."

Harry jumped up from his meditation rug and dashed for the telephone, grabbing it so frantically that he almost upset a lamp.

"Marcus, I'm here."

"Oh, hi. I'm... I hope I didn't call at a bad time..."

"No. Not at all."

"I'd like to meet about your offer."

"Great. When would you like to meet?"

"How about one hour."

"Fine. I can do that. Where?"

"At the Hollywood Walk of Fame. Let's meet at Bela Lugosi."

"Bela Lugosi?"

"You know, Bela's star."

Harry replied, "Sure. Whatever you want."

* * *

Harry arrived early and searched the sidewalk for Bela. He felt like a tourist, wandering with his head down, reading all the names. Stan Laurel...James Cagney...Big Bird...

Harry found Bela near a Thai restaurant at Hollywood and Vine. He firmly planted his feet inside the charcoal square, stepping on the five-pointed star rimmed with bronze.

"Hello, Bela," he mumbled at the sidewalk.

"Hello, Harry," said Marcus Stegman a few minutes later, walking toward him. He wore a black GWAR rock concert T-shirt, shorts and sandals. His toenails were long and garish. His ponytail was tied tight behind him. His eyes appeared tired and collapsed, sunken in small dark wells.

"Good to see you again, Marcus," said Harry, shaking his hand.

"I'm accepting your offer," said Stegman.

Harry nearly stumbled off the star. "Wonderful." He fought to remain calm.

"It's not like I have a lot of options out there," said Stegman, chuckling without a smile. "Besides, I'm not in this for the fame. I just love making horror movies. It's what I do. If it's going to have your name on it, I can live with that. I'm a Harry Tuttle fan, after all. That's why I came to you in the first place."

"I appreciate that," said Harry. "I think this is a great deal for both of us."

"The money," said Stegman. "It's the amount we discussed?"

"Yes, of course," said Harry.

"Good. And I'd like to ask for one more thing to seal the deal."

Harry gave him a careful look. "One more thing?"

Stegman nodded. "Yes. A special request."

"What is it?"

"Mr. Tuttle, I want your soul."

Harry cocked his head. Had he heard right? "You want... excuse me?"

"Your soul, Mr. Tuttle. I want the soul from your movie *Soul Snatchers.* I collect horror movie props and memorabilia. I've always loved *Soul Snatchers,* especially the scenes where the warlock takes the souls of his victims and you can see the spirits ripped from their bodies, against their will, like a skin being peeled off. It's an amazing image, like that painting, *The Scream.*"

"Sure," shrugged Harry. "The soul is just a prop we cast from a plaster molding. It looks better in the movie, with the lighting gels and effects. I think it's in storage. I don't even know if it's still in one piece, but you're welcome to have it, or any other movie props you want."

"Neat," said Stegman. "Thank you. I'll never forget the first time I saw *Soul Snatchers.* I was fourteen, sick with a fever, and I couldn't sleep because I had slept all day. I'm flipping the channels at one a.m., and there he was, the Master Warlock, the soul snatcher, sucking the essence out of his victims while they slept. And the way the souls screamed when they were removed. How did you make that horrible groaning noise?"

"We just recorded ourselves screaming and slowed down the audio. It wasn't very high tech."

"Yeah, well when I was fourteen, it scared the living hell out of me. It gave me nightmares for a week. I loved it."

Harry said, "Thanks. It's yours. Now let's talk about your movie. When do you think I could get the master elements?"

"Anytime. I can deliver them to your office tomorrow."

"Just so you know, I'm probably going to tinker a little. Remix the sound, change the music, make some minor edits, tighten a few scenes, create a new title sequence."

Stegman said, "Of course. Do what you must. I trust you."

"And remember, in your role as ghostwriter, nobody can know about your true involvement with this movie. I don't even want my business partner to know about it. This is between you and me. We're going to keep it very quiet. Everybody must be under the impression that I wrote and directed *Deadly Desires*. You need to promise me that."

"As your ghostwriter, I shall remain invisible."

"What about the people who worked with you on the picture?"

"It's a small, tightly knit group. We're friends. I'll talk to them."

"All of them will continue to receive credit. They have nothing to lose. Yours is the only name that will be replaced, but you will be paid handsomely for it."

"You bet."

Harry and Stegman shook hands and sealed the deal. "How cool is this?" said Stegman. "Two horror movie mavericks sealing a deal on Bela Lugosi's star. It's good luck."

"Is it?" chuckled Harry. "Bela's last movie was *Plan 9 From Outer Space*, the worst movie of all time. He became a drug addict."

"I'm not a drug addict," said Stegman sharply.

Startled, Harry looked him over. "I didn't say you were."

Stegman blinked a few times, and then babbled nervously to cover up the awkward moment. "No. Of course not. I just prefer to remember Bela's classic period. *Dracula*. *White Zombie*. *Mark of the Vampire*. *Son of Frankenstein*..."

"You really know your horror movies," Harry told him.

"They're in my blood," said Stegman. "You could say I'm

obsessed, and maybe a little weird."

"The same could be said about most of us in the movie business," said Harry. "That's why they call it la-la land. We're all a bunch of weirdos who never grew up, playing in the land of make-believe."

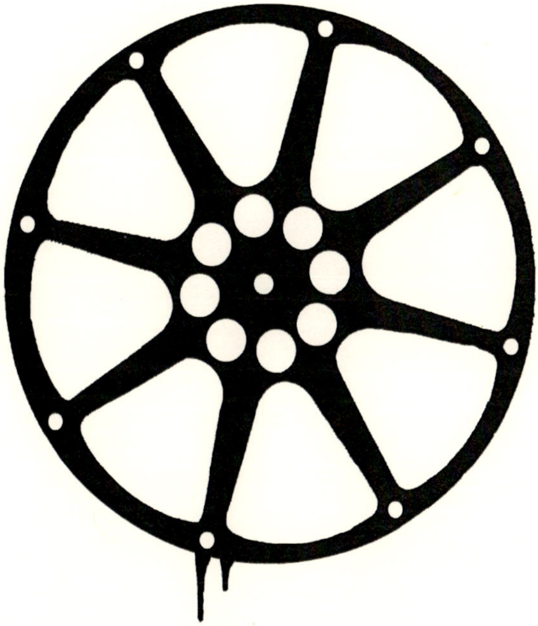

REEL TWO

14

In Pottstown, Pennsylvania, across the street from a closed pizzeria and shuttered beauty salon, Randy Furson began his first day as bartender at the Owl Creek Lounge. The pay was shit, but Randy was happy just to have a job. The owner of Owl Creek, Nick Macero, chewed on the end of an unlit cigar and taught Randy everything he needed to know in twenty-five minutes, including how to operate the clunky, old-fashioned cash register, the terms of the daily "Frosty Mug Special," and how to change the channels on the two color televisions hanging from the ceiling on opposite ends of the bar. Currently, the TVs were tuned to a sports network showcasing rodeo bloopers, watched in rapt attention by the grizzled regulars who sat together—but alone—at the counter.

Owl Creek wasn't much different than many other working class drinking establishments in the Philadelphia area. Two stained pool tables surrounded by a worn tile floor, dominated the back of the room. The walls featured historical framed photos of the neighborhood, and faded promotional posters of chesty cheerleaders in '80s hairdos, hawking cheap domestic beer. A jukebox mixed old country songs with older rock and roll. The limited menu featured barbecue ribs, a barbecue pork sandwich, grilled ham and cheese, and a popular two-dollar hot dog and potato chips platter. Diners couldn't get a good look at their food because the bar had no natural light. The windows had been sealed by brick for decades. Anyone entering the establishment needed to wait a moment for their eyes to adjust, to avoid advancing blindly into the darkness and crashing into one of the raised, round tables. More than one dice game had been interrupted this way, resulting in several patrons getting beat up before they had even tasted their first drink.

The ugliest and most prominent object in the room was a large, moth-eaten moose head securely fixed to the back wall. It happened to be located near the dart game, resulting in drunks gleefully inventing their own game that awarded points for striking Mr. Moose in key locations, including the eyes and nostrils.

Aside from darts, Owl Creek also offered two unintentionally nostalgic games: Pac Man and a bowling game that never worked right and received frequent abuse.

Owl Creek wasn't the worst dive bar Randy had ever seen—that award went to Shank's, where the walls were decorated with hubcaps and the floor smelled like urine—but it definitely carried its own remarkable lack of charm.

As the tutorial wound to a close, and all the liquors and taps had been discussed, Nick grew more serious and gestured Randy close.

"Above all, you gotta understand one thing," said Nick, still sucking on the end of the unlit cigar, soaking it dark with his saliva.

"What's that?" asked Randy.

"See that guy in the way back? Look quick."

"Big guy, bald?"

"Yeah."

"I see him."

Nick took the cigar out of his mouth and moved closer to Randy's ear, speaking in a firm, raspy growl. "Whatever you do, *don't bug him*."

* * *

Lenny grasped his rum and coke tight, and knew that if he continued to squeeze the tall glass it would explode, slashing open his oily, blackened hands and spilling blood.

Sometimes liquor helped to douse the flames of anger. But sometimes it fed the fury like gasoline.

All these months had passed, and he still obsessed with fresh rage over the most profane four-letter word in the world.

Nora.

Wife, bitch, whore. She had walked out on him in the middle of the night, leaving that snotty note, taking her things, vanishing in their car, delivering a shock as cold as a slap to the face and a hard knee to the balls.

Nobody treated Lenny that way. *Nobody*. Especially not the woman who had agreed to be his wife, for better or worse, richer or poorer, forever and into eternity, under the eyes of the Lord almighty and Pennsylvania state law.

In the beginning he was infuriated, but figured he would get over it. Stupid, slinky chicks were a dime a dozen; and he would replace her as easily as getting a new spark plug for his RV.

But it didn't work that way. Instead, the hostility grew. No one took her place. Chicks avoided him, even when he tried real hard to be civilized and mannerly. It was weird, but he could read eyes. People just looked at him funny. They didn't say anything outright, but he knew what they were thinking at the garage where he worked, and at the stores and restaurants he frequented.

Loser.

Everybody knew: His wife had run out on him, symbolically given him the finger and cut off his nuts; and now she was no doubt screwing someone new, and the two of them were *laughing* at him. Maybe at this very minute.

It drove him mad.

And he did some mad things, like shave his head bald. He needed the change, but his life stayed the same; only now he was just a humiliated *bald* big fuck.

Early on, he expected her to return. He could see the scene clearly: Nora coming back to her husband with tears in her eyes. Begging forgiveness. Recognizing the huge mistake she had made. He had figured it would take a week, then recalculated to two weeks, then a month for her to return, tail between her legs, wiser and obedient. But the event only played in his mind. She didn't reappear in the flesh.

As a result, each day his anger increased one notch. Every 24 hours, the severity of her punishment pushed up another degree. Crazy wench, did she know what she was doing to herself?

And God help the son of a bitch she ran off with. He would become so badly maimed and disfigured that he would never steal another man's wife again.

If only he could find them.

Early on, he had tried to beat information out of people, like Nora's boss at Dottie's Diner. After two black eyes and a broken tooth didn't release a confession, Lenny figured the asshole probably didn't really know.

But someone did, somewhere. She must have told somebody about her plan.

Her trail went cold at the Stuckey's parking lot where she ditched the Mercury. The early morning manager said he didn't remember seeing her at all. His story didn't change, even after his head was slammed into the wall several times.

Lenny felt no remorse for the wrongly pummeled.

He finished his rum and coke without pulverizing the glass in his hands. He felt the booze traveling in his veins, starting in his chest, and then moving in trails through his arms and legs. It was a good feeling, and he wanted more.

Lenny looked up toward the bar. He raised his empty glass. He kept it raised.

After a moment, Nick, the owner, noticed the gesture and quickly nodded. Nick nudged the new kid behind the counter and gave him instructions.

Inside of two minutes, the new kid delivered a new rum and coke to Lenny's table.

The new kid looked nervous. First day jitters. It looked like the freckles were going to leap off his face. "Here you go, sir," he said, placing the glass carefully on the table. "Can I get you anything else?"

"No."

"Sounds good," said the kid, and he backed off and left.

Lenny looked at his drink, marveled over how appetizing it looked, then took his first long pull.

The front entrance opened, always a noisy affair, and everyone in the bar looked over to see a skinny older man with a long neck and big Adam's apple. He wore a down coat, ripped at the seams, feathers protruding. He exchanged wordless nods of recognition with some people he knew at the counter, and ordered a beer. The new kid yanked on a tap and began to pour.

Lenny returned his attention to staring at his tabletop. His eyes followed scratches, lines of graffiti, carvings, unidentifiable stains and discolorations. He followed it like a roadmap to an alien landscape. He felt fuzzy in a good way. As he took swallows from his drink, he looked forward to the next glass. And the one after—

"Lenny!"

Lenny jumped. He almost jolted a spill out of his glass. He glanced up, not happy.

It was the scrawny guy with the Adam's apple. He had a face full of stubble. He looked familiar.

"Lenny, don't you remember me? Charlie Bing. We worked together for Sal, the roofing company, remember?"

Lenny vaguely recalled a scorching summer spent on residential rooftops, making repairs and doing resurfacing. He hated the job and the people. The work was seasonal. He quit or got fired when winter arrived and there was nothing to do. It was the first gig he landed after losing his job at the factory that made glass for television sets.

"Yeah, I remember you. You were the guy that was always talking and never shut up."

Charlie laughed and signaled thumbs up. "That's me, Charlie Chatterbox. See, how can you forget? So what're you up to these days, big guy?"

"I'm a mechanic at Berger's Auto Body."

"Great. People always gotta have their cars fixed. And how's that lovely wife of yours, what was her name, Laura?"

Lenny stared at him. Hard. "Nora."

"Nora, right. What a dish. She still working at Dottie's?"

"No."

"She's a sweetheart, way too good for you," Charlie chuckled. "Beauty and the Beast, right? I remember how she would bring you a sack lunch everyday and wear those little dresses. What a tart. So where's she working now, or do you have her chained up inside the house?"

Lenny didn't plan what happened next. It just happened. Somewhere deep inside a switch was turned on, and volcanoes erupted, bombs exploded, tanks discharged, and machine guns raged.

In a matter of seconds, Charlie Bing went from vertical and stationary to horizontal and mobile. His skinny body became a missile, crashing into tables on the other side of the room. He reached the ground for a moment before being lifted again, by his coat, and slammed into Pac-Man with a thundering crash.

"Lenny—!" said Charlie, his one and only word before fists pounded his mouth shut. Charlie's body returned to the floor. A series of savage kicks caused his long torso to curl like a worm pierced on a fishhook. For a short instant, there was a break in the beating; and Charlie used the opportunity to lift himself up on all fours and scramble like a lopsided dog. Lynyrd Skynyrd played on the jukebox. Charlie advanced maybe five feet before Lenny returned with a drinking glass snatched from a tabletop. The glass exploded against the side of Charlie's skull, sending spider claws of blood rolling down his cheek. Glass shards stuck in his scalp, but Charlie couldn't pull them out because his hands were busy defending himself from new punches. The palms-out reaction proved counterproductive when his fingers snapped under the ferocity of Lenny's battering fists.

"Is it funny?" screamed Lenny, eyes ablaze, punches continuing to the face, ribs and abdomen. "You still think it's funny?"

Charlie was too broken and semi-conscious to even shake his head "no." Unfortunately, the nonresponse only made Lenny madder...

* * *

Randy Furson remained frozen behind the bar counter, less than one hour into his new job, witnessing the worst violence in his seven years of bartending in the Philadelphia metropolitan area. He was astonished that none of the regulars rushed to stop the fight. A few of them simply left, very quietly, not allowing the big entrance door to slam behind them. The owner, Nick Macero, watched the proceedings with a frown. Randy kept looking at his face for a clue, *What should I do?*

Finally, Randy asked his boss, "Should I call the police?"

"No," said Nick, removing the wet cigar from his mouth. "Call an ambulance."

15

A jet airliner screamed overhead as Harry arrived at Los Angeles International Airport. Traffic packed the lanes. Harry drove into the lower level of the passenger terminal, inching along, and soon found Paul Jacobs curbside with a towering stack of luggage. Everyone else emerging from the baggage claim areas looked tired, crabby and disheveled. Paul, however, remained his slick and smiling self. His suit didn't have a single wrinkle. Harry pulled over, hopped out of the car, and waved.

"The world famous Harry Tuttle!" Paul shouted, embarrassing Harry. Nearby heads turned, followed by puzzled non-recognition.

Harry popped the trunk and Paul rolled his cart of luggage toward the car, approaching in big steps. "Good to see you, friend," he said, giving Harry a hearty handshake.

"Good to see you, Paul. Welcome home."

They began filling the trunk. "You are *huge* in Turkey," said Paul.

"That's great. How did the trip go?"

"Made us some good money, my friend. Major foreign rights deals. And I've been working the phones like you wouldn't believe. I think we're going to get into Redbox in a big way with *The Beastly.*"

"I don't know how you do it."

"It's called building relationships. Making friends in high places."

They emptied the cart. Before Harry could slam the trunk lid shut, Paul stopped him. "Wait a second." He opened a black duffle bag, fished around, and brought out a small jewelry box.

He handed it to Harry. "This is for you. A little gift from abroad."

Harry held the box. An Italian name in script graced the top. "You didn't have to get me a gift."

"Open it."

Harry opened the lid, revealing an extravagant wristwatch with a gold band. "Wow. Thank you. I don't have a good watch."

"Take it out of the box."

Harry removed the watch. Horns honked behind them.

"Turn it over," said Paul.

Harry looked at the back of the watch. He read the engraving: Scary Harry.

"Very cool," said Harry. "You really didn't have to."

"Yes, I did have to. I knew you needed a new watch. And I wanted to get you something special to say thanks for all you've done. Put it on."

Harry secured the watch on his wrist. "This is such a nice gift. I don't know what to say."

"Tell me about your new movie. I want to hear all about it."

"You don't have to hear about it—you can see it. It's done."

"Holy cow, Harry, you get more speedy with every release. You are the king of efficiency. That is why we love you."

They climbed into Harry's car. As Harry entered the stream of traffic departing from LAX, Paul said, "I've been telling everybody about the new picture. They love the concept. I met some Japanese investors who—"

"Actually," said Harry, "I scrapped the vampire picture. I didn't like the script. I came up with something better."

Paul's expression soured. "But I've been telling everyone we would come out with a vampire picture. Vampires are *in*. They're this year's werewolf."

Harry assured him, "You'll like this better, Paul. Trust me."

Harry dropped off Paul at his Brentwood Park home. After Paul unpacked and cleaned up, he rejoined Harry at the offices of PJ Productions.

Harry already had the DVD in the projection system in the screening room, ready to go.

"Don't I get to go through my mail first?" said Paul. "I've got a hundred things to catch up on."

"No," said Harry. "You have to see this movie. I'm really anxious for your reaction. It's a little different than what I've done before—more edgy and contemporary."

Paul nodded, then smiled. "I haven't seen you this pumped up in a long time. Well, all right. Let's do it."

Paul brought bottled water with him into the screening room and sat in the second row. He also carried a pile of paperwork.

Harry removed the papers from Paul's lap. "No multi-tasking," said Harry. "Shut off the phone. Hands off the BlackBerry. I really want you to watch this one. I'm going to kill the lights."

"I've got jet lag. If you turn off the lights, I might fall asleep."

"You won't fall asleep..."

The room went black. Harry started the movie.

On the large screen, a campfire ignited, followed by superimposed credits.

PJ PRODUCTIONS PRESENTS

followed by

DEADLY DESIRES

followed by

WRITTEN AND DIRECTED
BY HARRY TUTTLE

Soon, the storyline began. A full moon. Several tents. A sign in English and Spanish reading *Teotihuacan Camping Grounds.*

The 91-minute movie unfolded, and Paul watched it in its entirety in silence. Seated in the back, Harry heard no reaction from his typically verbose partner. He wondered if Paul had indeed fallen asleep.

When the picture ended, Harry waited a moment, then stood up and turned on the lights.

Paul remained still in his seat.

Harry approached cautiously.

As Harry stepped near, Paul turned to look at him.

"*You,*" said Paul in a low voice.

"I beg your pardon?"

"You mad genius." Paul began to reanimate, as if he was

shaking himself from a long spell, awakening from an epic dream. “Holy crap, Harry. For once in my life, I am speechless. This movie is amazing. This is your best ever—without a doubt. This is fantastic, kick-butt brilliant.”

“You like it?”

Paul jumped up from his seat. “Like it? Harry I *love* it. I have goose bumps on my goose bumps. This could hit big, really big. It’s youthful; it’s raw; it’s extreme; it’s in your face; it grabs you and doesn’t let go. I was totally captivated. You really outdid yourself on this one.”

Harry felt a wave of happiness wash over him. “Thank you, Paul...”

Paul declared, “We’re going to release this *theatrically*.”

“What?”

“This is the one, Harry. We’re going to transfer it to 35 millimeter. It’ll cost us 50 grand but be worth every penny. This baby is *not* going direct to video. We are putting *Deadly Desires* on the big screen, in the big movie houses for big crowds coast to coast. You wanted to get back into the big time, well congratulations, buddy, you are back in the big time.”

Paul affectionately threw his arm around Harry. “I have to admit, I haven’t always thought of our movies as having a lot of balls in the past, but this one—I knew you had it in you, pal. I just knew it. Congratulations. This one is your masterpiece.”

16

"Bravo! Bravo!"

Cal Stillwall's shouts rode the outbreak of applause that greeted the end of *Deadly Desires*. This wasn't polite, measured handclapping—it was a continuous roar of enthusiasm and approval. The investors had come to life.

Real Estate attorney Sara Connelly exclaimed, "I love it." Periodontist Alan Fisch said, "Four stars!" Elderly Ellie Kirby stuck two fingers in her mouth and let out a piercing whistle.

Paul bounded to the front of the room, beaming from ear to ear, gesturing for Harry to join him. Harry rose from his seat in the back row and staggered forward, shaken by the rapturous response from a group that had previously scorned him.

Jimmy Nancarrow, the car dealership owner from Santa Monica, said, "Now *there's* a movie I'm proud to put my name on."

Paul hugged Harry. "Is this guy awesome or what? I think you all underestimated him." Paul thumped a finger against Harry's temple. It hurt and Harry jerked his head back. "There's a brilliant mind in that skull," said Paul. "We should all feel lucky to be associated with him."

Paul gestured to Dick the Greek in the third row. "Dick, could you please stand? I have some big news for all of you here today. I hope by now all of you know Dick Stokapolis, a long-time investor in our productions."

Dick stood and faced the other investors proudly.

Paul announced, "Dick has agreed to fund the video-to-film transfer of *Deadly Desires*. This movie is going directly to the big screen."

The investors broke out into applause.

Paul became louder and more animated, as if addressing a pep rally. "We are going to have a big Los Angeles premiere next month, and all of you are invited! We'll roll out the red carpet. We'll invite the press. Jimmy, maybe you can help us rent some flood lamps so we can light up the sky. The candy counter will be on me. Free Goobers and Raisinets for everybody. Let's have a celebration!"

* * *

Deadly Desires held its premiere in downtown Los Angeles, on Broadway at the plush, intimate Kino Theater. The excited investors arrived armed with cameras, snapping pictures of the theater's elegant exterior and bright marquee. A few trade reporters attended, but the screening essentially became a party for PJ Productions, its investors, friends and family. They cleaned out the candy counter in 20 minutes.

Harry and Paul kept a watchful eye on Tom Cole, a reviewer from *Variety*. They made sure he had a good seat, unobstructed by tall people with big hair, and plenty of refreshments. Paul chatted nervously with Cole before the film started, shoving Harry at him, and complimenting the reviewer a few too many times on his exquisite prose and excellent taste. Cole left quickly after the screening concluded.

"Do you think he liked it?" Harry asked Paul.

The answer arrived the following week when a glowing review ran in *Variety,* captioned, 'DESIRES' DELIVERS SHOCKS ON A SHOESTRING.

Initially, Paul planned to generate a buzz with midnight screenings in New York, Chicago, and San Francisco, and showings at college campuses. But a buzz had already started humming.

Soon, Paul and the distributor could barely keep up generating enough prints to feed the demand. *Deadly Desires* initially appeared on a handful of screens in a limited number of urban markets, and then crept into more cities, as well as the suburbs of the film's initial markets. The box office figures showed muscle, and momentum continued to build. More reviews appeared, all of them good to great, and the word-of-mouth spread fast, especially among younger moviegoers.

The grosses grew. Paul fed money into further marketing and promotion. The number of screens climbed to a hundred. Before long, *Deadly Desires* entered the mainstream, raiding the multiplexes.

One morning, Paul phoned Harry at home and screamed into his ear, "We're on twelve hundred screens with a per screen average gross of four thousand, seven hundred dollars; and that critic from Chicago just gave you three-and-a-half stars, and he's syndicated! This is more than a cult following, Harry. This movie is going to be the biggest grossing indie of the year."

* * *

Harry sat inside the Village Coffee Shop at the foot of the Hollywood Hills, sipping his strawberry frappuccino, nibbling on a raisin bagel, and checking out the weekend grosses, latest rankings, and number of screens for *Deadly Desires*.

"Harry Tuttle!" shouted Frank Gleason, approaching the table with a big grin. "What a pleasure to run into you. I didn't know you come here. How are things?"

Harry had seen Gleason, a powerful Dreamworks executive, at the coffee shop many times in the past; and Gleason had always averted his eyes in a haughty manner that read, "I'm pretending not to see you." But now Gleason jumped to his side as if they were best friends.

Harry chatted with Gleason politely and accepted a heap of praise for *Deadly Desires*.

"I really love what you did with the handhelds and your lighting scheme, very stark, yet a richness, and those natural performances..."

Gleason continued schmoozing, and Harry found himself bored by the insincerity. He nodded while gazing out the window. He scanned the sidewalk for pretty women. Then he noticed someone familiar...

...and almost exclaimed "Oh shit!" out loud.

It was Marcus Stegman.

Stegman looked awful. His hair was longer, greasier. His clothes were dirty. He didn't look like somebody who had just been handed eight hundred thousand dollars.

Stegman talked with another, equally grubby young man in a tattered army jacket. The man handed Stegman something in a small plastic bag, shielding it from street view with his back.

Stegman was buying drugs.

"...on location in Mexico? Harry?"

Harry snapped his attention back to Gleason. "I'm sorry... I didn't mean to space out. I've been..."

"I know the feeling," said Gleason. "All this success kind of knocks the wind out of you, doesn't it? Well, enjoy it. Savor it. In this business, you can be king of the world one day and flat on your ass the next. Ha ha!"

Gleason left. Harry looked back at Stegman. Stegman extracted bills from a wad of cash in his hand.

Guilt hammered Harry. *I took advantage of a dope addict. I bribed him, stole his movie, and contributed to his drug habit. Way to go, Tuttle. You're getting famous at this poor kid's expense. Hope you feel just great when you accept your Oscar while he overdoses on crack.*

Just then, Stegman turned and faced the coffee shop window. Harry froze. But Stegman seemed to stare right through him. Harry realized that Stegman couldn't see him through the sun reflecting on the glass.

Stegman looked back at the filthy man in the army jacket and completed the transaction. Stegman coughed a few times, wiped his nose with the back of his hand, and walked away.

Harry stared down at the table. He looked at the expensive gold watch on his wrist, the gift from Paul, inscribed "Scary Harry." A generous gesture from his business partner to recognize and celebrate Harry's moviemaking bravura.

Harry wanted to rip the watch from his flesh.

17

Rachel returned to her apartment after a full day of auditions where she discovered she was (a) too short, (b) too cute, (c) lacked edge, and (d) looked too young for the roles she sought. She had learned long ago not to take such rejections personally—she knew it was simply a matter of casting directors finding the right DNA match for a character that existed on the written page. She wished that she was a better chameleon, able to fit into any mold. Her acting coach had worked hard with her to find a "wider palette of colors." A common criticism concerned her voice: soft and thin. "Too much bubble," said one of her instructors. "Where's the rage, the intensity simmering beneath the surface?"

But she wasn't naturally angry or intense, and it was a tough emotion to fake. She would try to harden her features, purse her lips, narrow her eyes; but it didn't look very convincing.

Once, her roommate Maria caught her trying to make moody faces in the mirror and burst out laughing.

"Maybe I should just do comedy," said Rachel.

"You're adorable. The camera loves you. You'll find your niche. Maybe it *is* comedy."

"What I really want is a romance."

"A romance movie, or romance in your life?" asked Maria.

"Both," Rachel had replied.

Maria wasn't home when Rachel stepped into the apartment. Rachel felt disappointed because she loved to commiserate with her roommate. Maria could reach back into her own well of audition stories, and usually top any humiliating rejections Rachel had experienced. One of the classics was the time a director dropped Maria from a music video for having breasts that were "out of proportion" with her hips.

Rachel made herself a peanut butter and banana slices sandwich—a favorite since childhood—and brought it with her to the couch with a bottle of Snapple. She aimed the remote at the TV and started surfing. She was always encouraged when she found bad acting—usually on the soaps—because it lifted her confidence. *Hey, I could do that.*

She flipped past—then back to—*Flick Picks*, a movie review program featuring Walter Wiggins, the renowned film critic for the *Los Angeles Star*. Unlike most critics, Wiggins was an entertaining presence himself, wearing flamboyant colors, waving his arms to punctuate his opinions, and speaking with an aggressive yet prissy voice. He was short and round, filling the screen so completely that it looked like he might push the glass out of the television. Rachel always enjoyed *Flick Picks*, keeping up with the new releases and catching glimpses of the stars in action. Also, for better or worse, she found that Wiggins' tastes in movies often ran parallel with her own.

Wiggins was finishing up panning a cardboard-thin comedy featuring a former Saturday Night Live comedian. "This is poo poo potty humor that wouldn't go over in a high school locker room. Flush it," he said, fanning a hand in front of his nose for emphasis. "I rank *Jock Itch*...a dud!" On the screen, a graphic appeared of a pile of Milk Duds.

Rachel giggled. For really bad movies, Wiggins sometimes added the sound effect of a falling bomb.

Wiggins faced the camera from a different angle and began his next review. Rachel had reached for *L.A. Weekly* to skim, but yanked her hand back when she heard Wiggins utter a familiar name, "Harry Tuttle."

"I know that guy," she said out loud.

"A while back, I opened one of my programs by bashing a movie by Harry Tuttle, a notorious director of super-cheap horror films that are mass-marketed like junk food to the indiscriminating public," said Wiggins.

Poor Harry, thought Rachel. *Why keep picking on him?*

But then Wiggins brightened his tone. "Well, believe it or not, from this crude craftsman, a truly good movie has arrived, *Deadly Desires*."

On the screen, a clip from *Deadly Desires* showed a handsome but fierce young man chasing a woman through the woods. The camera shook, offering jolting point-of-view shots. In a voice-over Wiggins continued, "Sure, it's got a minuscule budget; but in this instance the rough, trimmed-down scale of the movie works to a scary advantage. The story is a contemporary take on ritual human sacrifice."

In the clip, the man caught up with the woman. He grasped a strange-looking dagger in a close-up. The blade plunged toward the victim and the program quickly cut back to Wiggins, leaning forward and enthusiastic.

"Writer-director Harry Tuttle, amazingly, is the same man who made the unbearable *The Beastly* earlier this year. This time out, however, Tuttle has left behind the rubber monster suits. He's dealing with a more human kind of monster, based on themes of power and greed, for today's cynical society. The result is a truly frightening little gem. My recommendation for *Deadly Desires* is...Extra Large!" The screen showed a graphic of an enormous popcorn bucket, Wiggins' highest rating.

Rachel said to the screen, "Harry, I misjudged you." She now felt foolish over turning down the opportunity to appear in his next film. Why didn't she just grab the part? The role was gone now. *That'll teach you to be judgmental and snooty*, she told herself. *You never know who's gonna hit it big in this town.*

When Maria returned home, Rachel announced, "You'll never guess who just got a rave review on *Flick Picks*."

Rachel described the review for *Deadly Desires* and Maria said, "That movie's supposed to be really good. *He* did it? The same guy who made those bad videos?"

"I blew it big time," said Rachel. "He's such a nice guy, and he had a role all picked out for me; and I told him no."

"When you told him no, did you let him down easy?" asked Maria.

"Sure, I was polite. I wasn't mean. You know me."

"Then maybe you didn't burn any bridges. It's not too late. Call him up."

"I can't do that."

"Sure you can. Better yet, ask him out to dinner. He sounds like someone you should get to know better."

"I don't want to appear opportunistic."

"How do you think careers get made in this town? I'll bet he says yes. Who would say no to dinner with a hot and sexy young starlet like you?"

Rachel giggled. "Knock it off. I'm not going to call him, and that's that."

But 30 minutes of pestering later, Rachel relented. She called Harry. She still had his number from the note inside his package of DVDs. The box had been put aside with the intention of selling the discs to a used record store.

Rachel sat on her bed with her notes spread out in front of her—lines of dialogue in case she got tongue-tied. Maria dialed the number and thrust the phone at her, stating, "You're an actress. Here. Act brave."

Harry picked up on the third ring.

Rachel said, "Hello, is this Harry Tuttle?"

"Speaking."

"Hi, this is Rachel Stoller...you know, the actress...the flapper." Rachel saw that Maria was making faces. She cupped a hand over her eyes to block Maria from her field of vision.

"Yes, yes," responded Harry with enthusiasm. "Of course. How have you been? Still enjoying the Roaring Twenties?"

"Well, not anymore. I'm back in the 21st century. I'm doing a commercial for a new laundry detergent called Wipe Out. I do battle with a chocolate syrup stain."

"That's great. I'll have to watch for it."

After an awkward pause, she dove in. "Listen, I just saw your new movie, the one about human sacrifice, and I wanted you to know that I think it's really awesome. I loved it. It's my favorite movie of the year."

"Thank you," said Harry. "That's very kind. I really appreciate it."

"Dinner!" whispered Maria in the background.

Rachel said, "If you're not busy, I was wondering if you'd like to get together for dinner. I feel I was a bit distracted by the miniseries last time we met, and I thought it would be nice to get together again. That is, if you're interested."

Rachel bit her lip, listened, got the response she was looking for, and gave Maria the thumbs up sign. Maria danced a silent dance at the foot of the bed.

"I'd love to get together," said Harry.

18

Harry Tuttle sat at his desk reading the latest reviews for *Deadly Desires*. Nearly every write-up was positive. *USA Today*, *The San Francisco Chronicle*, *Atlanta Journal-Constitution*, *Rolling Stone*, *Newsweek*. The marketing people had an embarrassment of riches to choose from as they plucked the best blurbs for splashy, coast-to-coast newspaper ads.

"Nail-biting, edge-of-your-seat thrills."

"Dark and gripping...screamingly good."

"Terrifically terrifying."

"A small masterpiece."

Paul had just left the office to begin negotiations for the DVD release. "You won't believe the numbers we're discussing," he told Harry before heading out the door.

A few days earlier, Walter Wiggins, the influential movie critic from the *Los Angeles Star* had given *Deadly Desires* an "Extra Large" recommendation on his TV show, resulting in a big spike in box office grosses over the weekend. As if that wasn't enough, Wiggins called Harry directly the next day, to invite him to participate in a one-hour television special he was hosting on the new wave of independent filmmakers. "We'll chat, we'll show clips," said Wiggins. "You'll be one of four directors I'm featuring."

Harry said, "You really think people want to hear from me?"

Wiggins responded in his trademark haughty tone, "Mr. Tuttle, you've got a cult following. You're the master of minimalist moviemaking. Might as well grab your 15 minutes of fame while it's yours for the asking."

Harry couldn't believe it. Several months earlier, Wiggins had ridiculed Harry's entire body of work. Now he wanted to prop him up on a pedestal in primetime. Harry felt like he had entered a strange, alternate universe. Perhaps during meditation he had stepped into one of his fantasies and never returned. Things were too good.

Then they got even better. The icing on the cake arrived, and it was sweet.

Rachel Stoller called him up and asked him out on a date.

Harry had developed a crush on Rachel from the moment he'd first laid eyes on her at Richard Metherell's party in the Hollywood Hills. After she had gently rejected a role in his next movie, Harry had written her off as uninterested, unavailable, and way too good for him. She was on her way up; he was on his way down.

Now she was pursuing him. All because she had seen *Deadly Desires* and become attracted to the man behind the movie. She couldn't stop raving about *Deadly Desires* when they spoke on the phone.

Harry thought, *I've done a great job letting everybody else know I made* Deadly Desires. *Now if I could only convince myself...*

* * *

Harry entered date night with the jitters. Ever since his wife left him to shack up with another, better filmmaker, Harry hadn't gone out on many dates. For one thing, he worked long, tough hours. But more truthfully, his confidence had blown a gasket. He didn't have Paul's gift for pumping himself up with synthetic enthusiasm. When he felt low, it showed, and he wasn't much fun to be around. It wasn't a state that invited romantic companionship.

But now his mood had lifted. Success had returned from the grave like a zombie from one of his horror pictures. His life story had found a fresh romantic subplot. Rachel Stoller stirred his heart in new and exciting ways. She could heal the wounds from a broken marriage.

Even though Rachel had asked Harry out, he insisted on picking her up. She said fine, as long as she could pick the restaurant.

At six, Harry drove to Rachel's West Hollywood apartment building, circling the block four times for a space before finally double parking with flashing blinkers.

When Harry knocked on her apartment door and she opened up, he nearly said "Whoa" out loud. She wore a low-cut white top, with dark blue slacks and heels. Her blond hair, tossed forward, cascaded in clean sheets to her shoulders. The smile, just as he remembered it, was genuine and warm.

As Rachel disappeared for a moment to retrieve her purse, Harry met her Hispanic roommate, Maria, who gushed, "Mr. Tuttle, I loved every minute of *Deadly Desires*." She continued to fawn over him until Rachel playfully pushed her away and said, "Go get your own date."

In the car, Harry chatted with Rachel about the weather and potential for rain later in the week, silently cursing his banal dialogue even as he delivered it. As he drove to the restaurant, her perfume tickled his nose and his head swam laps, distracting him to the point that he could barely focus on the road.

On his car stereo, he played a CD by the Yeah Yeah Yeahs, a disc recommended by a shaggy clerk with a nose ring at Amoeba Music. Harry had asked for something hip and happening to help counter the fact that he was nearly 15 years older than his date.

As it turned out, Rachel had never heard of the Yeah Yeah Yeahs; and the restaurant she had chosen—a classic steakhouse—featured an older crowd and a live jazz band playing old standards.

"I love this music," she told Harry after they had been seated and handed menus. "It takes me to another era, when times were simpler, you know?"

They ordered cocktails, which loosened up the mood; and before long, they became so deeply engaged in conversation that the waitress had to return five times before they finally opened their menus.

"Where do you get your ideas for your movies?" she asked him.

"My mind is always ticking," said Harry. "I write things down on Post-it Notes. I have them plastered all over the house. Sometimes I'll brainstorm when I'm stuck in traffic. I keep a notepad by the bed in case I wake up with an idea in the middle of the night, but usually by morning, I can't make any sense out of what I've scribbled. It'll say something like 'Purple monkey doorknob' and I'll wonder, *what the heck does that mean?*"

She laughed and asked if he had always wanted to be a filmmaker. "Ever since I was old enough to watch movies," he responded. He told her anecdotes from his youth about making Super 8 movies with monsters and superheroes. He confessed to triggering a false fire alarm once at his high school, to get footage of the arriving fire trucks and police cars for one of his mini-epics.

"Have you always done horror movies?" she asked.

"That was my big interest when I was a kid, and I guess I've never grown up. That's how I got my start in Hollywood. Now I've done so many of them that I'm typecast. I've painted myself into a corner—with blood." Then he conceded, "Horror movies are just a good way to break into the business and make a mark. There's always a steady market for them, and you don't need big-name stars or big budgets to attract an audience. You can get away with being cheap."

He took another sip of his drink and felt a warmth wash over him. He confided, "But I'll let you in on a little secret... One day, I want to do a love story. I've got a script stashed away that I think is pretty good. I bring it out now and then to, you know, polish the dialogue."

"You should film it," urged Rachel.

"Audiences want action and violence and a lot of noise. Nobody's going to pay to see a love story."

"I would."

"Well...that makes two of us," he said.

Her warm eyes locked on him, and she smiled that smile that could melt concrete.

"I'm glad I met you, Harry," she declared. "I like you a lot better than the rest of the people I've met in this business. It's a weird scene out here. Everybody is so wrapped up in themselves."

"I completely agree," said Harry.

"I've met so many jerks and liars and bullshit artists. But not you. You're just this down-to-earth, regular guy who loves to make movies. You're not a phony like the others. I hate people who are phony."

Harry flinched. He felt a sinking feeling in his stomach. He was a phony. Rachel just didn't know it.

This whole date is based on a lie, he told himself.

"What's wrong?" she asked.

He shook the look of concern off his face. "Nothing. Just listening to the music. Is it Glenn Miller?"

"Moonlight Serenade."

"Beautiful," he said.

* * *

After dinner, they advanced to a nearby bar for another drink and continued conversation, before he took her home. She had to get up early for an audition—a nonspeaking role, "frightened pedestrian," in a Will Smith action movie. As Harry walked Rachel to her apartment building entrance, he felt a giddy feeling he hadn't felt since he was a teenager. *Do I kiss her?*

They stood close to one another, and she broke the awkward silence with, "I really had a nice time. I hope we can do this again sometime."

"I'd really like that."

"I hope you don't think I'm being too brash asking you out like this."

"Not at all," responded Harry. "I'm thrilled by it, if you want to know the truth. I've liked you since we first met. I've thought about you a lot since that party in the hills."

She smiled at that. "Really? What kind of thoughts?"

"Daydreaming."

"Daydreaming? About what?" She leaned closer.

Harry could feel himself blushing and wondered if she could see redness on his cheeks.

"Tell me," she said.

"That one day...things would turn out like this."

The look in her eyes told him she liked his answer. Harry saw his opportunity and seized it. He put his hand on her shoulder. They kissed, softly, a short but compelling introductory kiss, a coming attraction for things to come.

* * *

Harry drove home, sunroof open, stars above, humming "Moonlight Serenade," quite possibly the happiest man on earth. His head filled with ideas for where to take Rachel on their next date. He was already going through Rachel withdrawal.

As Harry pulled into his driveway, he didn't see the dark figure waiting for him on the front lawn. Harry stepped out of the car, continued humming, and headed up the walkway toward his front door.

A familiar voice greeted him from the shadows.

"Mr. Tuttle," said Marcus Stegman.

19

Harry stopped cold.

He turned and peered into the darkness.

Stegman stepped forward into the reach of the porch light. He wore an old fedora.

"Boo," he said. "It's your favorite ghostwriter. Did I spook you?"

"What are you doing here?" asked Harry.

"Just paying a visit to my friend and collaborator," responded Stegman. He looked like hell, a deteriorating version of his former self. His eyes had an eerie emptiness. His hair and clothes were unwashed. His fingers fidgeted, clenching at air.

Drugs, thought Harry. He had seen the symptoms before—Hollywood colleagues who succumbed to cocaine or worse, as they began raking in the big bucks, feeling invincible. Harry had tried coke exactly once in his life—it simply made him anxious and dry mouthed—and never again. He didn't understand the allure, but he understood the consequences.

"Did you see the article in *Variety* about our movie?" asked Stegman.

"Which...one?" asked Harry, cautious.

"*Cheap horror pic scares up boffo box office.*"

"Yes. Yes, I did."

"It looks like my movie—or should I say, your movie—has been doing very well."

Harry shot him a suspicious look. "It's been a success, yes. Is there something wrong with that? Marcus, we made a deal."

Stegman laughed, and the laugh became a hard cough. "Oh no, no. Don't worry. I'm not going back on our deal. I'm not in this for the prestige and headlines like you are. I'm in this because I love creating horror."

Harry nodded, still gripping his house key. He knew he wasn't going to open his front door until Stegman left the property.

"So..." said Harry, growing impatient. "What brings you here?"

Stegman looked incredulous. "What else? *Our next movie.* We have a big hit on our hands. The public will demand more. Don't you think?"

"I would imagine."

"So we're wasting valuable time. You want to continue the partnership, don't you? It helps us both, right?"

"Can't complain."

"Good. Because I've started working on the treatment and storyboards. You're going to love this. It's right up your alley. Get this: it's a horror movie about horror movies. Let me explain. The bad guy is a madman who murders people in tribute to his favorite horror films. For each victim, he takes on the persona of a different classic horror movie character. Michael Myers from *Halloween*. Jason from the *Friday the 13th* franchise. Freddy from *Nightmare on Elm Street*. Leatherface from *Texas Chainsaw Massacre*. And on and on. He's the ultimate horror movie killer! What do you think?"

Harry nodded. "It's an interesting concept."

Stegman stepped closer. "I'll do it for one million dollars."

Harry said, "I'll have to think about it. If it's as good as the last one...we could probably work something out. But this isn't the time for negotiating. I'm tired. Where do you get your energy?"

"Lots of coffee," said Stegman. "And unspent sexual energy."

"Maybe you should cut down on the caffeine and go get laid."

Stegman laughed louder than the joke warranted. Booming in the still night, Stegman's guffaw sent a chill up Harry's spine.

"You're funny," said Stegman, and he wiped his nose on his sleeve. Then he asked, "Do you like my hat?"

"Why are you wearing a fedora?" asked Harry.

Stegman took it off and handed it to Harry. Harry shrunk back.

"It doesn't bite; it's just a hat."

"I just asked about it. I don't want it."

"Read the name inside the rim."

Harry accepted it with three fingertips, cringed, and looked inside, expecting to find lice, or worse.

Someone had written something in ink on the inner band, long ago, but the letters were now badly faded after L-U-G.

Harry handed it back. "I can't read it."

Stegman placed the fedora back on his head. "It says *Lugosi*. This hat used to belong to Bela Lugosi in the 1950s. I bought it off eBay for fifty-six hundred dollars. I thought it was sort of appropriate, you know, since we sealed our deal on Bela's star."

Harry felt impressed, then worried. "So you're spending your money..."

"Hell, yes. On things I've always wanted. Props from my favorite horror films. Memorabilia from my favorite horror actors. This hat is going in my museum room."

"Don't blow all your earnings," said Harry. *Especially on blow.*

"I've never had money before," said Stegman. "I have a lot of catching up to do. Things I've always wanted to buy. You should see my new home theater setup and my DVD library..."

Harry nodded. Enough was enough. He didn't want to carry on a conversation in his front yard all night, with a coked-up kid. It was ruining his perfect evening.

"Listen," he said. "In the future, if you want to talk, set up a meeting. We'll go somewhere. Don't just show up at my house in the middle of the night."

"What's the matter?" said Stegman, rocking back on his heels. "Are you afraid of the dark?"

"Good night, Marcus," said Harry, turning his back on Stegman. He headed for the front door.

"Congratulations on your success, Harry," Stegman called out. "I'm glad to see it."

Harry couldn't tell if Stegman was being sarcastic or not. But he turned and replied, "Congratulations to you as well, Marcus. You deserve it."

Stegman nodded, saying, "Yeah, but you got the movie out to the public, into the multiplexes. I couldn't have done that. I don't have the connections you do. That's where you come in... partner."

Then Stegman bowed, dropping into a Transylvanian accent, tipping his hat. "Goot evenink."

"Good night," murmured Harry. He waited until Stegman was halfway across the yard before opening his door. He entered, locked up, then paused.

He swore he could hear Stegman cackling.

20

Diane Laughton, the five-foot-one producer of *Flick Picks*, led the way, walking swiftly in short steps, thick heels clicking aggressively on the tile floor. Harry followed her through a maze of pastel corridors, catching glimpses of editing suites, equipment storage rooms, and tape archives.

"We're so glad you could be a part of this," Diane said, ejecting words in a steely rapid fire, making a sudden hard left turn. "I haven't seen your movie but I'm told it's very good. You should experience a definite bump in ticket sales when this special airs. We're presold in most of the major markets. Washington, Chicago, New York, Dallas..."

Then she stopped so suddenly that Harry nearly crashed into her.

"Wally, he's here," she said.

They stood outside Walter Wiggins' small office at WKKG Studios. The big man was stuffed in a chair, surrounded by an explosion of clutter. DVD screeners, movie magazines, trade publications and press kits, merged across fallen piles on his desk. Signed publicity stills of medium-famous film stars decorated the walls. An empty bucket of chicken rested near the critic's pudgy grasp.

Wiggins rotated in his big swivel chair, turning to face Harry. He was breathing heavy, probably from the weight hanging off his squat frame, because he certainly wasn't exerting himself. He wore a purple and green checkered sports coat.

"Harry Tuttle," he said simply.

"Pleasure to meet you." Harry stretched out his hand and Wiggins shook it without getting up. Wiggins' hand felt greasy from the chicken.

Wiggins said, "We'll chat on camera for maybe an hour, then the boys in editing will slice and dice it to about nine minutes. You got my list of questions during the preinterview?"

Harry nodded.

"I changed a bunch of them, but don't let that throw you. Just keep your answers punchy, short, engaging. Tell us how you make wine from water. Be a poster boy for low-budget, independent filmmaking. Tell us what it's like to make a movie that's beating the pants off films that cost a hundred times more."

"I'll try."

"Just don't be boring."

Harry nodded.

"Why don't we get Mr. Tuttle in makeup," said the producer.

"See you on the set," said Wiggins, and his chair swiveled back to face his desk and food.

* * *

Essentially, the interview set was a minor variation of the familiar *Flick Picks* set, shifting the angle on the elements of a movie theatre interior. The scenery, which appeared lush and spacious on television, became thin and cramped in person. Wiggins' large, upholstered chair was repositioned; and a second chair, for Harry, had been added.

The soundman clipped a tiny mike to Harry's shirt collar and secured the belt pack. He guided Harry across the floor to his seat, telling him, "Watch out for the cables."

Harry sat down, slowly, eyes adjusting to the bright lights.

"Check sound," said the sound man, then instructing Harry to count to ten. Harry counted. A figure behind glass in the control booth signaled thumbs up.

"You're good to go," said the sound man, moving backwards and disappearing. Harry saw the director, a balding man with a headset, circling the room to huddle individually with crew members. Harry counted four cameras and examined the array of lights that dangled from a grid work of mounts in the ceiling. *Impressive*, thought Harry. *I wish I had all this.*

When Wiggins arrived with the diminutive producer at his side, everything was in place. The balding director stood behind Wiggins' chair, waiting for him with some last minute instructions.

Wiggins held up a hand before the director could speak. "I know the drill," he muttered in his raspy voice, and the director retreated into the shadows to join his crew.

"Well, Harry Tuttle, are you ready?" said Wiggins, climbing into his extra large theater seat with an "*oof.*"

"Yes, I am." Harry could no longer see the director or crew behind the bright lights, but he could hear them shuffling about.

"So am I. Let's get this over with. This chair always makes my buttocks fall asleep."

"Anybody need any water?" said a voice.

"No," Wiggins answered for both of them.

A second voice, the director, said, "Standby. Are we good? Quiet, please. Rolling. Ready. Counting down from five, from four, three, two and...*action*."

Wiggins turned and faced away from Harry. He began talking into one of the cameras, reading an introduction off the teleprompter.

"My next guest has been making movies for 20 years, but until recently you've probably never heard of him. He's Harry Tuttle, king of the low-budget horror movie. While movies like *Valley of the Zombies* and *Schizo Sisters* aren't exactly household names, Tuttle has quietly built himself a minor cult following with hardcore horror fans. But it wasn't until *Deadly Desires*, this year, that this no-name became a big name...and he did it without any stars, and without any film. Yes, you heard right. Tuttle's movies are recorded directly on digital videotape with handheld cameras and found locations, bringing a 'Reality TV' effect to the cinema. Is this the future of filmmaking?"

Wiggins froze for a moment and the director yelled, "And stop. Great, Walter. Do you want to run through it one more time for safety?"

"No," said Wiggins.

The cameras quickly repositioned. The lighting scheme changed, and within minutes the interview was ready to commence.

Wiggins faced Harry. He cleared his throat and adjusted his butt.

Harry felt butterflies. He wasn't used to being on the other end of the cameras.

"Mr. Tuttle, thank you for being here today," said Wiggins.

"It's my pleasure. Thanks for inviting me."

"How low is low-budget?"

Harry blinked. "Well...our movies typically cost about four hundred thousand dollars. Sometimes more, sometimes less. But we typically keep it under a million."

"Remarkable—because you're competing with the big boys who are spending twenty or thirty times that, just on marketing and advertising."

"That's why we have to create a really good product, submit to film festivals, and hope word of mouth will do the marketing and advertising for us."

"So what do you do for special effects? Ketchup for blood, that kind of thing?"

Harry laughed. "Not ketchup. It's Karo syrup and red food coloring. But we do get a lot of mileage out of a shoestring. We have a clip of an exploding car that we've reused in several of our movies. We use as many real locations as possible to avoid the cost of building sets. And we don't hire big name stars—we're looking to discover new talent."

"In fact, sometimes you put your investors in your movies?"

"Yes. It's a perk."

Wiggins chuckled, and Harry felt gratified somehow that he'd made the pompous man laugh.

"*Deadly Desires*," said Wiggins, pausing a moment to reflect.

"Yes?" said Harry.

"Knocked me out. Really a great film. As you probably know, I wasn't a fan of your earlier pictures; but now you've seemed to find a way to make the low-budget work *for* you, not against you. I was so captivated by the whole set up, the archeological site, the tombs, the Aztec empire, and how you took this ancient murder ritual based in fact, and brought it to the modern age with some clever twists and turns. It's really a sly morality play."

"Thank you," said Harry. He hoped Marcus Stegman would never see this TV special.

"So...the entire movie was shot on videotape, correct?"

"Correct."

"But it's showing in movie theaters. It looks like a film. How does that work?"

"Modern technology," replied Harry. "After it's shot in digital video, it gets stored on computer hard drives; and the footage goes through a process to add more grain and contrast to give it a film-like appearance. Then, typically, we go straight to DVD and cable TV, but the advance buzz on this one was so good, we decided to test market a theatrical release. We had a few prints made, taking the video and transferring it to 35 millimeter. It's an expensive gamble, but the showings did well, the reviews were good, and suddenly, boom, it's a hit."

"The beauty of this," said Wiggins, "is that it tells any kid in America that he or she can be a filmmaker. You no longer need to make this big investment in professional camera equipment and big crews. You can just go to your local Walmart or Best Buy, get a few things and get started."

"It's a mixed blessing," conceded Harry, "because you have a lot of product fighting for attention, and a lot of good work getting buried in the tidal wave of truly amateurish productions. It's like the publishing industry, with all these inexpensive self-publishing options, anybody can get into the marketplace without the traditional quality control filters."

"Indeed," said Wiggins. "You wouldn't believe how many self-produced, homemade DVDs I receive that go straight into the trash. I just don't have the time to wade through them all—even if there was a gem waiting to be discovered in the mix."

"It's hard to rise above the clutter," said Harry. "Often you need connections." He was thinking about Stegman again. He couldn't help it.

"I want to talk some more about *Deadly Desires*," said Wiggins.

"Sure," replied Harry.

"The performers—I really enjoyed the natural performances. I know these kids are all unknowns, but where do you find them? Do you put Help Wanted ads in the paper?"

Harry said, "Not quite. But close. I like to go to local colleges, meet with drama students. I have a few connections at acting schools. I'm not picky. I'm just looking for anyone who is young and eager, and can recite lines."

"And cheap."

"Of course."

"In *Deadly Desires*, the performances are all quite good, but there's one young woman who stands out in particular, Sandra Ross. Boy, she's good. Where did you find her?"

Harry drew a blank. There was utter silence. He hesitated for a long moment. Now they were getting specific about *Deadly Desires*. Now he would have to lie.

"Where did I find her?" said Harry, repeating the question to buy himself a few more seconds. "Well, word of mouth. Friends. I know her mother's cousin."

Wiggins nodded. "I thought she was splendid."

"Me too."

"What else has she done?"

Harry felt a dribble of sweat roll down his cheek. "You know, this must have been her first role. I really don't know..."

"Will we see her again in your future productions?"

"I wouldn't rule it out. As long as she doesn't raise her price."

Wiggins chuckled. "What does she think about all this newfound fame and fortune? From obscurity to the big screen. It must be every young kid's dream."

"She's very excited," said Harry.

"So you keep in touch with her?"

Harry felt his mouth getting dry. He wanted the water. Under the hot lights, this bombardment of difficult questions was beginning to feel like a police interrogation. *I never should have agreed to this interview. I'm going to blow it.*

"Sure," said Harry. "I like to keep in touch with all my actors and actresses. We're just one big happy family."

* * *

After the taping concluded, the bright lights snapped off and the studio erupted with a flurry of activity and voices. The soundman removed Harry's mike. Harry noticed his armpits had sweated through his shirt and hoped the camera hadn't picked it up.

Wiggins lifted himself out of his chair with a groan.

"Wally, great job!" said the director, walking up.

Wiggins ignored him, turning to Harry. "Good interview. I think we got what we need."

"Great. When will this air?"

"Two weeks. I have one more director coming in on Monday. Phyllis Ranger, does documentaries."

Harry was anxious to leave the studio and began inching away.

"Harry," said Wiggins. "Listen. For our segment, I'd like to spice it up with clips. Some short clips from your earlier work, funny ones that show the cheapness. Then a longer scene or two from *Deadly Desires*. Something with impact."

"No problem. You can use any of our stuff. We'll get you clearance."

"Also," said Wiggins, "I'd like to tape a quick interview with Sandra Ross. Just for a few sound bites when we go to the clips. I want someone from the film who can speak to your directing style and all that, maybe tell a cute story about the production, something behind the scenes. Where could I reach Sandra?"

"Oh," said Harry. He answered slowly, carefully, choosing his words in advance. "I'm not sure about Sandra. She—I'd have to get back to you on that. I'd have to check her availability."

"Don't worry about her availability. We'll set it up. I just need contact information."

"Sure. I'll get that to you."

"The sooner the better. If you can't reach me, give it to Diane."

"Right," said Harry, then speaking his biggest lie of the day, "No problem."

21

Harry drove with a map in his lap, prowling San Gabriel for the ranch house on Del Marino that belonged to Marcus Stegman.

Once he found it, he groaned.

The house and yard were a neglected mess, an eyesore in a neighborhood that worked hard to maintain its modest properties. Harry mumbled, "Stupid kid; all that money and he can't clean up the place?"

An occasional raindrop hit the windshield. The deepening gray skies promised more on the way. Harry turned off the engine and watched the droplets multiply on the glass.

Well, thought Harry, *here goes.*

He opened the door and climbed out of his car, followed the broken concrete walkway to the front steps. Tiny jolts of rain hit his neck and arms.

Harry pressed the doorbell, heard nothing, figured it was broken and knocked.

A young man with a wild, reddish beard answered the door in his bare feet. He wore a blue T-shirt and jeans. His eyes were bloodshot and glazed over. He looked familiar, but Harry couldn't place him.

"Harry Tuttle," the bearded man said in a deep voice.

"Yes. You know my name?"

"Of course." He turned and called into the house, "Marcus, it's Harry Tuttle." Then he gestured Harry inside. "I'm one of Marcus's roommates. I worked with him on the movie."

"Oh, hi," said Harry. "Nice to meet you."

"Same." They shook hands.

The living room—if you could call it a room for living—overflowed with filmmaking equipment. *So this is where the money goes...*thought Harry. Then he saw the large bong. *And there, too.*

"Mr. Tuttle," greeted Marcus Stegman upon entering the room, also in jeans and a T-shirt, his ponytail tied back behind his head. "Any trouble finding the house?"

"No," said Harry.

"You must come see my museum."

"Your museum?"

"Follow me."

Stegman brought Harry to a room in the back of the house, filled with shelves and cabinets of horror movie memorabilia. The walls displayed posters and framed lobby cards. A seven-foot replica of the monster from *Alien* stood in one corner. A dingy coffin rested on the floor. Harry saw Bela Lugosi's fedora sitting on the head of the Creature from the Black Lagoon. He also saw "The Soul" from *Soul Snatchers* prominently displayed. It made Harry proud for a moment.

"The Los Angeles Museum of Horror Movie History," proclaimed Stegman.

"Impressive," said Harry, taking it all in. On the counter next to him he saw a Hellraiser figurine, a voodoo shrunken head, spaceship models, ghastly rubber masks, a machete painted with blood, fake limbs, and an eyeball. It was like a toy store in hell.

Stegman identified several items, pointing around the room. "Glenn Strange's boots from when he played the Frankenstein monster in *House of Frankenstein*, 1945. Those fangs—from *Taste the Blood of Dracula*, Christopher Lee. Over here, Linda Blair's nightgown from *The Exorcist*. And this..." Stegman gestured proudly to a framed watercolor painting of a lighthouse on a rocky coast. "Painted by none other than Vincent Price. Did you know he was an artist?"

"Where do you find all this stuff?"

"Auctions. Online. Other collectors. All over. Places that specialize in movie memorabilia."

"You really should save a few extra dollars for a lawn service."

"I'll get to it. Jesus, you sound like my landlord. Here, I want to show you my home theater."

Stegman led Harry into a room turned into an entertainment heaven, with a 60-inch Plasma screen, state-of-the-art surround sound system, gigantic speakers, two rows of authentic theater seats, and a back wall of shelves jammed with hundreds of DVDs. The windows had been sealed shut to block out the light. It was more impressive than the screening room at PJ Productions.

Stegman boasted, "I've got every horror movie you could imagine. From Lon Chaney senior to junior, from *Dracula* to *Carrie*, from the classics to the obscure." He pulled a DVD case off the shelf. "This one here—bet you've never even heard of it. *Silent Scream*, 1980, Yvonne De Carlo, Barbara Steele. I need to watch at least two or three of these a day. It gets my adrenaline going, pumps the blood through my veins."

"It's quite a collection."

"Funded by you, Mr. Tuttle. Would you like to see a scene from your favorite horror movie? I'll bet I have it. I'll crank up the speakers for you."

"No," said Harry. "I don't have a lot of time. Listen. I came for a reason. We need to talk."

"Oh," said Stegman. "Sure. We'll talk. Have a seat. They're real comfy."

Harry sat down in one of the theater seats. It *was* comfy. Stegman sat next to him.

"So what's up?" asked Stegman.

"Well," sighed Harry, "I need your help with something. I did an interview earlier today with Walter Wiggins..."

"The short fat guy from *Flick Picks*," said Stegman.

"Yes. We taped an interview on *Deadly Desires* and talked about low-budget films, and now he wants to do a brief interview with one of the actresses, Sandra Ross. I'll also need some extras for the DVD, a featurette thing, so we'll probably want to interview her for that as well. We need to proceed very carefully—as you know, I don't want anything to happen—anything to be said by your people—that would compromise our special deal. Do you know what I'm talking about?"

"Of course."

"Everyone associated with this film needs to maintain the secret."

"Yes. Yes, I know. You met Terrance?"

Harry shrugged.

"The guy who answered the door—you know, from *Deadly Desires*. He has a beard and longer hair now, but he played Michael, the lead character. The killer."

It hit Harry all at once: Stegman's roommate was the star of *Deadly Desires*. "Oh my God, you're right. I barely recognized him. He looked familiar, but I didn't make the connection."

"You could interview him."

"Frankly," said Harry, "I'd rather not. He looks like he's high. I don't care what he does in his spare time, but if we put him in an interview situation...There's a lot at risk if he slips up."

"No, he'll be fine," said Stegman.

"They want Sandra Ross," said Harry.

"Sandra Ross."

"Right. I need to know where to find her. We've got to prep her before Wiggins contacts her."

Stegman nodded, giving it deep thought. "Sandra Ross. OK. Interesting."

"Do you have a phone number where she can be reached?"

"Sandra? No, I'm afraid I don't."

"Or an address."

"No address."

This stopped Harry for a beat. He said, "But I thought you said you were tight with these people. You said it was a small circle of friends."

"Not everybody," said Stegman. "Sandra was an outsider. Someone we recruited."

"So you don't know where she came from?"

"I know where she came from."

"You just don't know where she is now."

"I know where she is now."

"You know?" Harry's confusion rolled into exasperation. "Then why are you playing games with me?"

"I'm not playing games with you."

Harry asked again, firmly, "Do you know where I can find Sandra Ross?"

"Yes," said Stegman, "but it's not going to help you any."

"Then tell me where she is, for Christ's sake."

"You're going to need a shovel."

Harry paused. He studied Stegman's face. "What does that mean?"

Stegman smiled an off-balance, cracked smile. "You're not going to get an interview out of Sandra Ross," he said.

"Why? What happened to her?"

"You saw the movie. She was stabbed to death on the altar of sacrifice in the City of the Gods in Mexico."

"Yeah, right," said Harry quickly. "In the movie."

Stegman didn't respond, still smiling, eyes blank.

Harry broke out into a smile of his own. "Okay. Cute. So what are you saying? She's really dead?"

"It was an artistic decision, Harry."

"Right. Okay, joke's over. Good laugh. Now where is she, really?"

"I'm not joking, Mr. Tuttle," said Stegman.

Harry dropped his smile. He became very serious, studying Stegman for any clues; but the blankness offered none.

"Listen," said Harry, voice wavering. "Stop the games. You have to find her, Marcus. There's a lot at stake here. My career—"

"No can do," said Stegman.

"What do you mean, 'no can do'?"

"She's *dead*, Harry."

At that moment, Harry noticed Terrance and a creepy, dark-skinned young man standing in the doorway of the entertainment room, observing the conversation. Harry's eyes darted from them back to Stegman.

Harry felt his body grow prickly with perspiration. His breathing became tight.

"You're telling me you killed someone...and taped it...in front of a film crew?"

"There was no 'crew,' Harry. Just the three of us. And Sandra."

"But why?"

"That's a silly question. To make it more exciting, of course."

Harry exploded. The madness of the conversation had overwhelmed him completely. He jumped out of his chair. He clenched his hands into fists, stuck his face in front of Stegman and screamed, "To make it more exciting? *Are you fucking crazy?*"

"Harry, don't shout at me," said Stegman.

"What the hell is going on here? *What happened to Sandra Ross?*"

Stegman rose from his chair. He spoke vehemently, breaking out of his blank zone with a quivering, wild look in his eyes.

In that instant, staring into his face, hearing his words, Harry realized for the first time, that Stegman was over-the-edge, criminally insane.

"Listen to me, Harry," said Stegman. "The slaughter of Sandra Ross is the moment everybody remembers. Haven't you read your reviews? 'As electrifying as the shower sequence in *Psycho*!'"

Dumbfounded, Harry exclaimed, "But Alfred Hitchcock doesn't really kill Janet Leigh!"

"That's why our film is superior. Harry, you could spend millions of dollars on special effects and hire the best actress in the world; but you'd never get the same beautiful realism. The same fresh color in the blood. The same look in the eyes. The same sound in the scream." He extended a hand towards his video collection. "All of these movies, Harry, are ultimately flawed because they're phony. Our movie tops them all. It has the ultimate scare. It has *real* terror."

Harry stared into Stegman's eyes. "Dear God, you're insane."

"It's an insane world." Stegman again gestured to the DVDs. "Why else would so many people get so much gratification out of movies about killing? It's no big deal. I've just taken the concept one step further. Years from now, I won't be the only one. There will be others."

Harry's stomach turned over, churning; and his head pounded. His entire body shook. He had to get out of this mad house. He turned away.

"I've heard enough of this. I'm getting the police."

Stegman said, "I gave you popularity and respect and this is how you treat me."

Harry spun around. "I didn't want it at the cost of a human life!"

"No one ever promised that these things were cheap, Harry."

"What's to stop me from putting you in jail?"

"No," said Stegman. "The question is, what's to stop me from putting *you* in jail? After all, it's not my movie. I had nothing to do with it, remember. It's a Harry Tuttle movie. You better settle down, crazy man. Otherwise I might have to blow the whistle on you."

Harry took it all in. Then a monstrous tidal wave of panic hit him.

"Jesus Christ, I've taken credit for a snuff film."

And in that moment, he saw only red. He charged Stegman, grabbing him by the T-shirt, screaming into his face, "You can't do this to me, you lunatic! You've got to tell the people the truth—it wasn't me—"

Strong hands grabbed Harry and pulled him off Stegman. It was Terrance and the other creep, Stegman's movie collaborators in this house of horror.

Harry struggled to break free. Crimson faced, he continued to yell, "I could be locked up for the rest of my life for this!"

Stegman addressed his two roommates, "Take him outside. His head's a bit messed up right now. He needs to cool off."

They dragged Harry out of the room. Stegman disappeared from view. Harry screamed at him, "This wasn't part of the deal. *This-wasn't-part-of-the-deal!*"

The two men pulled Harry through the living room, past the camera equipment. As Harry squirmed he knocked over a big light, and it came crashing down. The roommates kept going, without hesitation, toward the front door.

They tossed Harry outside into the rain. He fell hard on his knees to the concrete, scrambled up, and spun back toward the door. It slammed in his face. The rain continued in sheets, and he became soaked.

Harry pounded on the door, screaming, words replaced by pure anguish. He punched at the door as if it was Stegman himself, until his hands couldn't take the pain; and then he howled into the sky like some kind of crazed monster from one of his films.

Harry Tuttle's life had just gone to hell.

22

On the television monitor, a young woman ran screaming for help in dark wilderness, stumbling through foliage, a sketchy silhouette under a full moon. Her scream was a traditional horror movie scream—big and full, but without much genuine fear behind it. In the next shot, closer, she tripped and fell. In an instant, a young man with a savage expression reached her and pounced. The footage became much tighter, the framing less controlled, dancing to keep up with the action. The woman, thrashing, became pinned under the man.

The man held a dagger. With a strong thrust, he jammed the blade into her side; and the woman made an ugly, deep-throated groan. Her eyes bugged with surprise and shock. The blade returned, swiftly, practically to the same wound; and then she screamed full force—this time a harrowing cry—different than her earlier, theatrical scream.

The woman exploded with a burst of desperate energy, catching the man with a slap that appeared full and unexpected, nearly toppling him. The camera fought to stay close. The blade returned to the flesh, striking her stomach, cutting through the white T-shirt, bringing a fast flood of redness.

The woman started sobbing, losing strength. The man panted, real panting, wheezing. One side of his face was red from the slap. With steady chops, the blade kept coming, catching her in the chest, the stomach again, and the neck. Her spastic movements fell limp and the killer took complete control.

The image abruptly froze.

Walter Wiggins had jabbed the "pause" button on the DVD player in his office. He leaned forward in his chair to get a better look.

The frame was an unnerving close-up of the wound to the woman's neck—a shot that lasted less than a second on screen, not enough to truly register—yet contained a chilling, clinical authenticity in freeze frame. Wiggins thought, *Why go to all that trouble for such a realistic special effect and then not let the shot linger so the audience can see it? Very unusual for such a low-budget film, where every penny gets showcased.*

He unfroze the image and continued watching.

The woman collapsed in a puddle of her own blood. The killer's hands dripped red. He straightened up and looked around, as if waiting for a cue. He nearly glanced into the camera lens.

The camera zoomed in on the dead woman.

Her eyes remained open, yet empty, and did not blink.

There was something about the image that chilled Walter Wiggins to the bone. He had seen thousands of movie death scenes over the years, but none like this.

Walter stopped the playback. He wondered if he was bonkers, or truly onto something big. While PJ Productions had provided him with a DVD transfer stamped "Reviewer's Copy," the movie had not yet been released on DVD to the consumer market. The movie was still in its successful theatrical run. At this time, few people had the opportunity to freeze frames or rewatch scenes to get a better look.

Wiggins watched the death scene one more time, reducing portions to super slo-mo, frame-by-frame playback.

It only strengthened his growing suspicions.

"Son of a bitch," he muttered.

Wiggins dug through a mess of mail and fast food wrappers on his desk, until he found his digital tape dub of the rough edit of the Harry Tuttle interview.

He slammed it into the player, connected to the same television, and switched the viewing mode from the DVD player to the tape. He fast-forwarded until he found the section he was looking for.

"—who stand out in particular, Sandra Ross," said Wiggins on the TV monitor. "Boy, she's good. Where did you find her?"

The question was met with an awkward silence. Harry struggled for words. The shot on him was close. The camera captured his discomfort.

"Where did I find her?" said Harry, blinking several times. "Well, word of mouth. Friends. I know her mother's cousin."

"I thought she was splendid," said Wiggins.

"Me too."

"What else has she done?"

Another long, awkward pause. Tuttle clearly did not want to talk about this actress. "You know...this must have been her first role. I really don't know."

A few questions later, Wiggins asked, "So you keep in touch with her?"

Tuttle looked like a deer caught in the headlights. He did not look at ease with this line of questioning. He had handled the earlier portions of the interview like a pro, chatting about the low-budget movie industry and his earlier pictures with relaxed charm.

But Sandra Ross made him nervous.

Wiggins punched buttons on the remote and returned to the DVD, back to the Sandra Ross death scene.

For the seventh time he watched her lying on the bare earth in the darkness, getting stabbed repeatedly while a handheld camera fought to keep up with the frantic struggle of life and death.

23

"A sabbatical?" said Paul Jacobs, repeating the word with a look of astonishment.

Harry nodded while tossing items from his desktop into a briefcase. "I'm taking some time off. I need a break. I won't be coming into the office for a while. I'm sure you can carry on without me."

Paul raised his voice. "But why now? You're finally getting what you've always wanted. Fame, recognition, respect. People are lining up to talk with you. Your movie is a hit, Harry."

"I don't like giving interviews."

"Don't like giving interviews?" Paul made a face. "That doesn't sound like you."

"I want a vacation. You took your vacation. Now I'm taking mine."

Paul's response hung for a moment. He stammered uncharacteristically before finding the words, "This makes no sense. You understand how the industry works. *Now* is the time for the publicity blitz. This opportunity won't wait. The train has left the station, Harry. Take your vacation another time. I'll pay for it. I'll send you anywhere in the world you want to go, just *not right now.*"

"I'm done doing PR for this movie," was all Harry could say.

"That's not going to fly, Harry. Because I just hired a public relations agency. We are lining up a week of media in New York. Print, radio, TV. The Today Show. Stern. Letterman. The movie's big, and we can make it so much bigger. We have to keep feeding this beast. Do you know how many screens we have this week? Have you seen the grosses?"

"I've seen the grosses," said Harry, trying to block out the irony.

"This baby is going global. We're going international in a big way."

"Great."

"I have big-time investors lined up to finance the next one—real money. We can get a major star. Do you want Matt Damon? Colin Farrell?"

"I want to go home."

"You can't go home!" thundered Paul. "We have work to do. We have *Maxim* magazine coming tomorrow morning at nine. We have *Entertainment Tonight* next week. We have to start on the DVD extras. There's the Toronto Film Festival. For God's sake, Harry!"

Harry snapped his briefcase shut and headed for the door. Paul followed.

"Just tell me what's wrong," said Paul. "Are you mad at me for some reason?"

"I'm not mad at you, Paul. It has nothing to do with you."

"Is it anxiety? The pressure of success? If so, I can get you pills. I know a doctor in Bel Air."

"I don't take pills."

"Harry, I don't understand. Six months ago you said you'd kill for a hit movie."

Harry spun around and nearly leapt out of his shoes. "I did not say that! I never said that!" He grabbed Paul's shirt. "Take it back."

Paul removed Harry's hands. "OK, OK. Settle down. Why are you being so hyper?"

Harry tried to regain his composure. *Long, deep breaths.* He wanted his meditation rug. He wanted out of the building.

Harry headed for the elevator. He stepped inside, turned around and told Paul, "I'm sorry. I know the timing is bad, but I have to take time off. I'm dealing with some personal issues. I can't explain them right now. I'll be back. I just don't know when."

And then the elevator doors closed, separating them.

* * *

Harry walked across the parking lot toward his car, relieved that he was done dealing with Paul. But Paul was nothing compared to the conversation that awaited.

"Harry Tuttle!"

Harry spun around to see Walter Wiggins squeezing from between two SUVs. He wore a mammoth Hawaiian shirt and green shorts.

"I was just on my way in to see you," said Wiggins.

"I'm sorry, but I'm late for an appointment," said Harry, turning away, heading for his car.

Wiggins followed as quickly as his stubby pink legs would take him. "You aren't returning my calls. I was in the area; I thought I'd drop by. I'm still looking for Sandra Ross."

The name struck Harry like a blow.

"Well, I can't help you," he shouted back. He reached his car and fumbled in a pocket for the key.

Wiggins reached him, panting.

Harry faced Wiggins. "Listen. You might as well skip it. She's not available. She's on vacation. She's on some island in the Bahamas. I don't have any contact information. I think she's in drug rehab. She's not allowed to do press at this time."

Wiggins said, "She's in drug rehab or on vacation, which is it?"

Harry realized that his lies were getting hurried, sloppy. The conversation needed a quick finish.

"Do me a favor," said Harry. "Just skip my whole segment, okay? I don't want to be on your show. Leave me out of it, or—or I'll have to sue you."

Wiggins looked him over. "Why so defensive, Tuttle? Is something wrong?"

"No."

"Well, I think there is." Wiggins moved closer to Harry. He lowered his tone and the words had bite. "I've been watching the DVD screener you gave me. I've been watching it a lot lately. The more I watch Sandra Ross's big scene, the more I think it might also have been her last scene. Do you catch my drift?"

Harry felt his bowels nearly release themselves. His skin went cold. Somehow, he managed to speak. "No. I—I don't catch your drift."

Wiggins smiled, smarmy and knowing. "Your movies were better when they had phony rubber monsters in them. What I think I see now scares the living hell out of me. Tuttle, I'm going to give you one week to bring me Sandra Ross. And if you fail...well, then you can tune in to Channel Five for the most shocking expose on a Hollywood director that the world has ever known. Care to comment?"

"You're crazy," said Harry.

"I don't think I'm the crazy one."

"Drop dead!" uttered Harry. He climbed into his car and shut the door on Wiggins. He started up the engine.

"I'll take that as a threat, Tuttle!" said Wiggins. As Harry backed out of the parking space, Wiggins cried out, *"I'm onto you!"*

* * *

Harry drove on Wilshire Boulevard with one hand on the wheel and one hand on his cell phone. He had to call Stegman. The maniac had created this mess, he had to get them out. He had to come forward.

As Harry fumbled with the cell phone, his brain everywhere but on the road, he ran a red light, causing a flurry of horns and a screech. He continued dialing, then realized—

—*shit, I can't have a phone record of calling Stegman!*

He promptly disconnected, threw the phone down, and began looking for a pay phone.

He pulled up into a parking space in front of Tom and Roxanne's, a modest diner that promised "Good coffee!" in the window.

Inside, scattered patrons sat on vinyl stools at the eating bar or in booths under local artwork. Pancake breakfasts mingled with hamburger lunches. Harry found a pay phone near a cabinet displaying pies.

He kept his voice lowered and his eyes alert for eavesdroppers.

"Marcus!" he hissed into the receiver. "It's Harry."

"Hi Harry."

"Shut up and listen. Wiggins suspects something. He's been examining the scene where Sandra Ross is killed. He thinks I did something to her. If I don't find her in the next seven days, he's going to break loose with some kind of investigative piece—about *me*!"

There was a pause on the other end. Then Stegman said, "Interesting."

Harry could barely contain himself from shouting. His face turned red as he squeezed out his response in a taut but restrained tone. "*Interesting?* No, it's *not* interesting, you maniac. Can't you see that I'm a dead man? You got me into this, God damn it; and you better help get me out."

"Wiggins can't prove anything," said Stegman. "He's bluffing."

"How do you know?"

"Trust me. Wiggins won't be able to pin anything on you. He has zero credibility. He's a fat little fool. Everything will be all right. So relax."

"*Relax?*"

"Take a Valium, Harry," said Stegman, followed by a click.

Harry stared at the receiver in his hand. He wanted to smash it against the wall. He felt like he was losing his mind.

"Hey, are you Harry Tuttle?" A chubby, grinning middle-aged woman came up to him, hair in a bun. "*The* Harry Tuttle?"

"Um..." Harry had to think it over. His mind was elsewhere. "Yeah...sure..."

"I love your movie!" she said loudly. She turned and waved to her three companions in a nearby booth. "It *is* him! It's Harry Tuttle! This guy's *famous*!"

Other patrons looked up from their meals, excited by the prospect of a celebrity in their midst.

"I'm not famous..." said Harry faintly.

"But you are! You are!"

A small circle of people gathered around him. Someone held out a pen and napkin for his signature.

The manager, a burly man, came out from behind the counter with a digital camera. "Do you mind if we take your picture for our wall? The meal's on us."

"I loved *Deadly Desires*..."

"Are you working on anything new..."

"I saw you on E!"

"Where do you get your ideas?"

"Is there going to be a sequel?"

"Do you think you'll win an Oscar?"

They continued to bombard him with questions, hands thrust out for handshakes, pens waving for autographs. But Harry just stood there, motionless, helpless, with nothing to say.

REEL THREE

24

Lenny stared, out of focus, at the dinner bill for about ten minutes, attempting math in his foggy skull, until he finally concluded *screw the tip, the service wasn't that hot anyhow.*

To help wash down the steak and fries, Lenny had consumed seven bottles of beer, draining each one in a short number of long swallows. He now blamed those beers for his troubles with math. He was decent at math. At least it wasn't one of the classes he had flunked back in high school.

English was another matter. Total agony. Those bastards had expected him to write long-winded essays on bullshit books. That one teacher, Mr. Huff, was the worst. Homework every night. Calling on unprepared people to humiliate them. Fuck *Oliver Twist!*

Lenny felt a sudden urge to go find and pound on Mr. Huff, but a small alliance of brain cells unsaturated by alcohol reminded him he was fretting over something that happened ten years ago on the other side of Pennsylvania.

Lenny counted bills out of his wallet and dropped them on the table in an impressive stack. He put the biggest bill on top. Most of the others were singles, stained with grease and oil from the auto body shop. He rounded the amount due to the next dollar. *There's your tip!*

Lenny shoved himself away from the table, causing a bottle to topple—no big deal, it was empty—and lifted his large frame from the chair.

He growled away the minor head rush and aimed for the exit.

"Thank you! Come again!" chirped the hostess, young but dogfaced, nice tits but fat legs; and he gave her a half wave.

Lenny stepped outside, and the sky was a lot darker than the last time he had seen it. The air was cooler. His legs started to move in one direction, but his car was in another direction. He nearly stumbled while trying to correct himself.

"Careful there, Lenny."

Lenny stopped and turned. The voice was bold and sarcastic. Who the f—

Pottstown Police Officer Roger Henry stood nearby on the walkway, hands on hips, watching Lenny with a smirk.

"Forgot where I parked my car," Lenny muttered.

Lenny and Officer Henry had a history. In fact, Lenny had a history with several of the local cops, but it was Officer Henry who always seemed to be lurking around a corner with nothing better to do than try and bust his ass. Meanwhile, bank robbers and crack dealers ran amok.

Henry had been the officer reporting to the scene of several ugly fights involving Lenny. The cops never seemed to witness or recognize the incidents that warranted the beatings; they only arrived in time to see the beatings, piling on him and dragging him off for overnight stays in the drunk tank.

Officer Henry had also nailed him for drunk driving. Twice.

"Going for a drive?" asked Henry, walking over, eyes fixed on Lenny's eyes, probably sniffing for booze.

"What's it your business?" snapped Lenny, then cursing himself because it came out sounding slurred and sloppy.

"I know you're already familiar with the drunk driving laws of the State of Pennsylvania, but I'd be happy to offer a refresher course," said Henry.

As an involuntary reflex, Lenny's upper teeth pressed on his lower lip and he began the "F" sound. But he stopped himself from uttering a short phrase that would have invited a whole bunch of new problems.

Henry stood very close now. "I just don't want you to do anything stupid, Lenny."

The restaurant sat across the parking lot from a large shopping mall. Lenny looked over Officer Henry's shoulder at the illuminated storefronts. Office Depot. Kohl's. Target. He hated the mall.

"I need to do some shopping," said Lenny. He moved past Henry, heading for the mall.

"Good idea," said Officer Henry. "I hope you mean it. I'd hate to see you behind the wheel of your car anytime soon."

Lenny walked about fifty feet before turning to look back.

Officer Henry remained out front of the steak house. Still watching him.

Lenny continued to the mall, grinding his teeth the whole way.

He entered through the electronic doors and the abrupt brightness made him angrier. It was Friday night and the place was busy with loud teenyboppers, the most annoying human beings on the planet, aside from crying babies, of course.

Lenny realized that he probably hadn't stepped foot inside

this mall since Nora left him. She liked the mall. She liked to browse and try on clothes she could never buy. She somehow found interest in entire stores devoted to soap, or sunglasses, or *calendars*, for Christ's sake.

Before they were married, he used to come here with her a lot. He put up with it. He'd put up with a lot of things during courtship so they could seal the deal.

After they married, he refused to go shopping. He simply hated it. She could go to the mall with her girlfriends as long as he preapproved any expenditures.

She was good about that, too. Obedient.

Lenny stopped walking. He realized he was starting to dwell on Nora again. He had promised himself he would stop obsessing over that bitch. That rotten little bitch who snuck out on him in the middle of the night. It still infuriated him. The beers at dinner were supposed to wash her out of his mind. Now she was back with the tide.

God damn it!

He noticed people staring at him and realized he had said that last thought out loud.

Lenny started moving again. He needed a destination, and it could not be his car; and it would *not* be the interior of one of these stupid stores.

Lenny came upon the mall's movie theaters. Ten screens of crap, but maybe there was something he could tolerate for two hours. Long enough to sober up a bit and make sure that imbecile cop disappeared.

If the movie sucked, he could take a nap.

His eyes scanned the movie titles. He recognized one of them as a Will Smith action flick receiving heavy promo on TV.

"Does this movie have a lot of ass kicking?" he asked the gray-haired woman behind the ticket window.

She said she didn't know, and she pointed out that the movie had started 45 minutes ago.

He looked back at the list of titles.

"What about *Deadly Desires?* What's that all about?"

"It's a horror movie, sir."

"About what?"

"I don't know, sir."

"Has it started yet?"

"Just got underway."

"Alright. One ticket for Deadly whatever."

Lenny entered the multiplex.

He considered buying popcorn, but then saw the prices, which pissed him off. He went looking for the right theater, which took several minutes, which pissed him off. Every corridor seemed to lead to some stupid Disney cartoon or faggy romance, which...

He finally found *Deadly Desires* and entered the darkened theater. The movie on the screen was dark, a nighttime scene. His eyes took a moment to adjust. He stood in the aisle until he could see.

The place was about half full. Lenny moved into a row near the back. He dropped into a cushioned seat and threw a leg over the seat in front of him. It was rather comfortable. Maybe he would nap. He hoped that Officer Henry remained perched in front of the steak house, waiting for his return. Let him stand there like a fool!

On the movie screen, some Hollywood pretty boy sat inside a camping tent. A lantern lit up his face. He was talking in low tones about an archeological site and old rituals.

"Human sacrifice was part of their culture," said pretty boy. "According to Mayan legend, priests would rip out the beating heart of their victims with a flint knife, and throw the bodies down from the temple to appease the god of death."

Lenny chuckled. Horror movies usually made him chuckle. They tried so hard to be spooky, but they were usually retarded. "The god of death," he muttered loudly.

Someone shushed him.

Lenny shushed back, fiercely.

The actor on the movie screen droned on and on about Aztecs and pyramids and how the pyramids were built.

Lenny started to shut his eyes.

Through the slits, he saw Nora.

He closed his eyes completely, then opened them wide.

Nora?

The pretty boy on the movie screen was talking to Nora. Lenny's Nora. She nodded, listening with big eyes, pouty lips.

Her hair was different, shorter and darker; and she had been dolled up, prettier; but it was definitely her.

His escaped wife. His Nora. In Hollywood. *Making movies!*

Lenny jumped up to his feet.

"You filthy whore!" he screamed at the movie screen.

People turned in their seats to look at him.

The screen showed a close-up of Nora. Her head was as big as the side of a house.

Lenny was going out of his mind. He jabbed a finger toward the screen. "*You bitch; you filthy bitch; you can't run from me; you no good slutty whore!*"

"Shut up, you lunatic!" someone shouted from a few rows away. Several people clapped in approval. The audience began buzzing.

"You shut up, asshole!" screamed Lenny.

One of the men in the audience stood up and turned around. "Listen, pal, if you don't shut up, I'm going to get the manager."

Behind the man's silhouette, the movie continued.

"Human remains have been found on this site as recently as five years ago," said the pretty boy. "The Mexican government keeps it very quiet. They don't want to hurt tourism."

"You're scaring me," said Nora. "Look at me, I'm shaking."

"Oh, hon, I'm sorry. It's okay," said pretty boy, and he reached for her. They embraced. "Relax sweetheart." They kissed. A big, sloppy movie kiss.

"*I'm coming for you, Nora!*" screamed Lenny. "Don't think you can get away with this." He began moving out of the row. Toward the end of the aisle, a seated couple didn't bring in their knees quick enough, and Lenny banged into them. The man said something unwise, and Lenny punched him twice in the face, fast and hard; and the man went quiet while his date screamed.

Lenny stomped out of the theater, back into the brightness. He turned toward the corridor walls where a succession of movie posters announced the current showings.

Lenny stood before the poster for *Deadly Desires*, hands clenched into fists. The artwork depicted a large blade, a full moon, and off to each side of the blade, a bunch of little faces of the people appearing in the movie.

Sure enough, there was Nora, sexed up, mouth open, a look of fear.

"You better be scared, you rotten bitch." He searched the movie credits for information. He didn't see Nora's name, but she probably had used a fake stage name, like all those fruity actors did.

"Sandra Ross" was the first actress listed. Could Sandra Ross be Nora Hurley?

No big deal, he would find her.

The most important information was readily available.

PJ Productions.

Written and Directed by Harry Tuttle.

"Harry Tuttle," said Lenny. "Hotshot Hollywood slimeball, stealing a man's wife." This Tuttle guy was probably screwing her. That's what all those movie directors did—screw hot young actresses in exchange for movie roles. The casting couch! How else would you explain a total nobody suddenly appearing in a major movie?

Lenny wanted to punch the movie poster. His insides felt like they were on fire. After many months of despair and aimlessness, he felt pumped up with passion, purpose, and a destination.

Hollywood, California.

"Nora," he growled at the movie poster, "you are a dead woman."

25

Harry stood in line at the Village Coffee Shop for his daily frappuccino and bagel, with one significant alteration to his morning routine: he was incognito. He wore sunglasses, a cap, and did not scan the room for familiar faces. Instead, he watched his shoes. For possibly the first time in his life, living in a community that thrived on attention, Harry Tuttle did not want to be recognized.

He just wanted to get his goods, retreat home, hunker down and stay out of sight until *Deadly Desires* blew out of the public consciousness and became yesterday's fad.

Unfortunately, the movie kept making good money and earning good notices.

Harry had spent many sleepless nights debating what to do next. Several times he'd climbed into his Audi, headed for the LAPD to reveal Stegman's crimes, but wound up back in his driveway.

He feared the police would not believe his innocence. They would arrest him as an accomplice to murder. Even if they didn't hold him accountable for the fate of Sandra Ross, he would still face devastation and ruin. He would be hit with fraud charges for *Deadly Desires*. His filmmaking career would come to a humiliating end. His reason to live would die.

Harry spent hours parked in his driveway, arguing with himself. In the end, he couldn't let go of the success.

"Harrrry."

Harry felt something like an electric shock travel up his spine. The voice behind him was shrill; it was nasal; it was...

"Julie," he said simply, turning to face his ex-wife. She stood behind him in line with her new husband, acclaimed British director Nigel Howard. Nigel was tall, which gave him the opportunity to look down his nose at Harry. He always had his lips pursed together in a weird, suppressed smile. Harry chalked it up to smugness.

They were the last two people on the planet Earth he wanted to talk to now.

"What's with the sunglasses? You have a hangover?" Julie asked.

"No. Just tired." He removed the shades and the room brightened, but not his mood.

"Congratulations, Harry," said Nigel. "I hear that your little movie is doing well." His accent somehow underscored the condescension.

"Yes," chimed in Julie. "Way to go."

"I wouldn't call it a *little* movie," said Harry, bristling. "It's been a pretty big success."

"Yes, but you know what I meant—the production."

Harry shifted the topic. "I understand you two are keeping busy with a 'little movie' of your own."

"*Army of Steel*," said Julie proudly. "It's going to be the blockbuster to end all blockbusters."

Nigel added, "We just finished five months of preproduction, and we're starting principal photography. We're shooting all over L.A. You won't be able to miss us. In fact, we'll be closing down a road up by your house."

"Thanks," said Harry. "The traffic's not bad enough as it is."

"Nigel's got a special effects army on this one, it's so huge," said Julie. "These guys are the best in the business."

Nigel nodded. "It's amazing what you can do with major studio backing. They gave me a $110 million budget. It's the greatest toy box a director could ever have. I feel like a kid at Christmas. We've got 200 technicians and about 500 different special effects. A lot of it is CGI, but there are also some live action stunts that are far superior to anything else out there."

"Well, I suppose the videogame crowd will go for it," said Harry.

Nigel didn't lose his smug smile. "This film will appeal to *all* generations, from eight to eighty. We have an all-star cast with a major draw for every demographic. We've got Tom—"

"I know, I know. I've read about it."

"Don't forget your biggest star," teased Julie, hitting Nigel in the arm.

"Ah yes, a sweet young thing named Julie Howard," said Nigel. "I heard she's pretty good."

Julie *Howard*. It stung Harry almost as much as *your little movie*.

"I'm going to be in *Vanity Fair*," said Julie, but Harry didn't have to respond because his turn had come up at the counter. He turned his back to them and ordered his frappuccino and bagel.

"To go, please," he said.

On his way out, he wished Julie and Nigel well with *Army of Steel*.

"Good luck with...what is it, *Deadly Dangers?*" asked Nigel.

"*Deadly Desires,*" said Harry.

"Yes, good luck with the monster movies," said Nigel. A quick movie clip ran in Harry's mind: a fist hitting Nigel squarely in his smug face. Nigel falling down. Harry pouring hot coffee on his head.

Harry walked out to his car. He climbed behind the wheel, shut the door, and sat there for a moment, munching on his bagel and taking sips from his frappuccino. The food and coffee made him feel better, but his mood promptly tanked again when he saw Julie and Nigel leaving the Village Coffee Shop, arm in arm.

I don't love her anymore, but why does it still sting?

Harry placed his coffee in the cup holder. He took out his cell phone. He dialed Rachel. They had a date planned for that evening, but he couldn't wait until then...

She answered on the third ring, and he told her, "I just wanted to hear your voice."

"Harry, that's so sweet," she said. "I'm glad you called. I'm so excited about tonight. I haven't been to a Lakers game in years."

"I checked our tickets. We have great seats." Paul had given them to Harry a few weeks ago, a freebie from a happy investor. "We'll be able to smell the players' B.O."

She laughed. "I'm just looking forward to one of those pretzels that are as big as your head."

They carried on with the light, cozy conversation for a few more minutes, until Harry's confidence levels felt restored. He confirmed the time he would pick her up, and they said their goodbyes.

Harry hung up and checked his watch. Eight hours until game time.

He shoved Julie to the back of his mind. He sidestepped the horrors of *Deadly Desires*. He continued to focus on Rachel. Her beauty, her sweetness, her purity.

Everything bad in his life became overpowered by the happiness Rachel brought him. And then he realized he might be in love.

26

Walter Wiggins stepped out of a side entrance to WKKG Studios as evening descended on Los Angeles. Even though he had a reserved parking spot close to the building, he was perspiring and out of breath by the time he reached his red Cadillac STS. Everywhere he went, he dragged along 250 pounds of human flesh on his short frame. He knew that a lifetime of sitting on his ass watching movies had done this to him. But he also knew that sitting on his ass watching movies all day paid handsomely—more money than any of his highbrow journalism colleagues would ever see. While they worked insane hours for pitiful pay to scratch out stories about city council bickering or ozone levels, he got to attend glitzy Hollywood press junkets and gab with the stars. If he was well fed along the way...so be it. The rest of them? Jealous.

Wiggins removed his checkered pink and yellow sports jacket and tossed it in the back seat. He stuffed himself behind the steering wheel and slammed the door. He twisted the key in the ignition.

The roar of his engine drowned out the sound of a second car engine that promptly kicked up nearby.

Wiggins flipped on his headlights.

Forty feet away, the other car flipped on its headlights.

Wiggins backed out of his parking space and headed for the parking lot exit.

The second car followed Wiggins out of the parking lot and into the street.

Wiggins didn't pay any attention to the second car. It was probably a member of the studio crew, or one of the office boys. Nothing to warrant a second thought. His mind was on more important things.

Harry Tuttle. Sandra Ross. *Deadly Desires.* And single-handedly uncovering the biggest, most shocking Hollywood scandal in the history of the movies.

Shooting down Sunset Boulevard, illuminated by the shining lights of L.A. nightlife, Walter Wiggins began rehearsing his acceptance speech for the Pulitzer Prize.

27

Maria opened the apartment door and greeted Harry. She wore a black leotard that clung to her trim, athletic build. She puffed a strand of hair away from her face.

"Rachel's getting ready; she'll be with you in a sec. I was just doing my stretching exercises. Come in—make yourself comfortable."

Harry walked to the couch and sat down on the center cushion. Maria said, "I heard you got great seats to the Lakers game."

Harry shrugged. "Yeah. I guess so."

"Look at you, all blasé." She told him about her friend, Michelle, a Laker Girl. "She's so lucky. What a great gig, you're on TV, like every night. It's amazing exposure."

"Oh shit," said Harry. His eye caught the new edition of *Entertainment Weekly* magazine on the coffee table in front of him. It was open to an article on *Deadly Desires*: a full-page photograph of Harry stood alongside the headline "The High Art of Low-budget." Harry promptly shut the magazine.

"Great article," said Maria. "Don't you think?"

"I don't know; I haven't read it," said Harry.

"Really?" She couldn't believe it. "If *Entertainment Weekly* magazine was writing about me, I'd want to read it. I'd buy every copy I could find. But I guess it's different when you're famous."

"I'm not famous," said Harry. "I'm just the flavor of the month. Six months from now, they'll be saying 'Harry who?'"

"I don't think so," she said. Then Rachel entered the room—and Harry's heart skipped a beat—because she was altogether gorgeous despite being packaged in a simple white blouse and jeans. Her warm blue eyes and genuine smile lit him up inside.

She hugged him, and he held her tight.

"Good to see you," he said.

"Good to see you, Harry."

Maria moved to another part of the room to give them space.

Harry told Rachel, "You're the only thing that's going right in my life."

"What's wrong?" She looked him over with concern.

"Things are just...crazy."

"Bad day at the office?"

"You could say that."

"You look a little tired."

"I am. I'm taking a break from work for a while."

"Good. You deserve some time off. You've been so busy."

"I want some of my privacy back. You don't realize how much you appreciate it until you lose it."

Rachel perked up then and said, "Hey, stay right there. I have something to show you. It's cool. Don't move."

"Okay..."

She bounded out of the room and returned moments later with something rolled up into a tube shape. "Look what I got."

Rachel unrolled the tube to reveal the movie poster for *Deadly Desires*: a garish montage of frightened faces, including Sandra Ross, split down the middle by a large blade.

Harry had to look away.

Rachel said, "My friend Jay works at Mann Theatres, and I begged him for it; and he finally gave in. I'm going to have it framed."

"Great," said Harry without emotion, looking across the room at a blank wall.

"Will you sign it for me?"

"Not right now—I'm not really—maybe some other time."

Disappointed by his bland reaction, she rolled up the poster. She examined him. "What's wrong? It's your movie poster. I thought you'd be flattered."

He stepped over and touched her arm, trying to sooth her confusion. "I'm just...I guess I'm tired of talking about that movie and seeing it everywhere. You know, I've made other movies."

"But not like this one," said Rachel. "Harry, this is the movie that brought us together."

"How do you mean?"

She put aside the poster and took Harry's hands. She looked into his eyes.

"After I saw the rave review on *Flick Picks*, I went to see the movie and I loved it. It was incredible. That's when I realized how amazing you are. Your other movies—well, they didn't have the same effect on me. But when I watched *Deadly Desires*, it scared me; it excited me; it stirred something up inside; and I thought to myself, 'I've got to give this guy a closer look.' And I'm glad I did."

Harry pushed out a small chuckle. "But it's really not that good. I don't know what all the fuss is about."

"You're so modest," exclaimed Rachel. "That one scene—the murder in the woods at the start with that girl—the way she's screaming and he keeps stabbing her—God, I get chills just thinking about it."

"We better get to the Staples Center or we're going to be late for the tip-off," said Harry. "Parking's going to be a nightmare."

They said their goodbyes to Maria and headed for the door. "I'll watch for you on TV," said Maria. "Call me on your cell phone and wave."

* * *

As it turned out, Harry and Rachel missed the first ten minutes of the game. They got stuck in a massive traffic jam, courtesy of road closings caused by the filming of Nigel Howard's action epic *Army of Steel.*

28

Hollywood Memories earned towers of praise among film buffs as the biggest and best movie memorabilia store in the Los Angeles area, and perhaps the world. While the building itself was relatively small, every square foot was crammed to the rafters with eye-popping collectibles covering many decades. Tourists and industry professionals alike flocked to the site to prowl the bulging shelves and overflowing boxes of lobby cards, publicity stills, one-sheets, animation cells, scripts, and books. Entire sections of the store were dedicated to classic icons such as James Dean, Marilyn Monroe, The Three Stooges, and Mickey Mouse. The walls behind the counter were covered in framed autographed portraits of TV and film celebrities, ranging from the famous to the infamous. It was not unusual to find Quentin Tarantino or Martin Scorsese deep in an aisle, immersed in motion picture artifacts.

The store's owner, Victor Grady, was widely regarded as the king of motion picture trivia. Anyone conducting in-depth film or TV research inevitably turned to Victor and picked his encyclopedic brain. He could rattle off the cast of unaired pilots, recite complete filmographies, identify old movies from the vaguest plot summary, and unearth fascinating factoids on bit-role performers. He had even revealed the early porn film appearances of a couple of well-known stars.

The *Los Angeles Star*, in a lengthy article about the store, gushed, "Victor Grady has probably not only heard of that obscure movie that you remember and nobody else has seen, he can also show you the poster, the lobby card set, early drafts of the screenplay, and perhaps an original prop from the filming."

The article quoted Victor stating, "Ninety-six percent of my brain's capacity is filled with movie trivia. Just don't ask me how to change the oil in my car."

Walter Wiggins often visited Victor to collect information on subjects he was researching. Victor never failed him, and Wiggins rewarded him with movie premiere tickets and piles of promotional materials he accumulated from the studios.

This evening, Wiggins had a new challenge for him. He hoped Victor wouldn't disappoint.

"Sandra Ross!" thundered Wiggins as he entered the store. Heads turned.

From behind the counter, half hidden by dangling T-shirts, Victor took up the challenge and responded, "*Deadly Desires*. New release. Sandra Ross plays the role of Helen Shaw, first victim of Michael Drake, who uses human sacrifice to propel his political career. Excellent film. Raw, like a documentary. Best of its kind since *Blair Witch Project*."

Wiggins made his way over to Victor, knocking into a cardboard standup of Sylvester Stallone and nearly upsetting a display of *Wizard of Oz* collectible plates. The aisles were too damn narrow for a full-figured man like himself.

"Okay," said Wiggins. "You passed the first test. Now tell

me—what else has she done? And where can I find her? I'm looking for any background you can come up with."

"Did you try the Screen Actors Guild?"

"They were no help. That's why I'm turning to the expert."

"I would imagine you've Googled her and tried IMDB?"

"Oh yes."

Victor lowered his eyes and concentrated. He was a graying man in his fifties, long gray sideburns, with narrow glasses perched on the end of his nose. He was permanently hunched—no doubt from ducking beneath all the movie memorabilia that crowded his every step. His shirt glistened with buttons of movie icons. He rattled when he walked.

"Sandra Ross..." mumbled Victor, still thinking hard. You could nearly hear the gears grinding away.

Finally, he looked back at Wiggins and said, "Crap."

"Don't tell me I've stumped the master," said Wiggins.

"Hold on a second." Victor retreated to an area of file cabinets lining the wall behind him. He scoured the labels on the drawers. "Let's see..."

While he conducted his search, another customer entered the store. Wiggins turned and glanced at him. He was a pasty, greasy young man in his twenties with rings under his eyes, a goatee, and long black hair tied in a ponytail.

Wiggins turned away. Sometimes when people recognized him they wanted to argue about one of his recent reviews. It was either "How could you recommend that movie?" or "How could you not like this movie?"

It was always tiresome. He couldn't help it if the public taste was inferior to his own.

The greasy young man busied himself looking at some Betty Boop mugs.

Victor returned to Wiggins with the press kit for *Deadly Desires*. "There might be some bios in here," he said, placing it on the counter.

Wiggins flipped open the folder. He frowned. "I've already seen this. It wasn't much help." The production notes were skimpy, the bios were sketchy, and the press release said nothing. The enclosed CD-ROM offered little more than a series of digital photos created from film frames.

"I've got some horror film magazines from the past few months—you know, *Fangoria*, *Shock Cinema*, that kind of thing—I'll bet there's an article in one of those. They cover the independents. Don't give up on me yet. I'll be right back."

Victor left the counter to go scour an aisle of film periodicals. As Victor left the counter, another clerk stepped forward, a chipper middle-aged man wearing a Groucho Marx T-shirt. "Can I help anyone?"

Wiggins shook his head no.

"Yes, please," said the pasty young man with the ponytail. He leaned against the counter next to Wiggins and pointed at something high on a shelf behind the clerk. "How much for the Oscar?"

The clerk had to climb on a stepstool to retrieve the statuette. He brought it to the customer to inspect.

"You don't see many of these for sale," said the clerk. "Anybody who received an Oscar after 1950 had to sign an agreement that they wouldn't sell it. And the Academy's been trying to buy back any pre-1950 Oscars that are on the market. This one here belonged to a film editor, Ronald Kelp, 1946. It's in excellent condition, one of a kind."

The customer lifted the statuette off the counter. "Heavy."

"Weighs nearly ten pounds."

"How much are you asking?"

"Thirteen hundred dollars."

"I'll take it."

The clerk appeared surprised by the immediate response. "Well...then...great. It's yours." He chuckled. "You can take it home and give yourself an acceptance speech."

"Funny," said the customer, not smiling. He looked over at Wiggins. Wiggins looked away before their eyes could connect.

Why on earth would somebody pay all that money for something they didn't earn?

Victor showed up a minute later, palms out to Wiggins, apologetic. "Nothing. Darn it, Walter, I couldn't find anything on her. You win, you stumped the master. I feel like you should get a prize. Do you want a gift certificate?"

"No," said Wiggins.

Wiggins turned on his heels and headed for the exit, moving carefully through the obstacle course of memorabilia.

"I'll keep looking," Victor cried out after him. "Something's bound to turn up."

"You've told me everything I need to know," said Wiggins. He opened the door and left the store.

The night air was heavy and still. Wiggins moved across the dark parking lot toward his car. His wheezing became amplified in the silence. His stout body heaved with every step. His mind reeled: a new actress in a hit film, and there's *no information on her whatsoever.* It only helped to seal his suspicions. Harry Tuttle had done something to her, for real.

As Wiggins approached his car, he reached into his pocket and pulled out his keys. The key chain featured Scooby Doo—an old promotional freebie from one of the studios. Before he could open the car door, he heard a voice behind him.

"Mr. Wiggins?"

Walter stopped, surprised, because he hadn't heard anyone coming. He turned and opened his mouth to reply. He didn't have enough time to utter a word.

The pony-tailed customer from inside the store rushed forward, holding up the Academy Award by its head.

The base of the statuette crashed into the side of the critic's skull, just above his left ear. He saw an explosion of stars. He let out a large, involuntary groan.

The base struck him in the head again, then a third time, and a fourth, wielded like a fierce hammer. Every blow brought a new eruption of blinding pain. Wiggins toppled off balance and struggled to remain standing. The next blow, the most brutal one yet, sent a network of searing cracks through the back of his head. Wiggins cried out, short yelps of pain and fear. The attacker's reply came in a crisp, flat monotone, "It's thumbs down for you, fat boy."

Wiggins collapsed hard. The sky became replaced by pavement, and then the blood in his eyes wiped everything away.

29

Harry's ears filled with screams. The Los Angeles Lakers had just sunk the game-leading shot with 2.4 seconds remaining, after chipping away for a good 15 minutes to close the gap with the San Antonio Spurs. The collective mass erupted in a frenzy. No one remained seated. Men danced. Women roared. High-energy music thundered on the P.A.

Harry could not feel more detached from it all. He joined the celebration mechanically, pumped his fist in the air a few times, whooped without passion, and clapped limply. Rachel, who could not name more than two L.A. players before the game, now cheered like a hardcore fan who had just witnessed the clinching of the NBA Championship.

The crowd continued to hum after the final buzzer. Following a ceremony of high fives, the Lakers disappeared into the locker room. Harry and Rachel wound their way in small footsteps toward an exit. Bursts of joy and laughter echoed throughout the cavernous corridors.

"What a game, I'm still shaking," said Rachel, throwing an arm around Harry and pulling him close. "Ooh, so are you."

They found his Audi in the crowded outdoor lot and

climbed in. Harry joined a long line of red brake lights going nowhere. She thanked him for the game and great seats.

"No problem," murmured Harry.

She stared at him for a moment as car lights projected odd patterns of illumination and shadow across his face.

"Is everything all right?" she asked.

"What do you mean?"

"You've been so quiet."

"I guess I'm a little distracted. You know, work has been crazy."

"Well, let me distract you from your distraction." As Harry's car idled, she leaned over and gave him a long, soft kiss.

Several inebriated fans walking past the car caught sight of the action and cheered.

Rachel pulled back gently and looked into Harry's eyes.

Harry smirked. "She shoots. She scores."

"So where's the postgame show?"

"We can go to my place. I like having home court advantage."

"Sure, coach. And feel free to send me to the showers."

He smiled in response, successfully aroused *and* distracted from his beguilement. A minivan behind them blasted its horn, and Harry realized the line had started moving. He tossed the Audi into drive.

* * *

The front door to Harry's home creaked open and no one entered. The darkened figures of Harry and Rachel remained in the doorway, leaned into one another, kissing. Fumbling to gain entry without disrupting the continuity, Harry's free hand reached in and waved for the light switch.

Rachel grabbed his arm and pulled it down.

"Don't," she said.

"You like the dark?"

"Don't you?"

"I love the dark."

They entered the house and shut the door. They knocked into an umbrella stand, backed into a wall, and continued kissing. Harry lost himself in the moment—and found a depth of passion he had not experienced since the early days of his marriage to Julie. The passion swept everything else out of his brain—the fear and the chaos, the future and the past.

He released words between kisses, "Want to—go—up?"

"Mm hmm..."

Despite the mutual agenda, it took them five minutes to disengage and start up the stairs. Harry knew where the night was headed and his thoughts swam in fragments, *Do I have condoms...I hope I made the bed...*

Harry closed the bedroom curtains, but the darkness was absolute; so he turned on a small table lamp. It lit up Rachel with a film-like grain. She smiled at him. He wished he could go grab a camera and record this perfect moment. They joined in a kiss.

Sometime during the kiss, she said his name. He realized the tone was an inquiry. "Harry...?"

"Hmm?" he responded.

"Why do you have a bottle of perfume?"

He stepped back, and she broke out in a small giggle and pointed.

On his dresser, mixed in with various masculine items like aftershave, an antiperspirant stick, and a men's comb, she'd spotted a bottle of Petals Perfume.

The design on the label had a funky 1970s look to it, with tall, rolling gold lettering.

"Do you like to smell pretty?" she teased.

"No..."

For a moment she turned serious. "Is there another woman in your life?"

"*No*," he said.

"Then..."

"I'll tell you," he said. "But you'll just think I'm weird."

"I know you're weird. I've seen your movies."

Harry picked up the squat, round bottle and put it in her hands. She examined it and said, "It looks old."

"It is old. They don't sell this anymore. You're lucky if you can find it on eBay."

"You collect perfume?"

"No. Just this one. It's a flashback in a bottle. Did you know—your sense of smell has the strongest memory of all your senses."

She nodded, looking at the clear liquid inside. "Sure. Sometimes a certain smell will remind me of a place—like my grandmother's house when I was a kid. I'll be able to picture everything, just from the smell."

"Exactly. Well, this perfume is my personal time machine," said Harry. "When I was growing up in Boston, my parents went out every Saturday night. I didn't have any brothers or sisters to play with. I had a babysitter, Karen. She was in high school. And she liked to talk on the phone with her boyfriend. She wasn't much into playing with a nine-year-old boy. So she would stick me in front of the TV on Saturday nights and let me watch whatever I wanted. That's how I got hooked on Creature Features."

"Creature Features?"

"Every Saturday night in Boston they had a horror film hosted by this guy, Ghoularie, on the local network. He showed films my parents would never let me watch. My parents were really straightlaced, and these films were way out there. Some of them scared the hell out of me and gave me nightmares, but they also excited me. It was like riding a rollercoaster. That's how I got my kicks. Horror movies were my adrenaline fix."

"Where does the perfume come in?"

"Karen, the babysitter, wore Petals Perfume. Too much of it. She was just a kid herself, you know? But this perfume—all these years later—one whiff and I'm back to those days, the exhilaration, the feeling of being scared but being safe. I was young enough for the movies to frighten me, but old enough to recognize that it was all make believe and I was not in any real danger. I craved the buzz. I couldn't wait until Saturday night when Karen would arrive, accompanied by this smell."

Her finger touched the opener on top of the bottle—a smooth, glass loop. "Can I...?"

"Sure."

She removed the top and held the small bottle under her nose. "Not bad," she said. "Has a rose scent. A bit heavy." Her eyes lifted from the bottle to meet his gaze. "Was Karen good looking?"

"Beautiful. But that's beside the point."

"Was it?" Rachel smiled. "Think about it. Your young hormones are kicking in, and there's this hot young babysitter in your house, in charge, putting you to bed at night. Heart going pitter-patter. Is it really the monsters? She's still a kid, like you, but her body is blossoming into an adult."

"Well," said Harry, "if you put it that way..."

As Rachel spoke, with her eyes on Harry, she unbuttoned her blouse with her free hand. “She’s probably talking dirty to her boyfriend on the phone, and you’re eavesdropping.”

“Only during commercials.”

Rachel’s blouse split apart to reveal the straight lines of her collarbones and the rising softness of her breasts.

Rachel dabbed perfume on two fingers. She traced the fingers between her breasts, just above the bra.

Harry smiled.

She placed the open bottle in his hand. He took it. She finished removing her blouse, dropped it to the floor, then unhooked her bra.

“Would you like to finish applying the perfume?” she asked. The bra joined the blouse at her feet.

When he didn’t react she took the perfume, dabbed some on his fingertips, and brought his hand to the warmth of her breast.

He came forward and kissed her. The smell invaded his mind and sent the blood racing through his veins.

After a few minutes, with the perfume bottle returned to the dresser, and Harry and Rachel advanced to the bed. The bed was already unmade—with his pajamas tossed on top—but she didn’t seem to mind. Her bare arms wrapped behind his shoulders and pulled him into her. He alternated between kissing and disrobing, the scent of the perfume doing crazy things to his head; and for a moment, it became all too much...

He straightened up. He needed a breather. *I have not gone this far with anyone since Julie left.*

“Are you OK?” Rachel asked, laying flat on the bed, her bare back against his sheets.

“Yes, it’s just been...you know...”

"Going too fast?"

"No," he said.

"I know." She sat up then on her elbows. "Do you have any wine?"

"Of course. Would you like a glass of wine?"

"I'd love it."

"Me, too."

"You're kind of tense."

"I know. It's just been a crazy couple of weeks at—"

"Forget about the office already!" she said. "God!"

"Right," he said. "I'll get the wine."

"Better bring up the bottle."

"Yes."

"The moon is full, Harry," she said with a Mae West-like purr in her voice. "I want to see you turn into a wolf."

He gave her a thumbs up—a queer gesture he immediately regretted.

The wine would help everything: the awkwardness, the tension, the distraction. He would not let Marcus Stegman ruin this perfect evening. He would block the bastard from his mind.

Harry hurried down the stairs.

He circled through the living room, feeling his way through the shadows, and entered the darkened den. He made a straight line for the small bar against a far wall, near his entertainment system. He opened the lower cabinet and removed a bottle of pinot noir, then he reached onto the upper shelf and removed two wine glasses. He rarely used the bar, not being a heavy drinker or entertainer; and it took him several minutes to hunt down a corkscrew in the shadows.

Now fully equipped to return upstairs, Harry turned away from the bar—

—and gasped out loud. He dropped everything to the floor with a crash.

Harry's heart thundered. His mouth went dry.

He could see the dark outline of a man sitting on the couch.

"Who—who's there?" said Harry.

There was no response. The shape did not move.

"Who are you?"

Continued silence. Who was this passive intruder? Or was the shape no one at all? Harry stepped quietly, cautiously, from the bar. His breathing tightened. He made it to the wall. His hand reached for the light switch.

Harry flooded the room with light.

Propped up on the couch, facing the television, sat Walter Wiggins. Wiggins' glassy eyes did not blink. His hair was crusted with blood. A portion of his face was bloated and purple. His mouth hung open. A long, unbroken strand of red drool dangled from his lower lip.

In his lap, somebody had placed a great big bucket of buttered popcorn.

Harry remained frozen, fear prickling his scalp as Wiggins watched him indifferently, nonjudgmental, dead.

As the sight before him sunk in, Harry fought very hard not to scream.

30

Harry burst into the bedroom and threw on the lights. Rachel sat up, naked on the bed, face scrunched in the sudden brightness.

"Harry?"

He was already picking up her clothes. "Get dressed. We have to go."

"What's going on?"

"It's my mother," he responded. Panic had pushed his voice an octave higher. He let the lie spill out, making it up as he went along. "She's been taken to the hospital. She's been in a car wreck. I—I just got a phone call."

"I didn't hear the phone."

"The downstairs line—it has a soft ring. I'm sorry, I'm just freaked out. Let me take you home. I can drop you off on my way to the hospital."

She quickly met his pace, scrambling to put on her blouse and jeans.

"Harry, I'm so sorry," she said. "Is she going to be OK?"

"They don't know. It could be serious."

"Oh God, how awful."

Rachel got dressed. Then she reached out and took his hands. Her face filled with sympathy. “Harry. You don’t have to take me home. Let me come with you.”

“No, no. I appreciate it. Someday I want you to meet my mother, Rachel. But not under these circumstances.”

“I can wait in the waiting room.”

“That’s very kind, but it’s getting late. I should take you home.”

“Please, Harry. It’s not a problem. I *want* to be there to support you.”

“Thank you.” He kissed her. “But no.”

He stayed close to her as they descended downstairs. He guided her to the front door, keeping the lights off.

In the entry hall, she stopped. She turned to him.

“Do you smell popcorn?”

“Popcorn?” said Harry. “Oh, popcorn. Yes, I had popcorn for lunch.”

“Popcorn for lunch?”

He opened the door and nudged her forward. “Yeah, let’s go.”

* * *

Harry drove her from Eagle Rock to West Hollywood, barely saying a word. At one point, his mind firmly centered on Stegman, he muttered, “That sick fuck.”

“What?” said Rachel. Her voice startled Harry out of his thoughts.

“The guy—whoever hit my mom—must be some kind of sick fuck,” said Harry.

She gave him a concerned look.

He dropped her off at the curb in front of her apartment building. "I'd walk you in, but..." he said.

"No, it's okay. I understand," she said.

He really wanted her out of the car pronto, but she sat there for a moment, studying his face. She put a hand on his knee.

"Call me from the hospital," she said.

"Sure."

"*Promise.*"

"Promise."

"I want to know how your mother's doing. Even though I never met her...I just want to know...I just...I really..." Then she said, "I love you, Harry."

The words rang in his ears like a sublime melody, yet he could not enjoy the moment. Too many emotions overwhelmed him at once, all crashing into one another. But he did manage to respond, "I love you, too," and he meant it.

Harry and Rachel kissed, and she climbed out of the car. She looked back at him and appeared genuinely sad.

He managed to smile, and it lifted a smile out of her. She gave a small wave and turned toward the walkway to her building.

Harry gunned the Audi back into traffic.

* * *

Harry moved through the house shutting curtains, snapping blinds.

Once he felt confident that no one could see in, he turned on the den light.

Wiggins remained motionless on the couch, a badly dressed, beached whale. His swollen face seemed to exaggerate and parody his chubby features. He looked like a grotesque cartoon.

Harry studied Wiggins for a moment, repulsed. He gingerly removed the popcorn bucket from his lap. Some blood had dripped into the bucket, creating a crimson topping.

I don't believe this.

Harry went up into his attic and found a couple of musty old blankets. One was gold, one was brown. He brought the blankets into the den, cleared a big space, and spread them out on top of one another at the foot of the sofa.

Then came the ugly part.

Harry had to move Wiggins onto the blankets. He grimaced, stretched out his arms, and placed his hands on Wiggins' fleshy shoulders.

In the back of Harry's mind, a horrible image erupted: Wiggins suddenly grabbing him, awakened into a zombie state, hungry for brains.

But Wiggins remained dead. Harry got a firm grasp on Wiggins' shirt. He pulled tentatively, without effect, and then yanked harder. Wiggins shifted, teetered, and toppled forward.

Wiggins hit the floor with a crashing thud, probably breaking bones.

The critic lay sprawled, face first, on the blankets. Harry moved to the floor. He adjusted Wiggins' position—moving his limbs closer to his body, handling the short, flabby arms and legs with revulsion. The head continued to leak blood. Blood stained the sofa, and now it was leaving a dribbly trail on the floor. Harry went into the kitchen and grabbed a handful of plastic grocery bags. He covered Wiggins' head with three bags, one after the other, and then tightly wound duct tape around them.

Shit, he's going to suffocate, thought Harry, followed by, *You moron, he's already dead,* concluding with, *THIS IS INSANE.*

Harry took a moment to compose himself, fighting back the urge to run from the house screaming. With a heavy sigh, he picked up the sides of the blankets and brought them into the center, covering Wiggins like a gift wrapped present. Walter Wiggins disappeared, becoming a lumpy brown mountain.

Harry used the duct tape to seal the blankets around the body, wrapping it continuously until he ran out.

Next came the hard part. Getting the body into the trunk of his car.

Harry pushed, shoved, and rolled the big brown lump across his den. He made slow but steady progress. His muscles ached and his back killed, but fear kept the energy fueled past quitting time.

Harry moved Wiggins out of the den, through the living room, into a corridor, across the kitchen, and through a side door that connected with his garage.

In the garage, Harry slid the body across the cement floor to the rear of his Audi. He gathered all of his remaining strength to get the chubby torso of Wiggins into the car trunk. With anguished exertion, he managed to get the corpse into a standing position, its weight leaning on him like a staggering drunk. He shoved Wiggins against the car. The top half of the corpse flopped forward, bending over the lip of the trunk. Harry adjusted his position and locked down his feet. He took hold of the lower half of Wiggins, clutching handfuls of thigh under the blanket. He lifted the lower half of Wiggins off the ground and fought for balance as his shoes slid on the cement. He sank under the torso, grappling with the ass, elevating it, grunting and wheezing, until something slapped his face.

Wiggins' arm had slipped out of the blanket, and it dangled near Harry's cheek.

The shock was disgusting enough to give Harry the extra shot of adrenaline he needed to shove the remainder of Wiggins off his back and inside the car. The rear of the Audi groaned and sank from the weight.

Harry panted for about five minutes, sweating, staring at the big brown package filling the trunk like a massive turd.

He wished his work was done, but this reality horror show was far from over. Harry said a silent prayer to any god that would listen to his pathetic, desperate dilemma. *Please let me get through this night.*

He tossed a shovel into the trunk with the body. Then he slammed the lid shut.

31

Harry Tuttle drove through Los Angeles swearing his head off with a dead, fat film critic in his trunk. Every time he hit a pothole, the body thumped in the trunk. Every time he braked at a red light, the corpse nearly crashed through the back seat.

Harry swore at Stegman, the lunatic, for snuffing Wiggins. He swore at himself, the idiot, for getting caught up in this disaster. He had known Stegman was a wacko from the start—but greed got the better of him. Why did he have to broker a secret deal that would bond the two of them forever?

Now he had no choice but to get his hands dirty and dispose of this body. Stegman knew what he was doing. It was his way of delivering a message, *You will not betray me, partner, because we are in this together.*

As the middle of the night dragged on and fatigue settled in, Harry imagined for a moment—just a moment—that this was all a dream sequence and a slow dissolve would take him back to bed, safe and sound, with Rachel's arms wrapped around him, her precious, soft face nestled close, eyes shut, mouth corners turned up in a thin, satisfied smile...

Then he hit another pothole, and the load in his trunk jumped; and he began swearing all over again.

Harry drove into the Santa Monica Mountains, climbed a path through monstrous sycamore trees, and reached the winding snake known as Mulholland Drive. Mulholland offered linkage to numerous branches of residential streets leading to luxury homes, buried deep in the hillside brush. Harry was looking for one home in particular, out of the way, hanging on the end of a skinny, private lane. The home of Herb Hunter, a famed music producer, known for his work with such stars as Elton John, Eric Clapton, and Phil Collins.

Harry didn't know Herb and had never been to his house before, but two important factors lured him:

1. Herb lived near a couple of Harry's old filmmaking friends, deep in the hills, so Harry knew the location.

2. Herb's house had recently burned down, and it was unoccupied, out of sight, and located on a large and rugged estate.

Thus, an ideal place to dump a body without witnesses.

Harry found the homes of his filmmaker friends, and a few minutes later, he arrived at Herb's private drive. Headlights punching through the dark, Harry followed the curving incline that took him out of view of the main road. Up ahead, he could see the silent, charred house—a blackened assembly of angular shapes. Harry pulled over to a grassy strip between the private drive and a cliff.

He killed the engine. He killed the headlights.

He swore a few more times, took a deep breath, and committed to silence. He forced himself out of the car.

Through the trees, Harry could see the sprawling, twinkling lights of Los Angeles spread out before him, peaceful. He felt a million miles away.

He circled to the rear of the Audi, holding his keys. Stopping at the trunk he looked around, turning a full 360. He saw nothing but dark brush in the stillness. Herb's skeletal residence loomed behind him, unlit, deadened like a haunted house.

Harry inserted the key into the trunk.

His horror movie imagination played a terrifying clip for him then: the trunk lid flopped open and a crazed, bloody Wiggins jumped forward, not dead yet, shrieking and clawing for his life.

"Stop it," said Harry quietly.

Harry counted to three, twisted the key, and heard a *click*. He pulled the key back out, gently lifted the trunk lid, and peered inside.

The big brown package remained unmoving, the shovel resting diagonally on top.

Let's get this over with.

Harry reached for the shovel...

...and heard a noise moving up the drive.

Harry froze. His limbs locked up like a mannequin.

A car!

Harry's hands fluttered wildly. His keys fell from his grasp as he snatched the lid of the trunk and slammed it down. Almost instantaneously he realized, *Holy shit, I just locked my car keys in the trunk.*

Lights reflected in the Audi's back window.

Harry internalized an agonized cry. He crouched low and scrambled to the front of his car.

The approaching headlights circled his way, threatening to pierce him out of the darkness.

Harry hurried into the brush.

The car pulled up and stopped on the grassy strip between the drive and the cliff, not far from Harry's Audi. A Bon Jovi song rocked on the car's stereo.

Harry stepped back several more feet...and then found himself sliding down a steep incline. He frantically grabbed at some brush. Several branches snapped until he got ahold of a strong root that held firm, preventing Harry from tumbling all the way down the mountainside.

Harry clung to the earth, swallowing back his panting. He couldn't shake the painful image of his car keys resting on top of Wiggins' wrapped corpse, just prior to the lid slamming down and locking.

I am in Hell.

The Bon Jovi song halted in mid-yelp and the car engine shut off.

Harry listened. He heard voices. He strained to hear...

Kids. Teenagers.

A girl...and a guy.

Of course, they had come here to enjoy an intimate encounter at a makeshift lover's lane.

Harry began pulling himself up the hillside. He hid behind heavy brush, stepping carefully to minimize the noise.

He lifted himself to a better position to get a look...

Two high school kids sat in the front seat, a skinny feminine shadow and a taller, broad-shouldered masculine shadow.

Harry saw a red dot passing between them.

"Killer weed," said the male voice, deep and satisfied.

"What about that car?" asked the girl, nervous.

"There's nobody in it. There's nobody here."

"I thought you said this was your own secret place."

"Chill out. We're alone."

Harry sat there and listened to several minutes of inane conversation as insects crawled on his hands and face. He remained still, fighting the urge to swat at the bugs. Eventually, the teenagers' dialogue became more sporadic, then nearly vanished altogether; and it didn't take a genius to interpret the scene. At one point, Harry heard an argument over whether or not the girl should pull down her leggings.

"Baby, I'm going out of my mind."

"I can see that," she giggled, little high-pitched hiccups, stoned.

The debate over the leggings continued. Harry had no choice but to listen and wait. Every minute felt like an hour. He prayed for them to leave.

Instead, another car arrived.

Oh great, thought Harry. *What could be worse?*

The teenage girl answered him, "Shit! It's a cop!"

"Hide the doob!" said the boy.

Harry quickly sunk deeper into the brush. He tossed branches over his head. His legs slid, then became snagged.

He heard the police vehicle pull up near the teenagers' car.

A door opened, then slammed shut.

"Hello," said an older male voice, not friendly.

"Hi Officer." The teenage boy stifled a cough.

"Would you like to tell me what you're doing here?"

"Just on a date, sir."

"This is a private drive. You cannot park here. Move along or I'll have to issue a citation."

"Yes, sir. We'll leave right now."

"Thank you."

The car engine kicked in, joined by blaring rock and roll. Harry listened to the music fade as the car departed down the drive.

Harry waited for the sound of the policeman's departure.

Instead he heard, "Hello? Who belongs to this Audi?"

Up above, Harry could see the dance of a flashlight beam. He shifted to get lower, but his foot slid and twigs cracked.

"Okay, who's out there?" shouted the policeman.

Harry grimaced.

"Yo!" said the cop.

Harry staggered up the grassy incline. He reached the top. A uniformed patrolman stared back at him, standing alongside the Audi. He had a square jaw and stern eyes.

He placed the flashlight beam on Harry.

"And what do you think you're doing?" asked the policeman.

"Taking a leak," said Harry.

"This is private property. It's not your personal toilet."

Harry just nodded as the policeman continued to inspect him, suspicious.

"Is there anyone else with you?"

"No. I'm alone."

"Alone," said the policeman, eyes narrowing. "Were you here so you could watch those kids?"

"Excuse me?"

"Peeping Tom. Lover's lane. Is that how you get your kicks?"

"No," said Harry, insulted, although it was better than the real reason he was here.

"Then do you want to tell me what you're doing?"

"I like the view."

"Like the view."

"I meditate."

The policeman sighed. "Alright. I think I've heard enough.

How about if you just get out of here. Because if I catch you here again, I'll find a good cause to arrest you."

"Yes. Absolutely, sir."

"I want to see you leave. Right now."

The policeman stood there. Harry didn't budge.

"Are you hard of hearing?" asked the policeman. "Get in your car. Start the engine. Move out of here."

Harry nodded, but still didn't budge.

The policeman started to lose his temper. "Look— "

"I can't," said Harry.

"Can't what?"

"I'd like to leave, but there's a problem."

"What problem?"

"I think I've lost my keys."

"Lost your keys?"

"When I was taking my pit stop—I think I lost them out there somewhere in the dark."

"I've got a flashlight. Do you remember where you were?"

Harry scratched at his bug bites. "I don't—really. I've completely lost track of where I was. It's really dark out here. Somewhere in that general vicinity..." He made a sweeping movement with his arm to indicate a large section of brush.

"Are you sure you didn't leave them in your car?"

"Pretty sure."

The policeman poked his flashlight beam inside Harry's car. He inspected the front and back. Harry held his breath. Finally, the officer said, "I guess you're lucky I came along, fella."

"I'm such an idiot," said Harry.

"Don't disagree with you there. Listen—you got a second set of keys somewhere?"

"At home."

"Where's that?"

"Eagle Rock."

The policeman exhaled loudly. "Well, isn't that grand." Then he turned toward his patrol car and waved Harry to follow. "Come on."

"Excuse me?"

"This is a major pain in my ass, but I don't think you have any other choice. It looks like I'll have to take you home to get your keys."

Harry said, "That would be fabulous. I'd really appreciate it."

The policeman simply grunted. He opened the passenger door of his patrol car and signaled Harry to get in. Harry thanked him several times.

During the drive to Harry's house, the policeman said very little and Harry had no conversation to offer, fearing that anything he said might trap him in a lie or confession. They listened to the crackle of voices on the police radio.

As Harry sat, he happened to look down at his shirtsleeves and noticed they were stained with blood. Wiggins' blood.

He folded his arms.

* * *

The police officer sat in his patrol car in Harry's driveway while Harry woke up his next-door neighbor, Susan Tyra, to get his back-up set of house keys. Then Harry entered his home to retrieve the second set of car keys.

Harry was deeply grateful that the policeman chose not to follow him inside. The floors and sofa remained splattered with blood.

During the ride back to the Hollywood Hills, the policeman opened up a little bit. He introduced himself as Officer Daniels, and they talked about the Lakers game that night.

To Harry, the game felt like weeks ago; but it was still fresh in the officer's mind.

"What a finish!" Officer Daniels exclaimed. "I wish I could've been there, you lucky bastard."

They returned to the site of Harry's Audi. Harry climbed out of the patrol car.

"Thanks. I really appreciate this," said Harry.

"I wanna see you leaving right behind me," said Daniels. "Got that?"

"Got it."

Harry hurried to his car. He climbed in, started up the engine, and signaled thumbs up. He threw the Audi in reverse and backed off the grassy strip, feeling the corpse roll in the trunk. He left the property.

The patrol car followed Harry on Mulholland Drive for several anxious minutes, before taking a sudden turn and disappearing.

Once the police car had left his rear view mirror, Harry let out a massive sigh of relief.

He checked his watch. Half past three in the morning.

He still had to dump this damn body before sunrise...

* * *

Harry followed Sunset Boulevard all the way to the Pacific Coast Highway, and then followed the coastline looking for a dark, secluded beach with quick access.

He found what he was looking for between Santa Monica and Malibu. An area without a barrier between the public parking lot and the beach. While driving on the beach was illegal, slamming over a small curb made it entirely possible.

The beach was unlit and unassuming. Harry drove onto a paved bicycle path. He turned off the headlights and rolled in the darkness to an isolated area out of view.

Harry parked, jumped out, and circled to the trunk. He unlocked it—*pocketed the key this time*—and tossed the lid open.

The big brown package awaited.

Harry retrieved his original set of car keys. He moved the shovel aside. He had to act fast. He wasn't going to bury the body. Just dump it.

Harry grappled with the big, heavy corpse, yanking and pulling, trying to shift the blubber up and over the lip of the trunk.

The duct tape began shrieking, tearing loose from the blanket, exposing sections of Wiggins. Harry saw part of his discolored face.

Harry gathered every ounce of his remaining strength to move the body over the edge of the trunk. The blanket became stuck on the latch. Harry fought to free it, while keeping an eye out for witnesses.

Then he saw something: a tiny light blinking far down the bike path.

Someone bicycling? At this hour?

Harry grew frantic, clawing madly at the body to bring the full mass out of the trunk.

The flickering light grew nearer.

Harry's wristwatch got caught on something—Wiggins' belt buckle—and he furiously yanked his arm free.

The weight of the body shifted away from the trunk. Gravity brought it crashing down to the sand. It rested in an awkward position, looking like a huge sack of laundry.

Harry slammed the trunk lid shut and jumped into his car.

The bike came closer.

Harry started up the engine, kept the lights off, and drove across the bike path. He rolled over the curb and bounced into the parking lot.

Within a minute, the Audi was back on the Pacific Coast Highway, joining other traffic, leaving Walter Wiggins far behind.

More than anything in the world, Harry wanted to grab a hot shower, scrub himself with soap, go to bed and sleep for a week.

But he knew he couldn't.

His next destination was a 24-hour pharmacy to load up on cleaning supplies. He still had a lot of messy evidence to clean up back home. He had bloodstained sofa cushions. He had blood on his den rug. He had a bloody car trunk.

He had a murder to erase.

REEL FOUR

32

As dawn splashed pink across the sky, the 8-ton behemoth charged at breakneck speed through the Mojave Desert, challenging any and all obstacles in its path. The other vehicles on I-40 West swiftly moved out of the way of the rampaging beast, or risked becoming roadkill. A wandering coyote that did not leave the payment quickly enough, exploded into blood and shattered bone.

Lenny Hurley gripped the wheel of his Gulf Stream Sunstream RV, kept his foot pressed hard on the accelerator, his eyes locked ahead, roaring toward Los Angeles with a singular mission.

He was going to kick Harry Tuttle's ass.

Shortly after he had seen his wife on the mall movie screen, made up like a whore, pretending like she was some kind of stupid actress, taunting and humiliating the husband she had abandoned, he knew he must find her, return her home, and deliver a severe beating to the man who'd stolen her away. The most unwise move of Harry Tuttle's career was parading another man's wife, half-dressed, in movie theaters from coast to coast for all to see.

No doubt, he was doing her. He was probably taking her to sleazy Hollywood parties rampant with fags, drugs, and loose sex. Lenny knew how those L.A. freaks and weirdos behaved. He would not allow Nora to become sucked into that world. She belonged in Pottstown with him, serving as a good wife, living a proper life.

Lenny had departed for Los Angeles the morning after discovering Nora's new life. He told his boss that he needed to take a week or two off to take care of some business.

"What kind of business?" asked Tex, owner of Berger's Auto Repair.

"None of your business," Lenny replied.

"You can't just take an unscheduled vacation right now. We're swamped. I don't have anyone to back you up."

"I need to go to California. I'm leaving today."

"Fine. Don't expect your job to be waiting for you when you get back," growled Tex.

A scuffled ensued and Lenny was fired. He didn't care. He went home, packed the RV with clothes, canned goods, soda, and microwave dinners, fueled up, and headed for the highway.

Approximately 2,700 miles separated Philadelphia from Los Angeles. He would reduce every mile to a blur. He loaded the passenger seat with maps, coffee and snacks, and tore through the states one by one, ripping them apart like tissue, stopping only for short catnaps at RV parks. Arkansas, Oklahoma, Texas, then New Mexico disappeared behind him. He came close to the Grand Canyon, but the landmark barely registered. He had bigger things on his mind.

Most of the drive flew by without event, but there was one rather irksome loss of time near Amarillo, where two leather-clad assholes on choppers wouldn't get out of his way; and one of them flipped the bird. Big mistake. Lenny promptly ran them off the road, and then pulled over for a chat.

Perhaps because there were two of them, they felt bold enough to challenge him, pounding on his RV door before he stepped out. When Lenny emerged, the bikers recognized their foolishness; but by then it was too late. The beatings had been ordered with no refunds available. The bikers got a full glimpse of his size, the fierce tattoos that curled up his neck, and his crazy hair. Lenny had stopped shaving his head, and the hair grew back unevenly, in patches like wild brush. It wasn't handsome, but it did send a signal: Danger. Untamed.

Lenny took care of business. One of the bikers received blows to his fat stomach until all the air had been punched out, and he lay gasping in the dirt. The other biker ate cactus.

When it became apparent that neither biker would be back on the roadway anytime soon, Lenny returned the flipped bird, climbed into his RV, and gunned it for L.A.

Total loss of time: eleven minutes.

"Fuck!" he screamed.

It continued to anger him from Texas to Arizona. When he reached Flagstaff, deep into the night, he pulled off the road for a short break to take a piss and stretch his legs.

The damp chill of Philadelphia was long gone, replaced by a hot, dry wind. The stars were brighter than he had ever seen. In this dark, he could see forever.

At that moment, he wished he could share the scenery with Nora. For once, his heart filled with sadness instead of anger.

Surrounded by barren desert, he had a weird urge to cry.

Must be the fatigue, he figured.

Before long, he was back on the road. When he crossed the state line into California, the sun was rising in the rear-view mirror, appearing like an orange fireball, propelling him faster. The sky opened up with color and renewed his energy.

He calculated another four hours to go until the ugliness of Los Angeles spilled across his windshield.

"Nora," he said. "The party's over. I'm coming to take you home."

33

Chuck Lear arrived early at Santa Monica Bay, scanned the horizon for swell and wind conditions, and grinned at the tasty wave formations. Yesterday, the waves broke too early, making them difficult to catch; but today the dawn brought some good sets. He had arrived before the crowds. He was stoked.

Suited up in his blue-and-black, three-quarters length wet-suit, Chuck sat on the white sand and began applying circles of wax to "Voyager," his trusty, nine-foot board with the rounded nose. He didn't have to report to his engineering job at Coastal Tek for another two hours. He couldn't wait to paddle out into his first wave of the day.

Chuck was a hell-bent surfing enthusiast who subscribed to the magazines, absorbed the videos, followed the daily conditions, and studied the sport's past, reading up on legends from the early 1900s like Alexander Hume Ford, Duke Kahanamoku and George Freeth. He looked forward to every new sunrise and each new swell.

As he waxed his board and took in the morning, Chuck noticed something strange and brown, not too far from where he was sitting. A big dark lump rested just off the bike path.

Chuck had seen it earlier and dismissed it as a brown trash bag, but the growing light revealed it to be something larger and stranger.

Just the sight of a discarded soda can spoiling the beach was enough to make him irate. This brown lump was really gnawing at him. What the heck was it?

Curiosity finally got the best of him. Chuck put down his board and wandered over to check it out.

The brown lump was a ratty old blanket wrapped around something with duct tape. Much of the duct tape had already torn loose. Chuck could see part of a colorful shirt inside. A big, sandy pile of laundry?

Chuck reached down and peeled back a section of the blanket.

He uncovered a portion of a man's face and a hairy, bloody scalp.

Chuck Lear screamed, sending nearby gulls scattering.

34

George Grubbis lay flat on his back on the hardwood floor of his bedroom. Sometimes it was the only way to relieve the pain from his bulging, herniated disc. His lumpy mattress fed the inflammation like a flamethrower. He needed a firmer bed.

Then again, he needed a lot of things.

What he did *not* need was the phone ringing at 7 a.m., especially given his troubled night of sleep. Every time he dozed off, Casper, his cat and sole companion, decided to walk across his chest.

He wished Casper could answer the phone and take a message.

The phone rang and rang and rang. George surrendered, accepted the pain, and sat up in slow increments. He cursed at the stings and moved across the bedroom on his hands and knees. He reached up and snatched the phone receiver.

"Yeah," he said.

"Mr. Grubbis, this is Rebecca Hirsch, at the 1100 block of Del Marino."

"Yeah," he said.

"Your tenant is causing problems again, and I am on the verge of calling the police—again."

"Yeah," he said. Last week, she had called the police to report horrific screams coming out of Marcus Stegman's house.

As it turned out, Marcus was blasting a horror movie on his super deluxe home theater, cranking his mammoth surround sound speakers like some kind of rock concert.

The cops found it funny. Rebecca Hirsch did not.

Her complaint this morning was not noise; it was the sight of Stegman's front lawn.

"Garbage," she said. "All sorts of garbage, and it blows into my yard. It's an embarrassment to the neighborhood. And now he's got this giant ant..."

"Yeah," said Grubbis. Then he realized he hadn't heard right. "Wait—what?"

"A giant ant."

"I don't understand."

"You better get him to clean up around his house, or I'm going to report this to the village. You're the landlord. You own the property. Go control the situation *please. Thank you.*" Her politeness was strained to the breaking point.

Grubbis hung up and Casper wandered over, white tail waving in a languid rhythm.

"Well, Casper," said Grubbis, "Looks like we're up."

Grubbis gobbled three ibuprofen tablets, got dressed, and filled Casper's bowl. He left to go see Stegman.

During the drive, he thought about Audrey Stegman looking down at him from the heavens with pleading eyes. *Please have pity on my boy. He's not right in the head. He's not a bad kid.*

It filled him with melancholy.

Grubbis arrived at the house, and indeed, there was a giant ant on the front lawn. It looked like a prop from some old monster movie. And that's probably what it was.

Stegman had spent huge sums of money on movie memorabilia. Grubbis did not ask where the money came from and did not care, as long as the rent was being paid. During Grubbis's last visit to collect the rent, Stegman had bragged about his growing collection and offered to show him artifacts from various horror films. "Do you want to see the tombstone from *Curse of the Mummy*?" Stegman offered.

"No," said Grubbis, collecting his rent money—in cash.

"One day I'm going to open a museum."

"Not on my property."

Stegman had just laughed. It was a weird, almost sinister laugh. Stegman kept getting stranger. His mind was frying in a saucepan soaked with drugs and alcohol. He was sinking ever deeper into brain damage.

It was depressing.

Even more depressing was the state of the ranch home on Del Marino.

In addition to the giant ant, random garbage filled the yard: a broken casket that looked fake, a shopping cart from a nearby grocer, fluttering newspaper pages, trampled fast food bags, and soda and liquor bottles. All buried in overgrown grass and weeds.

This was not acceptable.

Grubbis rang the front doorbell, then pounded on the door. No response. He was used to it. It didn't mean nobody was home.

Grubbis circled to the side of the house, kicking past more trash. He approached a small window. It was opened a crack, covered on the inside by a bedsheet, a pitiful makeshift curtain. Grubbis slid the window up. The effort produced pain in his back. He reached in, took hold of the bedsheet and pulled it down.

The inside of the house was a disaster, worse than ever before.

Movie equipment, monster memorabilia, food, dirty plates, magazines, books, spilled bags of trash, buried furniture, all mixed into a big, heaping stew. How could anyone even walk through this mess?

The sight repulsed him. Then a whiff of stench made him gag.

He stumbled away, gasping for air. He pulled up his shirt collar to cover his nose and mouth. He braced himself. He returned to the window.

He could see tiny spots of movement—flies—dancing circles around the room. On the wall closest to him he saw large, careless gouges, like scars. Above the gouges, where the wall met the ceiling, he recognized long brown stains that looked like water damage from a broken pipe or seeping rain.

This is my house, God dammit!

Grubbis felt enraged. The house probably had rats, too. Before long, the property would be worthless.

Then Grubbis noticed the most shocking sight of all—there was a naked, pink man, peacefully sleeping in the midst of all this squalor. He was sprawled on sofa cushions on the floor, scratching his hairy chest, long hair askew, probably wasted. It wasn't Marcus—it was the tall roommate with the red beard. A cockroach moved across his legs to his pubic hair. He slapped at it limply without opening his eyes.

It's a freaking mental institution!

Grubbis left the window. He left the house, the giant ant, the shopping cart, the trash, and climbed into his Toyota Camry. He itched all over. It felt like bugs were crawling under his skin. The stench still lingered in his nostrils.

Returning home, Grubbis picked up the phone and called Marcus.

An answering machine kicked in after five rings. Eerie organ music played in the background, a wolf howled, and Marcus Stegman welcomed the caller to the castle of Dr. Frankenstein, or some such nonsense, in a cartoony voice. Perhaps it would be cute coming from a 10-year-old on Halloween, but it was pathetic and stupid coming from a reputed adult. "Please leave your screams after the bell tolls. The grim reaper shall be with you shortly."

Sure enough, there were bells preceding the beep.

"Marcus Stegman," said Grubbis, "the game is over. I will be terminating the lease. You will have 30 days to vacate the premises. Anything you leave behind will be thrown away. I will be delivering the written notice shortly. If you do not leave voluntarily, you will be served with an unlawful detainer complaint; and the court will have you physically evicted. I'm done playing around. I'm through negotiating. What you have done to the house is a disgrace. Consider yourself thrown out on the street."

Grubbis hung up. Casper wandered over and rubbed against his legs.

Grubbis looked heavenward. "I'm sorry, Audrey," he said.

35

Brett Ludwig placed the Beretta 9000S pistol into Harry's hand. "Lightweight, compact, easy to carry, ideal for personal defense," he said.

Harry nodded, staring at the weapon, afraid to grasp it too hard.

"It's OK. It's not loaded. For God's sake, hold it like a gun, Harry," said Ludwig.

For many years, Ludwig had been Harry's primary source for replica, blank-firing guns—props for his various movies. These replicas faithfully matched the appearance of their counterparts, with important safety distinctions: the barrels were plugged and they could not be converted to fire live ammo.

However, being a hardcore gun nut, Ludwig also had access to the real thing. Aware of this, Harry had called him earlier this morning with an urgent request. Ludwig was happy to oblige. Harry had given him a lot of business in the past, and Ludwig was not about to disappoint a client.

Harry said he needed a firearm to protect himself against a crazed fan who was harassing him. That was all Ludwig needed to hear. He invited Harry to his Inglewood house and brought him into the "gun room," which was double-locked behind a sturdy door. The room offered a lineup of tables and racks filled with replica guns: pistols, revolvers, shotguns, rifles, machine guns. Ludwig led him past the phonies to a closet, also requiring a key, which stored the real thing.

After reviewing a few options, including a derringer, they landed on the double-action, 9mm "Baby" Beretta semi-automatic pistol.

"Brand new, from the manufacturer. Never been fired," said Ludwig. "Comes with two 10-round magazines."

Harry sighed. "I'll take it," he said. "Do you take credit cards?"

Ludwig gave him a long look. "Here's what we'll do. In the paperwork, the receipt, it's for one of the prop guns. You understand?"

"Understood."

Harry bought the gun. He felt better, as if he had regained some control. He was up against a maniac who had killed—twice—and brought the most recent victim into Harry's den. If Stegman broke into his house again, threatened him in any way, Harry would shoot him. It was as simple as that.

Ludwig packaged the gun and Harry paid the bill.

As Ludwig led Harry to the front door, they passed Ludwig's wife in the living room. She sat on the couch in her pink robe and pink slippers, drinking a glass of orange juice, watching the morning news.

Harry gave her a nod and smile. She stopped him with a frantic wave.

"Did you hear about this?" she said, pointing to the television.

On the screen, a sober-faced reporter was broadcasting live from a beach site surrounded by yellow tape, police, and curious onlookers.

"—where police have identified the body of film critic Walter Wiggins. Wiggins apparently suffered massive head trauma, but the exact cause of the injury remains unclear. Police continue to search for clues at the scene. The body was found wrapped in blankets earlier this morning by—"

Ludwig erupted with shocked laughter, causing Harry to jump. "Hah! Maybe somebody didn't take too kindly to one of his bad reviews."

Harry forced out a chuckle even as his entire body broke out in a sheet of cold sweat. "What a crazy world," he said, dazed. His words sounded like someone else talking to him.

"You know, I never liked that guy," said Ludwig. "He only liked artsy, foreign shit. Hey, didn't you just do an interview with him?"

"You did?" said Ludwig's wife from the couch, interested. "You knew Wiggins?"

Harry responded, "Oh boy, look at the time. I've really got to run." He brought up his wrist to glance at his watch—

—only there was no watch.

Harry froze.

He didn't remember taking off his watch.

Then, images replayed in his mind from the prior night—sluggish, dark, dreamlike—dumping Wiggins' body at the beach—the bicycle headlamp approaching—getting his watchband caught on Wiggins' belt buckle—frantically tearing his arm free and jumping back into his car to drive away.

I left my watch with the body.

The watch Paul had given him. The watch inscribed with Harry's nickname.

Harry felt absolutely paralyzed. He couldn't take his eyes off his bare wrist.

"You OK?" said Ludwig.

"Yes," said Harry. "Yes. Yes." The cell phone in his pocket rang out then, the spaceship tones from *Close Encounters of the Third Kind*.

Harry fumbled until he had the phone flipped open in his hands and could read the caller ID.

It was Rachel.

Shit. There was no way he could talk to her now.

"Nobody," he said, snapping the phone shut and returning it to his pocket.

"They're interviewing the surfer who found the body," said Ludwig's wife, pointing to the TV screen.

Harry left the house.

As he climbed behind the wheel of his car, the cell phone starting ringing again.

"Damn it!" said Harry. He flipped it open to see who it was now. It was Paul.

Harry answered the phone, nearly shouting, "*What?*"

"Hey, buddy," greeted Paul. "Listen, we've got a bit of a situation here at the office."

Harry shut his eyes. "What is it?"

"There's somebody here to see you, and I don't think he's going to leave until you talk with him."

"Who the hell is it?"

"Leonard Hurley."

Harry snapped, "*I don't know who that is, Paul.*"

"You should. He says you stole his wife. He's got this great big RV filling half the parking lot. He says he came all the way from Pennsylvania to personally kick your ass."

"He what?"

"What the hell is going on, Harry? What is it you're not telling me?"

"Nothing. Absolutely nothing. I don't know. It's just some lunatic."

"Yeah, well, he says he's not budging until you show your face. And I tend to believe him. He's as big as a freaking house. Harry, you better get over here."

Harry said nothing. He slumped in his car seat. He prayed very hard for a meteor to strike the earth.

Paul's voice buzzed in his ear like a persistent gnat. "Harry? Harry, are you still there? Harry?...*Harry!*"

36

Harry pulled into the parking lot outside the offices of PJ Productions. A sprawling, tan and white RV sat on a diagonal across several parking spaces. An enormous man filled an orange lawn chair alongside the vehicle, looking at the Sports section of *USA Today*.

Harry parked nearby, keeping his eyes on the man, who did not remove his attention from the paper.

Well, thought Harry to himself, let's see what the hell he wants.

Harry stepped out of his car, shut the door, and walked over. He let his shoes scrape the cement as he neared, hoping the sound would at least cause the man to look at him. The man's face stayed behind the paper.

Harry cleared his throat as he approached. "Hello?"

The big man lowered the newspaper. His eyes fixed on Harry. His expression did not offer a greeting—just a cold and hardened stare. He had short, messy hair, a natural frown, and tattoos of snakes crawling up his thick neck. Muscles bulged beneath his white T-shirt.

The stranger did not speak, so Harry struggled for words,

badly underrehearsed.

"Hello...I'm wondering...I received this phone call...I don't know what...OK, let's start at the beginning. My name is Harry Tuttle."

The words *Harry* and *Tuttle* ignited an explosion.

The man shot out of his chair, dashing aside the newspaper and grabbing Harry by the shirt collar. He shoved Harry backwards about five feet, then smashed a fist into his cheek.

Harry saw stars. Gasping, he struggled to escape, but the next blow came fast. The man struck Harry under his eye, a blinding jolt that rattled everything in his skull. Harry cried out, and the next blow sent him down hard to the concrete.

As Harry reached the ground, a large black boot greeted him, kicking him in the chest, propelling him backwards, tumbling, blue sky spinning.

Harry tasted blood in his mouth. The boot returned—in the ribs this time—and the sky twirled again, then became gray cement. Harry lay crumpled face down on the pavement, throbbing from a multitude of shocks.

Harry fought back the pain. With effort, he turned around, facing his attacker.

The large man stood over Harry, blocking out the sun.

Harry braced for the next blow.

The man simply said, "Where is she?"

"What?"

"Wrong answer."

The boot returned to Harry's side, crushing the wind out of him, leaving him gasping and scraped across several more feet of cement.

"Let's start over," said the man. "Where is she?"

"Y-your wife?" said Harry, trying to recollect what Paul

had told him on the phone.

"Yes."

"Let me...think..." said Harry, trying to find words that wouldn't trigger more strikes. "I'd like to help...Can you...give me just a little bit more information?"

"Nora Hurley," said the man firmly, accent on every syllable.

Shit, thought Harry to himself, *I have no idea who Nora Hurley is.*

"Nora Hurley," said Harry, sitting up on the pavement. How long could he buy time before the next attack? He could feel his lower lip swelling, blood dribbling to his chin. "Nora Hurley..."

"You gave her a fake name for the movie, asshole," said the giant. "Sandra...something."

"Sandra Ross?" said Harry immediately.

The giant said "*Yes*."

"She was your wife?"

"She *is* my wife, asshole," spat the giant, and Harry braced for another blow; but the giant didn't move.

"I'm sorry," said Harry. "I'm a bit dizzy right now. My ears are ringing."

"What's my wife doing in your movie? That's what I want to know. She's no actress. She just comes out here and you make her a star overnight? How come? Did she suck your dick?"

"No," said Harry. "No, no. She did not. That didn't happen."

"Then how come you cast her?"

Harry chose his words carefully. "She gave a...very realistic performance."

"She looked like a whore."

Harry didn't have an answer for that. He slowly rose to his feet. His legs shook. He kept one hand wrapped around his aching ribs.

"I want to help..." said Harry. "I really do. What can I do..."

"You can bring me back my wife."

Harry said, "Sure, I'd love to. There's just one problem. I don't...know...where she is."

The husband's eyes narrowed. He obviously didn't like the answer. He stepped closer.

"I am not leaving until you return her to me. I will camp out here, and I will hammer the shit out of you every time I see you, until you bring back my wife."

"Please understand," said Harry. "After we wrap on a movie, I don't always keep tabs on—"

The giant's hands rushed forward and grabbed Harry by the throat. He shoved Harry backward, throwing him into a Pontiac Grand Prix. Harry crashed into the passenger door, setting off a shrieking car alarm.

Harry realized he had a small window of opportunity to escape: he remained standing on his feet, and the giant did not have a hold on him.

Harry dashed through the narrowing space between the Pontiac and the angry giant.

"I'm not done with you!" thundered Harry's attacker.

Harry hurried to his car, grateful that it was unlocked. In a single, rapid, seamless motion, Harry pulled on the door handle, opened the door, leapt inside, slammed the door shut, and secured all the doors.

The doors locked with a "chunk!" just as the giant slammed against the side of the car.

Harry started up the engine. The giant pounded on the

glass.

Dear God, he's going to shatter the window.

"Bring me back my wife you wife thief!" screamed the giant. He began circling to the front of the car to block its advancement.

Harry threw the car into reverse and floored it.

The Audi shot back, crashing into a parked Ford Taurus, shoving it back. Harry slammed his car into drive, yanked the steering wheel to the right, and spun away from the rushing madman. The Audi roared out of the lot, entered Wilshire Boulevard and nearly hit a delivery van. Several vehicles braked and honked. Angry drivers waved fists or middle fingers, but they were the least of Harry's worries.

Harry swerved into an open lane and sped away from the office building.

Several blocks later, Harry pulled over to the side of the road.

The pain from his beating continued to throb. He examined himself in the rearview mirror. His face did not look pretty. Swollen, purple and bloody, he looked like something out of one of his movies. But this was not makeup.

Harry felt a rising anger over the unwarranted attack. Fury and humiliation washed over him for becoming such a helpless punching bag.

Harry's eyes landed on the plain brown package on the floor of the passenger seat. The Beretta semi-automatic pistol.

In that instant, Harry imagined a vivid and explosive scene where he returned to the parking lot. He could feel the words erupt from his throat, "You want to rumble, crazy man?" Then he would blast away the maniac who beat him bloody.

Now who's the tough guy?

Harry could imagine every angle, every edit of the sequence. The storyboard unrolled in his mind. Start with a point-of-view shot of Harry from the madman's perspective... don't reveal the gun in the frame until it's too late...maybe just the audio, an abrupt, shocking *bang*. Then a wide shot: the attacker goes down, humbled and neutralized, bullets searing his flesh. Close-up on Harry's battered but satisfied face. The roles have been reversed. The madman, bleeding, begs for mercy, but it's too late. Show no mercy; receive no mercy. Harry feeds him more lead...

Harry continued to contemplate the scene. He really wanted to bring it to life. He wanted to feel the satisfaction of revenge, the power of bloodshed.

But he knew he couldn't.

He picked up his cell phone.

He dialed Marcus Stegman.

"Marcus, it's Harry."

"Comrade..."

"Don't talk. Just listen. We have a...No, *you* have a problem. Remember Nora Hurley? Well, Nora Hurley's husband is parked in an RV outside my office; and he's not going to budge until he finds out what happened to his wife. He's angry and he's violent."

"Is he."

"He's getting suspicious," said Harry. "We need a plan."

"I'll talk to him."

"Talk to him? I don't think that's going to work."

"Sure it will. Trust me."

"Trust you?"

"Do you know what your problem is, Harry? You worry too much."

Harry was speechless. He stared at the phone for several seconds, before ending the call with an angry jab of his thumb.

37

The bedroom in the rear of Lenny Hurley's 1988 Gulf Stream Sunstream RV was barely big enough to fit a bed. As Lenny slept, his large body covered the mattress, head crushing the pillow, fists gripping the sheets. A curtain separated the bedroom from the rest of the living quarters. The window shades were drawn tight, blocking out the parking lot lights.

Three hard knocks stirred him awake. His eyes opened. He listened to a lengthy silence, and then the knocks returned. Three again, evenly spaced, forceful.

"Who the fuck," he said, quickly sitting up, planting his bare feet on the carpeted floor. He wore a gray, sleeveless T-shirt and faded blue sweatpants. They didn't smell too good. Neither did the bedsheets. The RV could get stuffy at night, plus he sweated a lot when sleeping. However, finding a Laundromat had not been high on his list of priorities.

He looked at his watch.

Three-fifteen a.m.

That made him mad. He expected the encounter to be ugly.

He ripped the bedroom curtain aside and headed up the thin aisle, past the mini bathroom, past the dinette table and compact kitchen area, and between two facing sofas.

Lenny reached the door and looked out a small window. He wanted to get a good look at his visitor.

A skinny young man, dressed in black, with a ponytail and goatee, waved at him.

This better be good.

Lenny unlatched and opened the door.

"*What*," he said, filling the single word with maximum menace.

"Mr. Hurley, I'm sorry for disturbing you at this hour."

"It's three o'clock in the morning, asshole."

"I know. But I wanted to see you as soon as I could. My name is Marcus Stegman. I understand you're looking for Nora Hurley."

Lenny stared at the stranger, startled by hearing her name out loud.

"I am," he said. His tone switched from annoyed to anxious. "Do you know where she is?"

"I am here to reunite you with her," beamed Stegman proudly. "May I come in?"

Lenny nodded. "Let me get the lights." He felt excitement pushing away the fog of sleep, his heartbeat drumming. He snapped on some fluorescent lighting, then waved the stranger inside.

Stegman stepped into the RV. "I figured you wouldn't want to wait until morning," he said.

"I just want to find her. Where is she?"

Stegman asked, "May I have a seat?"

"Sure. Go ahead."

Stegman sat on one of the small sofas and crossed his legs. Lenny sat on the other one, across from him, still studying the stranger.

"Your wife made a movie called *Deadly Desires*," said Stegman. "Her scenes were filmed near Mexico City."

"I know about the movie. That's why I came here to their offices. Nobody will tell me anything. How do you know Nora?"

"I know Harry Tuttle."

Lenny asked, "Did he fuck her?"

"No," replied Stegman. "I'm pretty certain he did not."

"Then why won't he tell me where she is?"

"I can tell you where she is," said Stegman. "She's still in Mexico."

"What's she doing there?"

"Not much."

Lenny felt confused. The conversation was weird. This man showing up in the middle of the night was weird. But he had information on Nora. "So she's in Mexico..." Lenny said.

"Do you mind if I ask you a question?" said Stegman, fixing him with an odd, thoughtful gaze.

"What."

"Have you ever been in a movie?"

"In a movie? What do you mean?"

"Acting."

"*Acting?* Hell, no."

"The reason I ask... I'm sorry, I couldn't help noticing. You have classic movie star features. Handsome, chiseled face. Great build. Strong jawline."

"*Are you some kind of fruit?*" Lenny felt ready to pounce.

"No, no. Hear me out. I'm a filmmaker," said Stegman, "and I'd like to put you in my next movie."

"What does this have to do with Nora?"

"My new movie is about a crazy killer who loves horror

films," continued Stegman. "He kills his victims in tribute to his favorite movies. For each murder, he becomes a different character. He's obsessed."

"Why are you changing the subject?"

"Did you ever see *Texas Chainsaw Massacre?* Either the original or the remake?"

"I don't know what you're talking about."

"A shame," said Stegman. "Because they're both classics."

Lenny stood up, scowling. He towered over Stegman. "Okay, I've had enough of this shit. You have exactly one minute to tell me where I can find Nora, or you are going to be *my* personal massacre, you goddamned freak."

"I can send you to Nora right now," said Stegman.

"Then *do it*," demanded Lenny.

Stegman smiled. He faced the door.

He called out, "*Action!*"

A mighty roar erupted. A tall, red-haired man burst into the RV, gripping the handle bar of a screaming 16-inch chainsaw.

Stegman flattened himself against the wall, and the bearded man charged forward, the cutting bar extended in front of him. A second young man entered the RV, armed with a large video camera with a mounted light. He followed the action, equipment propped on his shoulder, watching through the eyepiece.

Stunned by the surreal scene, Lenny had no time to think—only time to react. His impulse was simple: he made a fist and threw it forward, punching at the attacker who came at him.

The chainsaw cleanly severed Lenny's right hand at the wrist, and his fist fell to the carpet with the thud of a softball.

Lenny screamed.

Behind the rotating chain, he saw the crazed man with the red beard grinning with excitement.

Behind the man with the red beard, he saw a big, round camera lens and a bright light.

Behind the camera, he saw part of the cameraman's face, neither grinning nor shocked, just focused and businesslike.

Then he saw nothing at all, ever again.

38

To load the magazine, remove it from the pistol by depressing the magazine release button.

Harry studied the pages of the Beretta product manual he had downloaded and printed out from the Beretta web site. The document contained diagrams and detailed information on loading, firing, ammunition, and maintenance. A good, immediate primer for a novice like himself.

Harry sat at his kitchen table. His eyes moved back and forth between the gun illustrations on paper and the three-dimensional, very real gun resting near his salt and pepper shakers.

The firing chamber of the pistol is the portion of the barrel into which the cartridge is fed...

The telephone rang.

Harry stood up and grabbed the receiver off the wall. He studied the caller ID.

Paul.

"Shit."

Harry took a deep breath and answered. "Hey, Paul..."

"The wacko in the RV is gone," said Paul. "I came in early

this morning and the lot's empty. But there's no telling when he might come back. Listen, should we call the police?"

"No," said Harry immediately. "Let's not get the police involved. It's not worth their time. Just some nut..."

"Who *was* that big ape?"

"The husband of an actress from one of my movies. The crazy jealous type. He thought I was screwing his wife."

"Were you?"

"No! I never even met her. How could— "

Paul cut in, "Never met her and she was in your movie?"

Harry jumped to correct himself. "Barely ever met her. It was a real small part. A couple of lines. I don't remember. I'm getting old."

"Harry..." Paul hesitated, troubled. "Are you OK? We go way back. I can tell when something's not right, and you're just not yourself anymore. You've got this big hit movie; you refuse to do any publicity. You never come around the office anymore. You..."

The doorbell rang.

Jesus now who is it? thought Harry. He interrupted Paul, "I gotta go. There's someone at the door."

"When are you coming in so we can talk?"

"I don't know. I'll let you know."

"Let's set up a time— "

"OK, gotta go, bye." Harry hung up.

He picked up the pistol from the kitchen table. He headed for the front door, staying away from the windows.

Harry stopped at the peephole in the front door. Still gripping the gun, he shut one eye and pressed the other to the hole.

Rachel.

Harry's heart sank. She had left several messages on his cell phone and home phone. He had not called her back.

Harry quickly took the gun into the living room and tucked it under a chair cushion. Then he returned and opened the front door, just as she started to retreat down the walkway to her car.

"*Rachel.*"

Rachel saw him. She headed toward him and began to smile. But then an alarmed look took over.

"What happened to you?" she gasped.

"What—?" Harry didn't realize right away, but then saw the shocked way she stared at his face. "Oh, that. I got mugged."

She brought up a hand and gently touched his cheek. He flinched.

"Mugged?" she said. "When did this happen? Where?"

"I was running an errand...last night...downtown...location scouting...it doesn't matter. I'm fine. Just a little banged up. Heh, you think I look bad, you should see the other guy..."

She wasn't laughing. "Harry, how come you haven't returned my calls?"

Harry worked to keep the lie machine cranking, but for a moment he was entirely distracted by the beautiful porcelain face, sympathetic blue eyes, and the way her shining blonde hair hung like soft sheets down to her shoulders.

"I'm sorry," he said simply.

"Is everything OK?"

"Just busy."

"How's your mother?"

"My mother?" He gave her a puzzled look. "She's fine. Why?"

His nonchalant response startled her. "The car accident..."

Harry fumbled to catch himself. "Oh—yes—well, she's on the mend. Banged up a bit, that's all."

"How long will she be in the hospital?"

"Not very long. They'll have her out of there in no time. She's a tough lady."

"Did you hear what happened to Walter Wiggins?"

Harry forced himself to think clearly before responding. "Yes. I did. On the news."

"Can you believe it?"

"It is pretty incredible."

"You were just with him."

"I know. We taped that interview."

"All of L.A. is talking about it," said Rachel. "I bet they catch who did it. They said the killer left tire tracks on the beach."

Harry shuddered and thought, *Note to self: replace tires.*

"Anyway, I still haven't told you my big news."

"What's that?"

She broke into a huge grin. "Are you ready? Here it is: I just landed my first big movie role!" Rachel raised her fists in a victorious gesture.

"Oh. Okay." Harry nodded, half listening. His mind remained on tire tracks. *Maybe I should ditch the car altogether.*

"Harry?"

"Yes."

"Did you hear me?"

"Yes. Movie role."

Rachel's upbeat mood deflated. She looked him over. "You're not listening. Well, maybe it's not a big deal to you; but it's a big deal to me. I have been working my butt off for years to get a role like this and you don't even want to hear about it. I guess you just don't care. I'm sorry to bother you. I'll go now." She turned.

"No, Rachel..."

Rachel headed down the walkway, sandals clicking.

Harry quickly followed. "I'm sorry. I know I'm distracted. I'm a little dazed from the mugging, that's all. Really, I'm excited for you."

She stopped and turned. "Are you?"

"Yes. I am. In fact, let's go out tonight and celebrate. We'll have dinner at Buzz. We'll drink champagne. We'll get crazy. I'm sure this is the start of big things for you."

She looked at him, skeptical.

"C'mon, what do you say?" said Harry. "A night on the town to celebrate your new movie. I'll pick you up at eight."

She searched his eyes for sincerity and finally smiled. "Okay."

He reached out and hugged her. It felt good to wrap his arms around her and hold on tight. He shut his eyes. He tried to shed the horror of the past few days. He wanted to lose himself in this one moment, holding this beautiful, sweet woman who mattered more to him than anyone else on the planet. Why did everything have to be so complicated when something this simple—not fame, not wealth—made him happy?

He kissed her. He apologized. She accepted.

They remained holding one another for several more minutes and Harry felt some of his strength returning.

39

The damn giant ant remained in the yard. Grubbis passed it on his way to the front door. He gripped a white envelope in his arthritic fingers, special delivery for Marcus J. Stegman.

A thirty-day written notice of the termination of the lease.

There was patience, and there was foolishness. Grubbis was not about to make the transition from one to the other. The hourglass had run out. The time had come for Marcus to face the music.

Even though Stegman had gotten a lot better about paying his rent, he had gotten much worse about keeping the property in acceptable condition. The yard remained littered with crap, the inside had become a feast for bugs and rodents, and the neighbors complained regularly about noise and strange goings on.

In heaven, looking down at the inevitable, Audrey Stegman probably wept for her baby. That made Grubbis feel bad. But her baby would be fine. This was best for him. He needed to be kicked out of the nest.

Yes, that's what the house had become—a literal nest. Grubbis planned to hire a cleaning crew after Stegman moved out. They would scrub the place down, throw away sack after sack of garbage, make extensive repairs and bring the home back to a level of respectability. And then, maybe some nice, young, decent family would move in. Somebody responsible with a steady job and solid morals. Churchgoers. No more of this crazy horror nonsense. He would screen the applicants carefully. He was too damned old to deal with any more loonies.

Grubbis lifted his gnarled fist to knock, then paused. The front door was already opened a crack.

He pushed it open halfway and peered inside. Mountains of camera equipment, food dishes, newspapers, and dirty clothing filled his eyes. Stale stink rushed to his nostrils.

"Hello?" said Grubbis.

He listened for a response.

Then he heard a voice. It was his *own* voice talking back to him.

"...the game is over. I will be terminating the lease."

Stunned, Grubbis pushed the door all the way open. He stepped forward.

He continued to hear his voice sounding through the house. "You will have 30 days to vacate the premises. Anything you leave behind will be thrown away. I will be delivering a written notice shortly. If you do not leave voluntarily..."

It was one of the messages he had left on Stegman's answering machine.

Grubbis advanced forward on a path that had been created through the debris. He moved out of the living room and entered a corridor.

He heard his voice become louder, angrier. Now the words came from a previous answering machine message.

"I will not stand for this any longer! Damn it, you have disgraced my property."

Then Grubbis heard a second voice responding to the taped comments, "But this is my home. I have nowhere to go!"

The new voice did not sound like Marcus.

What the hell?

Grubbis reached one of the bedrooms. He looked inside. Marcus Stegman and one of his roommates — Garon, the dark-skinned one with the earring — sat huddled around a table of computer equipment. They did not see Grubbis. They focused on a large monitor.

On the monitor, a video clip played, showing the red-haired roommate, Terrance, on the phone.

Terrance was conducting a phone conversation with fragments of messages Grubbis had left on the answering machine during the past week.

"*Hey*," shouted Grubbis into the room. "That's my voice."

Stegman and Garon turned from the monitors to look at him.

They did not act surprised. In fact, Stegman smiled. "Hello, Mr. Grubbis. We've been expecting you. I received your messages. They were great."

"What are you doing with my phone messages?"

"You want to see?" said Stegman. "Come over, I'll show you."

Grubbis entered the room cautiously.

"This is my editing suite," said Stegman. "State of the art. Like the big studios have. I've been working on the eviction sequence. Grab a chair."

"I'll stand, thank you," said Grubbis.

"We put you in our new movie."

"I don't want to be in your friggin' movie."

"But you're perfect. You've got the perfect look, the perfect voice, for the cranky old landlord."

"You can't do that without my consent."

"Too late. We've got you. The messages you've been leaving on my answering machine—they're the perfect fidelity to use as audio for the other end of a phone conversation. I created sound files from the tapes, did some editing on the PC, and now you're part of a phone call with our main character, Boris. Look."

Stegman moved the mouse, clicked a few buttons on the keyboard, and played the scene from the beginning.

On the monitor, the red-haired Terrance answered the telephone. He interacted with portions of Grubbis's answering machine audio as if it was a live conversation.

"Magic!" said Stegman. "It's like the two of you are really talking to each other."

"Cute," said Grubbis, unamused.

On the monitor, the red-haired man said, "You can't do this to me. This is my home." Grubbis could be heard responding, "I tried to cut you slack, but enough is enough. You have created a public nuisance, health violations, property damage, harbored strange people at all hours..."

"Please, I beg of you..." said the red-haired man.

Stegman stopped the clip. He turned to Grubbis and smiled. "See? Seamless."

"You think this is all some big game?" said Grubbis.

"What's in your hand?" asked Stegman. "Did you bring the notice?"

"Yes, I did."

"Goody," said Stegman. "Let's film you delivering it. That's the next scene."

"You are deeply disturbed, boy," said Grubbis.

"This will take two minutes. Here's how I see it." Stegman jumped up, animated, and began describing the shots, holding up his hands and framing the scene.

"There's a knock at the door. 'Boris' answers. It's you, the landlord. You come in. You say, 'I am serving you with a 30-day notice to terminate your rental agreement.' Boris is speechless. Shocked. You hand him the notice and you leave. And that's it."

"Let me get one thing straight with you," said Grubbis, looking Stegman squarely in the eyes. "This-is-not-a-movie. This-is-real-life. You really will be evicted. Does this make any sense to you?"

Stegman nodded. He hung his head. "I know. I know it's for real. I promise you I will move out...for real...if you help me tape this scene."

Grubbis knew at that moment that he had never dealt with a more bizarre request, or a more bizarre tenant; and he had encountered his share of oddballs in the past 35 years. Like the woman who collected snakes and lizards...the performance artist who lifted weights from nipple rings...the old Hungarian guy with wooden teeth and a 17-year-old wife.

But Stegman took the cake. The champion freak.

"Let me get this straight," said Grubbis. "If I let you film me serving this notice, then you will go away *for real*?"

"Yes."

"Fine," said Grubbis. "Nobody's going to see your stupid little movie anyway."

Stegman clapped his hands and said, "Awesome." He turned to Garon. "Go get the digital camera and the tripod. I'll wake up Terrance."

"So what do I do?" said Grubbis.

"Go back outside. Stand on the front steps. When you hear me yell 'Action,' knock on the door. Terrance will answer the door in character, as Boris. You step into the house and deliver the termination notice. Explain it to him and hand it over. Tell him he will be evicted, then leave."

"I guess I don't have to ask, 'What's my motivation?'" grumbled Grubbis.

"This will be quick," promised Stegman.

"Good," said Grubbis. "It better be."

Grubbis left the room. He headed toward the front door, kicking at some of the junk in his path.

"Just give us five minutes!" called out Stegman.

"Fine," said Grubbis.

Grubbis stepped outside the house and closed the front door. He waited.

He stood there, hands at his sides, doing nothing. His back started to flare up again.

He felt like a fool. But one thing was for certain: He would be serving the notice and it was no prop. It was the real thing. And if these idiots didn't vacate the property willingly, he would pursue court action. Nothing would derail this train.

After 10 minutes, Grubbis became struck with an awful feeling that he had been deceived. They had made him step outside with the notice, shut the door, and probably snuck out the back way. The whole "let's film you" story was an elaborate scam to lock him out of the house and avoid being served.

Grubbis was prepared to leave when he heard a voice inside cry out, "Action!"

No scam, thought Grubbis. Just insane.

He exhaled a big sigh. "Time to be a movie star," he muttered. He knocked on the door.

"Come in!" shouted a voice.

Grubbis took hold of the doorknob, turned it and pushed open the door.

Nobody was there to greet him.

Grubbis stepped into the messy living room. He noticed the large black camera on a tripod facing him, with the dark-skinned Garon behind the lens. Bright lights had been set up nearby, causing Grubbis to squint momentarily.

So where was this "Boris" character who was supposed to receive the notice?

"Hello?" said Grubbis. He looked around and finally held up the envelope and waved it. "I have come to serve you with a lease termination notice. You have 30 days to vacate the premises." After a pause, he added, "Where are you?"

The door behind him shut with a slam.

Grubbis turned. He faced Terrance, who wore a white hockey goalie mask and a large flannel shirt. He carried a machete.

I don't remember this being part of the scene, thought Grubbis; and he just stood there, baffled.

Terrance took several swift steps forward. He thrust the machete into Grubbis. The blade entered his gut with such force that it kept going until the tip emerged from his backside.

George Grubbis put the entirety of his strength and being into a shrill, anguished scream.

* * *

In the house next door, Rebecca Hirsch heard the screams coming from the Stegman house. Loud, agonized cries for help, like the others. Only this time she knew better than to call the police. Those crazy boys at the Stegman house were cranking up their horror movies again on the home theater system.

Still, the noise was a nuisance. She had complained before to the property owner, but obviously he hadn't done anything about it—or the garbage that remained scattered all over the front lawn. She wondered why the landlord was so indifferent to his tenant's behavior.

The screams continued, so Rebecca turned on her stereo to drown them out. She played a CD by Cher. The song "Love and Understanding" filled the house and brightened her mood. The screams left her mind, replaced by Cher's soaring vocals, a majestic melody, a catchy beat, and a dancing string section. When she thought she could still hear the screams, she turned the music up louder...

40

Harry picked up Rachel at eight at her West Hollywood apartment. She greeted him at the door with a hearty embrace. Maria waved from the couch and said, "You guys have some celebrating to do."

"Check it out—brand new dress," said Rachel, striking a quick pose, and Harry was happy to indulge.

"I splurged," she said, twirling, elegant in turquoise: light, sunny, leggy, strapless.

"You look like a movie star," said Harry.

The drive into Beverly Hills for dinner hit a roadblock. Literally. Streets had been closed for the filming of *Army of Steel*. What should have been a straight route became a maze of turns and dead ends. Harry followed a long trail of brake lights.

"You can't throw a rock around here without hitting one of their shooting locations," grumbled Harry, inching forward in the traffic. "It's like they own L.A., just because they have a $110 million budget."

Rachel said, "Tomorrow they're taking over Farmers Market to shoot a big action scene."

"And I'm lucky to get a permit to film at 2 a.m. in an empty parking garage."

"I wonder if the movie will be any good."

"With all the marketing they've committed to it, I'm sure it will be a big success with ten sequels. There will be videogames, Happy Meals, breakfast cereals, pop-up books, pillow cases..." Then Harry caught himself and said, "I'm sorry to sound so bitter. I just..."

He glanced at her and she was beautiful, and in the moment, he became candid.

"I used to be married," he said. "I apologize. I haven't talked much about it. But my ex-wife is Julie Howard. She's married to Nigel Howard, the director of *Army of Steel.* Basically, she left me for him. I think she was tired of playing minor league ball and wanted to get a taste of the majors."

"Honey, you're major league," Rachel told him. "The budgets don't mean anything. It's the talent."

"You would think so. But she thought I was a failure."

"What does she know?"

Harry thought about it and replied, "Nothing, actually."

The traffic started moving, finally, at a decent clip.

"Let's change the subject," said Rachel. "I'm sure you don't want to talk about your ex-wife all night. Hey—here's something. Did you hear about that guy they found dismembered in his RV?"

Harry ran a red light.

Car horns blared and a Jaguar flew by, missing them by inches.

Rachel shouted, "Watch the road!" and burst out laughing after Harry made it across the intersection without an accident. "You want me to drive?"

Harry felt his hands sticking to the steering wheel with

perspiration. "What—what about the dismembered guy?"

"It was in the news," she said. "They found an RV parked in a trailer park on Long Beach with a dead guy inside, all cut up with a chainsaw or something. Isn't that gross? It sounds like one of your movies."

"No it doesn't!" said Harry, a tad too defensively.

"Who would do such a thing?'

Harry wanted to go back to talking about his ex-wife.

"Real life is always scarier than anything you could put in a horror film," said Rachel. "Don't you think?"

Harry replied, "For dinner, I'm leaning toward the swordfish, or maybe the spinach ravioli..."

They arrived late at Buzz, but not late enough to lose their table. The smiling maître d' led them across the art-deco bistro to a private booth in a back corner. After the edgy drive, the soft amber lighting and pastoral classical music helped to sooth Harry's nerves.

Rachel sat across from him, and he studied her as she studied the menu.

He thought about their last date, the Lakers game followed by the beginnings of a bedroom scene. He wanted to pick up where they left off. He wanted to spend the entire night with her close.

They ordered appetizers—lobster crepe with asparagus, marinated portobello mushroom with ratatouille—and Harry selected a bottle of champagne.

"Champagne?" said Rachel.

"Of course," said Harry. "We have to celebrate your new movie role. I'm ready to hear all about it. No distractions. You have my undivided attention, so let's have the details." He adopted a glib announcer voice. "This is E! Entertainment here.

Miss Stoller, tell us how you landed your big role."

"Well," smiled Rachel, "I had the audition on Monday. I got the call on Tuesday. We film the scene a week from Friday. But here's the part I've been holding back—I wanted it to be a surprise. I'm working with someone who knows you."

"Someone who knows me?" said Harry, intrigued. "Well, gee. I know a lot of people in this town. It's a director?"

"A director. He says he knows you really well."

"You want me to guess?"

"Sure."

"Boy...it's not Nigel Howard, is it?"

She laughed. "No, no."

"What's the genre?"

"Just like you. Horror. Suspense. Low-budget."

"Hmmm..." said Harry.

"I told him we were having dinner here tonight and I invited him to drop by," said Rachel. "So if you can't guess, I'm not telling you who it is until he gets here."

"It's a he. So it's not Scarlet Dean."

"Right. It's a he."

"James Newman?"

"No."

"Bill Gagliani? Thomas Willis?"

"Nope."

Then her eyes lit up as she looked over Harry's shoulder and saw someone approaching the table. She told Harry, "You're almost out of time."

Harry just smiled and shrugged. "I don't know. I give up. Who is it?"

Harry felt a hand drop on his shoulder. He turned.

"Hello, Harry," said Marcus Stegman.

41

The champagne arrived as Stegman leaned over to kiss Rachel on the cheek. He said, "Hello, darling."

Stegman had cleaned up and dressed up. He wore a crisp, white shirt, fashionable dark slacks, and spotless new shoes. He had shaved off the patchy goatee and neatly pinned the ponytail behind his head. He looked sane...even handsome.

Harry's fingernails dug deep into his palms. Several times he started to speak, but he couldn't find words to express the cacophony in his mind. Stegman and Rachel together created a horribly wrong, impossible image, a Photoshop creation, perhaps, but not a moment in real life...

"Could we have another glass for our friend?" asked Rachel, and the waiter said, "Certainly."

The waiter filled three glasses with bubbly.

Rachel lifted up her glass. "A toast."

Stegman lifted his glass. "To a new star."

Harry didn't touch his glass. He wiped a hand across the air. "Hold on. Hold everything. *Wait*."

Rachel and Stegman stared back at him.

"Somebody...please explain what's going on," said Harry.

Rachel looked at Harry, puzzled. "What's to explain? I answered an ad in *Backstage*. It was for a movie. Marcus is the director. I had an audition on Monday."

"And she passed with flying colors," said Marcus, beaming. "She was *perfect*, Harry. I cast her the next day."

"What movie?" said Harry, nearly breathless. "What role?"

Stegman sighed. "Harry, you know about my new movie. I told you all about it. How soon you forget. It's a tribute to horror films. It's about the ultimate, obsessed horror fan who kills people in character as his favorite horror film killers. I'm going to pay homage to all the greats, the classics of the twentieth century. And Rachel—she will be in a scene that honors the greatest of the greats. A little film called *Psycho*."

"Yes," said Rachel. "We're going to recreate the shower sequence, one of the most famous movie scenes of all time."

"No," said Harry, very quietly at first, but then his voice kept rising and tightening. "No. *No*. NO!"

Rachel looked shocked.

Stegman feigned shock. "Comrade, what has gotten into you?"

"I'm not your comrade." Harry stood up and faced Rachel, addressing her forcefully. "You will not make a movie with this man."

"Why?"

"Because," said Harry. "Because...because his movies are crap."

"Harry!" said Rachel, stunned.

"Dear me," said Stegman. He put down the champagne glass. "Rachel, I feared this would happen..."

"Harry, this is your friend," said Rachel.

Stegman's face saddened, a hurt puppy dog expression.

"But friends can still harbor rivalries. I fear that Harry's hostilities stem from professional jealousy. That's OK. I admire a competitive spirit. We all want to be the best. We all want to hire the best actors and actresses. We all want to make the very best movie possible."

"That's not it," said Harry, but he was stuck because the real reason could never see the light of day.

"We should be supportive of each other and promote our genre. There is nothing to be gained from being adversaries," said Stegman. "Harry, I have always treated you with the highest admiration and respect. I would do anything for you. Say, that reminds me. Did you get my package?"

"Package?"

"Sure. The other night. A great big package. Rather roundish. I had it delivered to your house. Did you like it?"

"What are you— " Then Harry realized: *Wiggins.* He exclaimed, "I don't want anymore 'presents' from you!"

Stegman turned his attention to Rachel. He turned on the charm full power. "Rachel is vibrant and beautiful and one heck of an actress. I'm sure there is plenty of her to go around, isn't there Rachel?"

"Harry, I still want to do a movie with you too," she said.

"It's not about doing a movie with me," said Harry. "It's about *not* doing a movie with *him*."

"This is how you treat your old friend from film school?" she asked.

"Friend? Film school?"

Stegman shook his head sadly. "Perhaps I should go."

"No," said Rachel. "Please join us."

"No," said Harry. "Please leave."

"*Harry,*" said Rachel.

"You're intruding on our dinner," Harry told Stegman. "I want you to leave now. Get out of here before I have you thrown out. I'm serious. Get out. Now!"

Stegman turned to face Rachel. "I'm so sorry. This is all so...unnecessary. Perhaps it's just not in the cards for us to work together. A missed opportunity. Oh well. Maybe some other time. Enjoy your dinner."

He gave Harry a hard look. "Goodbye, Harry." Then he left.

Harry watched him go. He didn't sit back down until Stegman had left the restaurant.

Rachel was livid.

"What's the matter with you?" she said in a tone harsher than Harry had ever heard from her before.

"Believe me, you do *not* want to work with that man."

"Why?"

"Because you're better than him."

She fell back against her chair in disbelief. "What does that mean?"

"He makes...cheap little horror movies."

"That's what *you* do!"

"Right. And remember when you turned me down, you said it wasn't the vehicle you were looking for."

"That was then; this is now," she told him. "Low-budget horror movies are all the rage, thanks to *you*. You made them a hot property. They're popular like never before, and I want to be part of the action."

"It's a bad way to launch a career."

"It wouldn't kill me to do this film, Harry."

Harry swallowed hard.

"It's just one short, simple scene," she said.

"Right. The shower scene from *Psycho*. I hate to tell you, but it's already been done before, and it's been done very well, I might add. What's the point? Where's he going to film it? In his house?"

"The Stardust Motel."

"Stardust Motel? That place went out of business and closed down weeks ago."

"So he's renting the space. He probably got a good deal."

"If he's even asking permission."

"This conversation is ridiculous."

"His movie is ridiculous. I'm telling you, Rachel, honestly, from the heart, *don't do this movie*."

She studied him. "You really are jealous, aren't you? Just like in the car tonight, talking about Nigel Howard. All this jealousy is not healthy, Harry."

"I'm not jealous about Marcus Stegman."

"Then why are you so adamant that I not work with him? I really resent being told who I can and can't work for."

The appetizers arrived. Neither one of them glanced at the food. Harry felt sick to his stomach. "Let's just drop this," he said.

"No. I'm not going to 'just drop it.' You've been acting weird all week, and I think I deserve an explanation."

"There's nothing to discuss. Can we forget this?"

"No, we can't." She stood up and snatched her purse. "I've had enough of this. I'm leaving."

"Where are you going?'

"I'm going home," said Rachel, and she left the booth.

Harry quickly got up to follow.

He caught up with her just outside the restaurant's entrance. "Rachel—"

She spun around to look at him. "What."

"Please. It's very important that you stay away from Marcus Stegman."

"God!" she said. "Is that all you're concerned about? That I might act in his movie?"

"Promise me you won't be in his movie."

She nodded. "All right. All right. Fine. I won't be in his movie. But here's another declaration: this relationship is over."

She turned from him and headed down the sidewalk, weaving past the valet parking attendants. Harry followed.

"Rachel—"

"I don't want to go out with you anymore, Harry," she said, not looking back at him. "Let's face it, we're not having fun. Why don't we just break up now, cleanly, OK?"

"Rachel, that's not what I want."

"It's what *I* want. I'm sorry, Harry."

"Rachel," he called after her. "You don't understand!"

She stopped abruptly. She faced him, ice cold. "I don't understand? Then explain it to me. Now."

She looked hard at Harry. He shrunk back. "I can't," he said.

"Fine. Then it's over."

Rachel reached the street corner and hailed an oncoming taxicab. Within a minute, she was headed down Rodeo Drive, without him.

Harry watched the cab vanish into the night. He couldn't move. His entire insides felt like they were crumbling.

42

"How was dinner?"

Rachel didn't answer. She hurried past Maria and made a straight line for her bedroom.

"Rachel, what's wrong?"

"N-n-nothing," she said, but a sob escaped from her throat. Not a very convincing answer.

Rachel entered her bedroom and slammed the door. She heard Maria call out, "What's going on?"

Rachel didn't reply. She pulled off the expensive strapless dress she had bought from a boutique on Melrose Avenue and dumped it on the floor. She put on her frumpiest pajamas, the ones with the tear at the shoulder seam. Then she climbed into bed and brought the sheets up high.

Maria knocked lightly. "Do you want to talk about it?"

"No."

Maria entered anyway. She opened the door a crack and slipped in, holding out a bag of chocolate chip cookies. "You sure?"

"We broke up," said Rachel, sitting up, reaching for a cookie.

Maria came over and sat with her on the bed. "Oh no. How come?"

"I don't know," Rachel sniffled. She bit into a cookie. "That's the weird part..."

Over the next hour, Rachel ate most of the cookies and used up all of the Kleenex. She told her roommate about the evening's disastrous dinner date.

"He became all possessive and jealous," said Rachel. "It was a side of him I've never seen before. It scared me. There was all this weird tension. He was so adamant about me not appearing in this movie."

"Well screw him," said Maria. "You have your career to think about. Who is he to tell you what to do? You don't need somebody like that in your life. You're independent."

"I can't believe I'm crying like a 14-year-old," said Rachel.

"Get it all out of your system," said Maria, "because tomorrow's a new day. We'll just forget this creep like he never happened, and start over."

"I wish it was that easy."

"Trust me," said Maria. "It is."

* * *

Rachel slept deep into the following morning, the outside world removed by drawn shades. During scattered waking moments, she refused to look at the clock, rolled over and returned to sleep. Day, night, who cares. She had no motivation to get up and do anything.

When Maria creaked the door open at ten-thirty, Rachel told her to go away.

"You got flowers," Maria responded.

Rachel sat up and rubbed her face. "Flowers?"

"Come see."

Rachel left the bedroom and stumbled into the light of the living room. A large, colorful bouquet sat on the coffee table in a vase.

"They just arrived," said Maria. "There's a note. Read it. I'll bet they're 'sorry flowers' from Harry. That prick."

Rachel took the small, pink envelope from the table and opened it. She slid out a rectangular note.

"What's it say?" said Maria, trying to glance over her shoulder.

"It's not from Harry," said Rachel. "It's from Marcus Stegman."

Maria smiled. "Ah, a new man in your life."

Rachel read the note aloud, "Shine bright, my star. Looking forward to an exquisite performance. Marcus."

Maria slapped a hand on her chest. "God, that's so sweet. I've never gotten flowers from a director. Even the ones I've slept with."

"I told Harry I wouldn't do this movie."

Maria wrinkled her nose. "So what? You guys broke up. It doesn't matter what he wants. It's what *you* want."

Rachel put down the card and admired the flowers. "God, I'm so confused."

"Make the movie, if that's what you really want to do. If you pass this up, you might never forgive yourself."

The phone rang.

Maria picked it up off a table. "Hello?" She listened, then said, "Just a moment."

Maria passed the phone over, mouthing, "Marcus."

Rachel answered. "Hello?"

The voice spoke in her ear as smooth as silk. "Hello, Ms. Stoller. It's Marcus. I hope you are doing well this morning."

"Thank you for the flowers."

"Good, they arrived. You're most welcome. It's the least I could do after last night. I felt so bad you had to sit through that argument. Harry and I, we've had our ups and downs over the years. Sometimes, I think he just gets a little...controlling."

"I've never seen him get like that before."

"It's unfortunate," said Stegman. "You never know what's going to set him off. But that's not the reason I called. I have a rather urgent matter. The shooting schedule's been moved up for your big scene. We just found out that we must tape this afternoon, rather than next week, because we're going to lose the location."

"I haven't rehearsed..."

"You'll be great. Rehearsal is for amateurs."

Rachel took a deep breath. "You want to film me, the scene, today?" She looked at Maria for a reaction.

Maria signaled thumbs up with a vigorous nod.

"Well...OK," said Rachel.

"Great. Thank you for being so flexible," said Stegman. "You remember where we're filming?"

"Yes. The Stardust Motel. I know the location."

"Can you be there in...one hour?"

"One hour?" said Rachel, startled.

Maria continued to nod vigorously, thumbs still up.

"I guess so," said Rachel. "Sure, one hour. I'll get dressed fast."

"Fabulous," said Stegman. "I can't wait. This will be the centerpiece of the movie. You are going to give the performance of a lifetime."

"I'll try my best," she said, almost giggling at his hyperbole.

"See you in one hour, Ms. Stoller."

After Rachel hung up, Maria told her, "Way to go. You made the right choice. C'mon, girl, high five me."

Rachel smacked her the high five.

* * *

Rachel showered and enjoyed the irony of showering to prepare for the filming of a shower scene. She dressed in her favorite hot pink sleeveless top and snug jeans, fully aware that it was all going to come off anyway, for the cameras.

Freshened up, Rachel grew excited by her good fortune: handpicked to pay homage to one of the great movie moments of all time. A chance to become a part of the *Psycho* legacy.

She had never expected her big break to be a shower scene, but that was fine with her. The timing was right. *Might as well show off this body while it's still trim and youthful,* she thought to herself. *Preserve it on film, because as soon as the flab arrives with the varicose veins, the clothes stay on.*

She realized then how badly she wanted to do this. She was going to give it her all. Harry's cranky protests faded away. They no longer mattered. He was simply jealous.

Maria gave Rachel one more high five as she headed out the door. "A star is born," called out Maria.

The word "star" resonated with Rachel as she drove down Sunset Boulevard in her MINI Cooper Convertible, top down, inviting the sunny skies in. Rachel let the wind blow her hair, accelerated the car, and propelled her career toward stardom.

43

The fax machine hummed. Paul Jacobs walked over and received the latest sales report from B&B Distributors. He scanned the numbers, knowing they would be big, but they were bigger. "Amazing," he said out loud. The success of *Deadly Desires* had revitalized demand for all of PJ Productions' output. The DVDs were flying off the shelves—everything from *Slash* to *Swamp Monster*. The entire library would soon need to be repressed.

Best of all, the sales prospects for a *Deadly Desires* DVD were monstrous. Paul had already entertained several offers that filled his eyeballs with dollar signs. The DVD needed to be a top priority while the property was hot. It would be the real moneymaker. The theatrical release was just a taste of the profits to come.

Paul needed Harry to record a director's commentary, pronto. He needed outtakes, bloopers, interviews with the cast. Harry had to get back to work and support the success. The neurotic recluse bit was wearing thin. Paul would have to get stern. After all, it was his company. It was time for Harry to face the fame.

The phone rang. Paul picked it up. The University of Illinois wanted to hold a four-day Harry Tuttle film festival. Could Harry appear on the final night for a Q&A with the audience? They could pay $5,000 plus travel and expenses.

The phone rang again. The latest numbers were in from overseas. *Deadly Desires* had moved up one slot to become the third highest grossing film of the week in Italy, edging out Adam Sandler, while holding steady at number two in Germany.

The phone rang again and caller ID listed *Rolling Stone* magazine. Paul needed a break. He let voicemail grab it and heard the request, "...would like to interview Mr. Tuttle for a feature story..." Paul left his desk to get more coffee.

Alongside the coffee maker, a small radio played. Paul filled his mug and added half-and-half from the little fridge, while listening to the day's headlines.

As Paul took a long sip, the newscast began discussing the latest development in the Walter Wiggins case.

Paul leaned in to listen.

The anchor announced, "We have new information to pass along in the Walter Wiggins murder investigation. A source close to the investigation reports that a broken wristwatch was found with the body and may have belonged to the killer. According to the source, the watch has a gold wristband and sports an engraving that says, 'Scary Harry.' Investigators handling the case are still— "

Paul sprayed a mouthful of coffee across the room. He slammed down the mug.

He stared in shock at the radio.

"Holy shit! *Harry*."

44

Harry sped toward West Hollywood in his silver Audi, wheels squealing around a corner as he entered La Brea Avenue. He had awakened this morning devastated and aching over the prior night's blow-up with Rachel. He had searched deep in his soul and decided it was time to come clean.

Enough bullshit. He was going to tell Rachel *everything.* And then he was going to the police.

He dreaded Rachel's reaction most. The humiliation would be crushing. But she needed to know.

He was not a great director.

He did not create *Deadly Desires.*

He was still the same old loser she had rejected at the start, the maker of terrible, cheesy horror movies. Everything that excited her about him was a lie.

Deadly Desires was all Marcus Stegman, from beginning to end, and Harry had taken credit for another man's movie. It was a desperate effort to boost his sagging career and medicate his midlife crisis.

Then, with that confession out of the way, Harry would tell Rachel the twisted truth about Stegman: The real killings masquerading as film art. The brutal fate of Sandra Ross.

And the real reason he did not want Rachel to shoot the scene for Stegman's new movie.

Her life was in jeopardy.

A fresh bouquet of flowers bundled in cellophane sat beside him in the passenger seat. They might not mend fences. She might throw them back in his face. But if he could stop her from filming that "Psycho" scene next week, it was worth it. Even if she never talked to him again. Even if he spent the rest of his life in jail.

If he could save her from this madman, that was good enough. He no longer cared about his career, his reputation, his legacy. He was done giving priority to a fake world.

There was Hollywood and there was real life, and it was time for real life to finally take over.

Harry parked as close as he could get to her building, given the dreadful West Hollywood parking, and hurried up the sidewalk, clutching the flowers.

In the lobby, he buzzed all the units until someone let him inside. He took the elevator up to the third floor, walked fast down the hall to Rachel's door and knocked hard.

After two minutes, Harry saw the peephole darken and a voice behind the door said, "What do *you* want?"

It was Maria, the roommate.

"I need to see Rachel," said Harry.

Maria opened the door halfway and faced him, dark eyes cold, a hand on her hip in a confrontational pose.

"She doesn't want to talk to you," said Maria.

"I'm sure she doesn't," said Harry, "but I need to speak with her. It's very important."

Maria gave him a smug smirk. "Too late. She's gone. Not

home."

Harry's heart sank. Then, looking past Maria, he saw a large bouquet of flowers in a vase on the coffee table. The colorful assortment dwarfed the bouquet in Harry's hand.

"Who sent those flowers?" said Harry.

"None of your business."

"Was it *him*?"

"I think I'll close the door now," said Maria, and she started to do so.

Harry slammed his hand against the door to prevent it from shutting. He shoved it back open and entered the apartment.

"Hey!" said Maria, stumbling back a few steps.

He brushed past her to examine the flowers on the table. He saw the card resting near the vase and picked it up.

"That's none of your business," said Maria, coming at him.

But Harry had already read the card. "Marcus Stegman," he said aloud. He tossed his flowers on the sofa.

"That's right," said Maria. "She's involved with another director. Someone who treats her with more respect. A real man. Because of you, she sat up half the night crying. It's over, Harry. Why don't you just give it up and go away."

Harry returned Maria's hard stare. "Tell me where she is."

"Screw you," said Maria.

"I'm not leaving this apartment until I get a chance to talk with Rachel. It's crucial. She *cannot* film that scene next week."

Maria laughed out loud then.

Harry looked at her strangely.

Maria said, "You're too late, bozo. The shooting got moved up to today. She's already filming her big scene *right now*. Guess you can't stop her after all. So boo hoo to you." She picked up Harry's flowers from the couch and slapped them back at him.

Harry let the flowers drop to the floor, stunned. He thought for a long moment, recalling the previous night's conversation. "The Stardust Motel..."

Studying Harry, Maria read his thoughts. "No. You're not going to..."

"How long ago did she leave?" asked Harry, grabbing Maria by the shoulders.

"I'm not telling you anything."

Harry let go and spun away from her, heading for the door. "I can still stop them."

"No you won't!" thundered Maria.

She raced him to the door. She tried to block him.

They struggled for a moment and she grabbed hold of his shirt. He tore himself free, heard the fabric rip, and stumbled into the corridor.

"You will not ruin this for her!" shouted Maria.

Harry headed for the elevator, saw that Maria was coming at him, strong and fierce, and realized he couldn't wait. He was better off rushing down the stairs.

He threw open the stairwell door and began to descend. She entered the stairwell and shouted from powerful lungs, "*Stop*! Somebody stop him! Murderer! Rapist! *HELP!*" Her voice echoed loud, crashing off the walls, all the way down.

Harry didn't look back, taking the steps two at a time, grabbing the rail for support. As he reached the ground floor, Maria let loose with a final, mighty scream from above.

"SOMEBODY STOP THAT MAN!"

45

The Stardust Motel rested on a weedy plot of land just south of the Santa Monica Freeway, situated near a dead commercial strip of shuttered storefronts and barely alive, unbranded fast food joints.

Rachel stood in the parking lot, an uneven stretch of cracked blacktop, empty save for a single white van. The motel rooms surrounded the parking lot in a U-shape, two layers of red doors and darkened windows. Litter blew past her feet.

This was not a good part of town, and Rachel felt uneasy that no one was here to greet her. Nothing indicated that she had entered a filming location. Perhaps she had gone to the wrong Stardust Motel? But the phone book only listed one...

She heard the hum and rumble of trucks on the freeway and felt alone in the stark surroundings. Even if this was the right location, she wondered if she had still made a mistake. She started to step back from the motel when a voice greeted her.

"Rachel."

She turned. Marcus Stegman approached, beaming. He wore all black, ponytail tied so tight behind his head that his pale face looked like a skull.

"Where are we filming?" asked Rachel.

"Room 10."

She shrugged. "Oh...OK."

He smiled, tuning into her concern. "We're using a real motel room. I know—not very glamorous. But why build a set when you can use the real thing? The motel is between owners at the moment. I worked out a financial arrangement to borrow one of the units for some filming. Got a good deal, too. It always helps when you are negotiating with a drunk." He laughed heartily.

Rachel just nodded. "So where should I go?"

"Just follow me."

Stegman led her across the lot to Room 10 on the first floor. He opened the red door and gestured for her to enter. Stepping inside, Rachel faced a bare bones crew consisting of exactly two people: a tall, redheaded male and a shorter, dark-skinned man with an earring. She saw two halogen lights on stands, and two video cameras.

A large portion of the wall separating the bathroom from the rest of the room had been torn down, exposing the shower to allow for easier filming.

Stegman entered behind Rachel and shut the door. "Gritty realism. It doesn't get any better than this. This place even has cockroaches."

"Great," said Rachel. Her shoes felt spongy on the crusted carpet. A wall of bad smells smacked her: cigarettes; body odor; and heavy, uncirculated air. The wallpaper and furniture looked old and funky.

Stegman introduced Rachel to Garon and Terrance. She shook their hands, nodded, smiled. They seemed nice enough, if a bit freaky.

"Don't let the modest set-up fool you," said Stegman. "We have the best state-of-the-art digital equipment that money can buy. Terrance here will play the lead. Garon and I will operate the cameras. We're a lean, mean, movie-making machine."

"I guess that's the formula that made *Deadly Desires* such a hit," said Rachel.

"Exactly," said Stegman.

"So where are my script pages?" asked Rachel.

"You don't need any. Really, the scene is very simple," said Stegman. "You are Betsy Brewer, a weary business traveler from Chicago. You want to take a quick shower. You disrobe; you climb into the tub, and you begin your shower. Then Terrance here..." He gestured to the tall redhead. "Terrance plays the killer. He's Boris, the psychotic horror fan. Boris has come to this seedy motel, driven by an obsession to commit murder in the same manner as his all-time favorite horror movie scene. He enters with a key stolen from housekeeping. You don't hear anything over the rushing water. You just keep soaping yourself, up and down." Stegman rubbed a hand in a circular motion across his chest and then down to his groin to demonstrate.

Rachel cringed at his enthusiastic display.

"So I take a shower," she said. "OK, got it. Then what?"

Stegman walked over to the twin bed, which was covered with camera equipment, cables, and supplies. He reached into a black bag and took out a large knife. Light hit the blade and it glistened.

Stegman held up the knife. His voice grew dramatic. "All of a sudden, Terrance *yanks* back the shower curtain. You see him and scream. You scream with all your might. But you are helpless. He's upon you in seconds." Stegman began making stabbing motions in the air. "He lunges the blade at your naked flesh again and again...hacking with brutal force...a cold-hearted killer. Viciously, he slashes you to death and your screams turn to whimpers. You collapse, emitting a final, choking gasp. Then you die."

Stegman smiled and dropped his hand. "And that's your big scene. Think Janet Leigh, Alfred Hitchcock. Except now it's Marcus Stegman and Rachel Stoller."

Rachel nodded, eyes focused on the knife still in Stegman's grip.

"That's a very realistic looking knife," said Rachel.

"Of course," said Stegman.

Rachel held out her hand and asked, "Can I see it?"

46

Harry slammed the brakes in front of his Eagle Rock house, threw the car in park, jumped out and raced across his lawn. He reached the front door, unlocked it fast, and entered.

Running into his den, he pulled open his bottom desk drawer, grabbing files and papers, throwing them on the floor, searching for the Beretta semi-automatic. He found a box of cartridges, then remembered tucking the gun under a sofa cushion in the living room when Rachel visited. He retrieved it, tossing the cushion across the room.

Harry removed the magazine from the pistol and loaded it with ten rounds. He pushed the magazine into the pistol grip until it *clicked*. Then he loaded the first live cartridge into the chamber. He activated the safety lever, stood, and placed the gun under his shirt, into the waist of his slacks.

Then he rushed back outside.

As Harry crossed the front yard to his car, a blue Mercedes screeched into the driveway. Paul Jacobs scrambled out. He waved frantically. "Harry! We have to talk!"

Harry swore and kept going.

Paul dashed toward Harry and caught up with him just before he reached his car door.

"Harry, Harry," said Paul, blocking him, lit up in panic. His hands fluttered like wild birds. "How could you do this to me? To our *company*?"

"I can't talk," said Harry, trying to reach past Paul for the door handle.

"No," said Paul. "We *have* to talk! On the radio they said they found a watch—" He grabbed Harry by the shoulders. "*Listen to me.*"

"Let go of me, Paul!"

Harry tried to shake him off, but Paul was all over him.

"They found a watch with Walter Wiggins' body," said Paul. "They described the watch and it's *yours*. The one I gave you!"

Harry pushed at Paul, but Paul maintained his grip on Harry.

"I'll explain everything later, but not right now," said Harry. "Please let go of me. I really have to go."

"Harry, you could be locked up for life! This is *big trouble!* What did you do to Wiggins?"

"Paul, stop it—"

"I won't stop it!"

Harry finally pulled the Beretta 9000S semi-automatic pistol out from under his shirt. He pointed it into Paul's chest. "I said *let go of me*, Paul. I really mean it. I have to leave!"

Paul's eyes bulged. His panic reached a new stratosphere when he saw the gun. "Oh my God! It's true! You've snapped! You've gone crazy!"

Harry again tried to get into his car, but Paul continued to block his path, grabbing for the weapon.

"Give me that gun, Harry, before you hurt someone."

"Paul, *let go.*"

"I'm serious. Give me the gun."

They struggled for the pistol. Harry finally reached back and slugged Paul in the jaw, knocking him down into the street. It was the first time Harry had hit anyone since junior high.

Paul sat on his butt for a moment, stunned, holding his chin.

"Ow," he said.

Seizing his window of opportunity, Harry yanked open the car door. He jumped in, slammed the door and locked it.

Harry started the engine.

Paul jumped up and rushed toward the Audi. Harry floored it in reverse, shooting backwards about 50 feet, creating a long arc ending on a neighbor's lawn. Then he threw the car in drive and tore down the street, roaring away from Paul.

Paul screamed, waved, and danced in the rearview mirror like some kind of spastic puppet, limbs flying everywhere.

Harry kept going.

47

Stegman reached out and took Rachel's hand. He turned it over. He pressed the knife blade into her palm.

The blade retracted into the handle.

"See? Painless," he said. "Doesn't break the skin. Can't cut a thing. Check it out."

He let her hold the knife for a moment. She ran her fingers along the side of the blade, delicately at first, then applying pressure. She touched the tip. "It looks so real."

"Just a prop. Made by a professional theater prop manufacturer."

"Impressive."

She handed the knife back to Stegman. He passed it on to Garon.

"We should get started," said Stegman. "We're on a strict schedule, and we need to move quickly."

"I'm ready when you are," Rachel told him.

"Great," said Stegman. "Let me explain the shot sequence. First, we'll shoot you entering the motel room. Then you call home to touch base with your family. After that, you decide to take a shower. You disrobe. You climb in the shower. Then the killer attacks."

"Pretty straightforward," she said.

"Garon, please present Ms. Stoller with her wardrobe," said Stegman.

Garon brought Rachel a 3-piece pinstripe skirt suit, polyester, with a black and lilac color scheme and lace trim camisole. Price tags dangled from the clothing.

Ugh, thought Rachel. *Ugly*.

Stegman noted her expression and promised, "You'll look lovely. We have nylons and pumps, and a matching purse."

"What kind of company do I work for?" she asked.

Stegman seemed to make up an answer on the spot. "Ah... office supplies."

"Great."

"If you'll get dressed into character, we'll prepare the lights and cameras for your first scene."

Rachel, holding the business suit, glanced around the room. The interior bathroom wall was gone. "Where...do I get dressed?"

"Rachel," chuckled Stegman. "There's no dressing room here. No one has a trailer. We're family. Go right ahead. Don't mind us. We'll be seeing you in your birthday suit soon enough anyway."

Rachel was feeling increasingly creeped out by the whole thing. Her initial excitement had been replaced by an attitude of, *Just get it over with.*

Maybe Harry was right. This guy was an amateur hack and not one of the exciting new breed of low-budget film directors. The whole set-up felt unprofessional.

Had she jumped at this role simply to snub Harry and make him jealous? To awaken his passion?

Way to go Rachel, she told herself. *Another brilliant career move.* She unfastened her blue jeans and slid them down to her ankles, as Stegman and Garon reviewed lighting levels.

She caught the other fellow, Terrance, checking her out. She smiled weakly at him, before taking off her pink top.

The business suit felt baggy. The padded shoulders gave her a bulky, masculine look. The shoes were small and hurt her feet.

I suffer for my art, she thought. To complete the businesswoman look, she put her hair up, something she rarely did. She didn't like the way it enlarged her face. *I should count my blessings. If I actually was a businesswoman, I'd have to look like this every day.*

"All right, Mr. DeMille," said Rachel. "I'm ready for my close-up."

Stegman chuckled with appreciation at the classic film line. He said, "Come here; let me get a good look at you."

She walked over, grimacing *ow ow ow* with every step as the shoes pinched her feet.

"You look fabulous," said Stegman. "Classy. Beautiful. Strong. Fuss with your hair a little. Let's see a few strands out of place. A rumpled look. You just flew into town. You're jet-lagged. You sat next to a fat man who coughed on you the whole flight. You're feeling dirty and exhausted."

She pulled hair loose with her fingertips until Stegman said, "Perfect! Now we are ready."

He proceeded to film the first short sequence: Rachel entering the motel room, tired, loaded down with a laptop, suitcase, business bag, and purse. She dumped everything on the bed and let out a heavy sigh.

"Cut!" said Stegman. "Awesome!"

They shot two more takes, and then set up the next scene: Rachel on the phone, calling home.

Stegman gave her a loose framework for the one-sided dialogue. He told her to improvise, keep it real, keep it short. So she gave him several variations of "Hi honey, it's Betsy. I'm in Los Angeles now. Just wanted to touch base. I'm wiped. I think I'm going to take a shower. Tell the kids I love them. Bye."

"Love it!" he said after the second take. "You nailed it. On to the next. Now it's shower time." He walked over and tossed his arm around her shoulders.

Don't touch me, she thought to herself, but said nothing.

"This next scene is simple," he said in a reassuring voice. "You feel icky. Your clothes are sweaty and dirty. You want nothing more than to peel them off. Turn on the shower. Get the steam going and disrobe."

"How far do you want me to...disrobe?"

"You're taking a shower," he said. "All the way, of course."

"I mean, what's going to show on the screen?"

"Oh, don't worry about that. We'll be tasteful."

She looked over at Terrance. His eyes sat on her, eager, like a wolf. She sighed. She had shown off her body before. She had revealed almost all in lingerie ads. She had worn a bikini in a TV beer commercial. She hadn't bared everything for the cameras, but it wouldn't be a big deal.

She just regretted that her first time would be this movie. It was like losing her virginity on a careless one-night stand, to someone she didn't really like.

"Let's do it then," said Rachel. *The show must go on.*

Rachel kicked off the shoes and entered the exposed bathroom. She watched and waited as Stegman, Garon, and Terrance repositioned the lights and the cameras.

Suck in your tummy, she reminded herself.

When the scene was ready to roll, Stegman walked over and gave her words of advice in a soft tone.

"Forget the camera. Just become Betsy, the weary traveler. Let the clothes fall from your body. You're very tired, so pace it slow. Every muscle aches. The suit peels off gradually, like a second skin. On your face, relief. You are overjoyed to remove this sticky, stale business suit. You feel freedom. Freedom at the end of a long, hard day."

"OK, I get it," she said flatly.

Stegman turned and headed to his spot behind one of the cameras. "Great! Alright guys, let's roll!"

As the cameras rolled, Rachel reached into the shower and turned on the spray. The water hissed loud. She let down her hair and shook it loose. She began undressing. She didn't look at them, but she could feel three sets of eyes on her body as each item of clothing slid off and struck the floor.

She stopped at the panties.

She glanced out at the lights and cameras, squinting in the brightness. "That should be enough, right?"

"Cut!" said Stegman. He moved out from behind a camera. He came up close to her.

She folded her arms over her naked breasts.

"Rachel, honey," said Stegman. "No one showers in their underwear."

"Right, but—"

"Let's do it again," said Stegman, returning to the crew. "*All the way this time.*"

She stared after him, wanting to object, maybe offer up some choice profanity; but she bit her tongue. She stayed professional, despite the fact that these people were amateurs.

She swallowed her pride and told herself, *Rachel, just get this nonsense over with.*

"Turn off the shower," said Stegman. "Put the outfit back on, let's start from the top."

"From the top?"

"Yes, please."

She redressed.

They filmed the sequence twice more, both times all the way to the end, the white cotton panties sliding down her legs to her ankles, Rachel stepping out with one foot, kicking them away with the other foot, followed by a long, discomforting pause before "Cut!"

She could feel the three of them leering, Terrance in particular. His eyes coated her body with a filth worse than anything she could accumulate from a long day of business travel.

As bad as the scene was, the next one was worse.

The cameras and three-man crew moved closer and they filmed her showering, curtain open. It went on too long. Was this a hygiene documentary?

"Lather your breasts please," directed Stegman in a plain tone, as if he was saying *walk across the room and open the door.* Rachel reached a zone where she refused to think about her surroundings. She simply adapted to the awfulness. It would all be over soon enough, and hopefully no one would ever see this movie.

Be a true actress and forget everything around you. Forget the mechanics of moviemaking, forget the baggage of the situation, forget these slimy people and just become the character, living inside the moment.

Finally, Stegman yelled, "Cut! We got it." Rachel turned off the water, stepped out of the tub and wrapped herself in a large bath towel.

"One more scene to go, and it's the biggie," said Stegman.

"Yes," she said. "Now you kill me."

Stegman looked at her, cocked his head and smiled. "Indeed. Now we kill you."

"Let's just get it over with," said Rachel. "I'm getting soggy."

"Maybe we can do this in one take," said Stegman.

"That would be nice," agreed Rachel.

He put his arm around her again. She clung tighter to the towel to keep it from dropping.

"Here's the sequence," he said. "You're still showering. However, we're going to shut the curtain and pull the cameras back so that Terrance can be in the shot. We'll film a point-of-view shot, over his shoulder, as he steps up to the shower curtain. Then everything will happen very quickly. He will rip the curtain to one side. He will attack with the blade. He will stab you to death."

"Cool," said Rachel.

Stegman leaned closer to Rachel. He brushed some hair from her cheek. "From you, Rachel, I want full, unmitigated horror. The horror of being confronted by a mad slasher with a blade. The horror of your naked vulnerability, alone and cornered in a strange motel, hundreds of miles from home. Show me the horror of seeing your entire life flash before you as the blade strikes. The horror of realizing you will never see your children or husband again. The horror of unbearable pain and agony as the knife penetrates your bare flesh. The horror of feeling the flow of your own warm blood draining from your body. The horror of death, unexpected, unrelenting, uncompromising. Give me all you got, Rachel Stoller. Give me goose bumps. Make me *believe*."

"I will," said Rachel.

"I know," said Stegman.

Stegman stepped back to the cameras. He looked to Terrance.

"Are you ready for your big scene, 'Boris'?"

Terrance nodded without a word. He held up the knife. Rachel looked at her assailant and his weapon. The knife blade glistened in the light.

From behind one of the cameras, Stegman called out, "Back into the shower, Ms. Stoller, and please close the curtain."

Rachel reached in and turned the water back on. During filming, the spray had turned from hot to lukewarm. Now the heat was gone entirely.

"It's cold," she said, feeling the icy spray on her hand.

"We'll film quickly."

"I mean really cold."

"I'm sorry. We can't do anything about that. Please get in the shower. We need to get rolling."

She examined the tub for a moment, which was a mistake, because she got a good look at the mold spores and rusted soap tray.

After this shower, I'm going to need a shower, she told herself.

"Please, Rachel!" said Stegman.

Rachel dropped the bath towel to the floor and stepped into the tub, under the spray.

She let out a small shriek as the freezing water struck her.

She heard one of the men giggle.

She hated them.

She shut the shower curtain. The blue curtain lit up from the glare of the halogen lights.

Stegman cried out, "We are filming in five...in four...three... two...and *action!*"

Rachel grimaced under the cold spray and reached for the bar of soap. She ran the soap up and down her arm several times, the same motion, wishing the deadly assault would hurry up.

Terrance's shadow approached the shower curtain. She could see the dark outline of his arm and the knife.

The shadow grew larger and larger until it nearly engulfed the shower curtain.

Any second now...

As the anticipation mounted, Rachel felt a wave of genuine fear ripple through her body.

The curtain ripped open with a loud *whoosh*.

She dropped the soap and delivered a scream, throwing up her hands.

Terrance, wild eyed, thrust the knife at her.

She felt an immediate, unexpected sting—a burst of pain in her forearm—and staggered off balance—*this isn't supposed to hurt—he's going to leave a bruise—*

Then she saw the blood.

Rachel's screams exploded.

The knife came at her again, and it was for real.

Rachel twisted to get out of the way, and the sharp blade caught her hip, cutting deep, sending huge shockwaves of pain—

—and she stumbled back into the tile shower wall, hitting it hard, catching a glimpse of her blood joining the water spraying at her feet—

—and Terrance came at her again with the knife, missing this time, hitting the empty space between her arm and side—

—and Rachel struck his face, a large and wet slapping sound; but he didn't flinch, stabbing again with the knife; and she jumped as she saw the blade come at her, but there was nowhere to go—

—and it scraped across her stomach, a thin line of red, the bloodied blade retreating, then returning, and she screamed with everything in her—

—and then the top of Terrance's head exploded.

48

Harry stood inside Room 10 of the Stardust Motel, his arm straight and steady, his gun still aimed at the precise location where Terrance had been standing seconds earlier.

He swung his arm and aimed for Garon next.

Garon stepped back from his camera, hands up, palms out.

Harry turned and aimed for Stegman.

Stegman spread out his arms—halfway between a surrender and a greeting. "Harry...?"

"I'm not done," said Harry. "If either one of you moves, I'll kill you next."

Harry's appearance stunned them all. He had pulled into the Stardust Motel lot minutes earlier, unsure of where the filming was taking place. His frantic search didn't last long.

Rachel's screams identified the room.

Harry had stopped her assailant in mid-attack. But now, as she shut off the water and staggered out of the shower, Harry could see that her face was covered in blood.

"Oh my God," said Harry. "Rachel."

"It's OK," sputtered Rachel. "Most of it is his blood."

She wiped herself with bath towels and held a washcloth to

the worst wound, the cut on her hip. It bled through. Her left forearm seeped blood, and there was a slight but long red slash on her stomach.

"You've been cut..." said Harry, stepping toward her, alarmed.

"Don't worry about me," she said, voice shaking. "Whatever you do, don't take your gun off *them*."

"Get dressed and we'll get the police," said Harry. "We'll get you to the hospital."

She found her jeans and pink T-shirt. She put the pants on slowly, cringing as the denim rubbed past the gash on her hip.

"Very heroic, Harry," said Stegman. "Very Hollywood."

"Shut up," said Harry.

"No. I mean it. This is just like a movie. The hero arrives in the nick of time to save the girl. I cannot underestimate your intuition for dramatic turnabout and plot points. It's the scriptwriter in you."

"Maybe we need more violence," said Harry. "What's to stop me from shooting you next?"

"Because the threat is over," replied Stegman. He held out his arms. "Look at me. I'm defenseless. You hold all the cards. A true hero would never shoot an unarmed man."

"This isn't the movies," said Harry, but he knew that Stegman was right. He couldn't do it now. The danger had ended.

"Rachel," said Harry. "Do you have your cell phone?"

"In my purse."

"Call the police."

"Right." She stepped toward a small table and picked up her purse. As she reached for the phone, a voice called out from outside the motel room.

"Harry!"

Rachel froze.

Everyone looked at one another.

"Who said that?" said Rachel.

A stretch of silence followed. Then, a second time, the voice cried out, "Harry!"

"Somebody's looking for you, Harry," said Stegman.

"Who would be looking for you here?" Rachel asked Harry.

Harry heard the voice a third time, much closer, and the realization hit him. He had been followed. "Paul?" he said.

Paul Jacobs burst into the motel room, out of breath, his tie askew. He walked halfway into the room, stopped in his tracks and gasped. His eyes took in the bizarre and gory scene: the crude movie set with the exposed bathroom and blood-splattered wall, bloodied Rachel, Harry holding out the gun, Terrance's dead body, Stegman and Garon.

Paul's expression shifted through a series of bewildered reactions as he fought for words, finally landing on, "What the hell is going on here?"

Harry stepped toward him. "Paul, don't—"

"Harry look out!" shrieked Rachel.

But it was too late. In the moment of confusion, Harry had turned his back on Garon, a huge mistake. Garon lunged at him, grabbing Harry's wrist and slamming him into the wall. Harry lost control of the gun and it fell from his hand.

Garon kneed Harry in the stomach, doubling him over. He grabbed the gun. He pointed the weapon at Harry's head. Then he aimed it at Paul, and then at Rachel, instructing her to drop the purse.

Stegman beamed. "Thank you, Garon. And thank *you*, Mr. Jacobs, for that bit of distraction. I don't know what you're doing here, but your entrance was much appreciated."

"My God," said Paul. He looked at Harry. "Do you mind telling me what in heaven's name this is all about?"

"You want to know what this is all about?" said Stegman, stepping back, finding his center stage. "A long story, to be sure. But I can explain. Do you have a minute? Well, of course you do. You're not going anywhere."

Garon slammed the motel room door and secured the bolt.

Stegman walked over to Harry and threw his arm around him. Harry squirmed and Stegman tightened the grasp. "Mr. Jacobs. Ms. Stoller. Now that I have your undivided attention, I have an important announcement to make. This man, Harry Tuttle, whom you admire so much, is a *fraud*. He's a loser. His talent, his recent success—it's all one big lie. Why don't you tell them, Harry? Tell them the truth about *Deadly Desires*?"

Harry said nothing, refusing to look at Stegman.

"All right then," said Stegman. "*I* will tell them. You see, Harry Tuttle's popular little movie, *Deadly Desires*, wasn't created by Harry Tuttle at all. No sir. It was all me. Writing, directing, production. I made the picture and then sold it to him—at his request—for a very large sum of money to help boost his sagging ego. The only contribution he made to that film was a new set of credits. It was our little secret, wasn't it, Harry?"

Harry quickly spoke up and elaborated. "What I didn't realize was that this lunatic had spliced a real-life murder into the film. He'd killed a woman named Nora Hurley on camera in Mexico, and made it appear as part of the storyline. Then he killed Walter Wiggins when Wiggins became suspicious about the picture."

"I didn't kill Walter Wiggins," said Stegman. "I believe it was a fellow by the name of Oscar."

Harry ignored the comment and kept talking. "He dumped Wiggins' body in my house. He did it to frame me so I wouldn't go to the police. I freaked out. As I was getting rid of the body, I lost my watch. The police found it. That's what you heard on the radio, Paul."

Paul, dazed and overwhelmed, said, "This is way too weird."

"Now he's killing people for his next movie," said Harry. "He was going to make Rachel his next victim. When I found out they were filming today, I got here as fast as I could to stop him."

"And that brings us up to date," said Stegman. "I'm so glad we've had a chance to air this all out. Harry, I'm happy that your closest friends now know the truth, that you are a no-good fraud and phony. All the praise you have received is bullshit. You have no real talent. And they can take that information with them to the grave. Garon, the time has come to dispose of the troublemakers. The truth stays in this room."

Garon nodded and stepped forward with the gun. "Shoot them?"

"Yes, all three. Cleanly. Quickly. Execution style would be nice."

"You got it."

Paul said, "Wait a minute..."

Rachel begged, "Please..."

Harry said nothing. His eyes were fixed on the nearby video camera locked down on a tripod. He could see the movement, hear the faint whirring. He stared hard and confirmed the feeling riding high in his gut. He knew this equipment well, and one thing was for sure.

The camera was still rolling. It had recorded everything, including Stegman's confession to the murder in Harry's film.

Garon stepped up to Rachel with the gun. He gave her a long look, then turned to Stegman.

"Let's save her for last," he said. "She showed us her hot little body. She's got spunk. We've got the bed. How about some fun with Betsy Brewer before knocking her off?"

Rachel spat in his face.

Garon turned to her, eyes blazing. He wiped the spit gob off his cheek. He said, "You will regret that. I swear to it, you bitch."

With all eyes off him, Harry seized his opportunity.

He pounced on the video camera. He pounded the eject button and pulled out the digital tape cartridge.

Stegman whipped around to see what was happening. He hesitated before realizing, "For Christ's sake, we've been taping ourselves. Garon—*shoot him!*"

Garon spun away from Rachel and aimed the gun at Harry.

Paul plowed into Garon, shoving his aim off target. The gun fired into the ceiling.

Harry ran for the door, Stegman chasing after him. He reached Harry and grabbed him with both hands, pushing him backwards into the dresser. Harry felt a sharp pain in his back.

"Give me that tape!" snarled Stegman. Harry pulled free, but now Garon came at him too, and Harry realized that there was no way he would be able to maintain possession of the tape much longer. But...

Paul was open.

"Paul! Take it!" Harry flung the cartridge past Stegman and Garon.

Paul caught it by surprise. He looked at the tape. He looked at Harry. He looked back at the tape. He looked back at Harry.

"*RUN!*" screamed Harry.

Garon fired a shot at Paul. It missed and exploded one of the lights, showering white sparks.

Paul yelped and ran for his life. He dashed across the room, jumped on a chair, and dove through a plate glass window, shattering it to pieces.

49

Paul landed on the walkway with tinkling glass, wrapped up in drapes, still clutching the video cartridge. The drapes helped prevent him from getting sliced up by the broken window, but the fall to the cement hurt like hell; and he yelled.

Picking himself up, Paul ran for his car.

He heard the motel room door slam open behind him, and an angry shout.

Paul didn't turn to look. He kept going, running across the parking lot toward his Mercedes, fueled by panic and a single thought, *I don't want to die.*

As he ran, the video cartridge tumbled from his grasp and his foot kicked it across the blacktop. As Paul bent down to retrieve it, he heard the crack of gunfire and the zip of a bullet overhead.

Paul grabbed the video while still on the run, losing as few steps as possible. He reached his car, unlocked it, and scrambled inside. He turned to see if someone was pursuing him and his fears were confirmed.

Garon came running at the car, fast, gripping the gun.

Paul started his car and floored it. The Mercedes shot past

Garon, almost hitting him. Paul tore out of the parking lot with his foot flattened on the accelerator.

Garon took aim and fired at Paul.

Paul's back window shattered.

The Mercedes sped down the street, away from the motel, blowing past two stop signs.

Paul checked the front seat. The tape remained at his side, safe and sound. He planned to leave this wasteland and head into downtown L.A. to find a policeman, any policeman.

After several blocks, Paul began to breathe easier. He wiped the sweat from his forehead. He said out loud, "I made it, I made it," and a wave of relief washed over him.

Then he saw a car approaching fast in the rear-view mirror, a white van with Garon behind the wheel.

50

Stegman attacked Harry, face pink with rage, long hair free of its ponytail, wild and flowing. The two directors battled inside the cramped motel room, and Stegman unleashed a brutal beating on the older director, pounding him with punches. Rachel fought to stop Stegman, hitting him from behind; and he finally grabbed her by the shirt and threw her into the camera equipment, toppling tripods and sending lights crashing to the floor.

Harry punched Stegman squarely in the mouth, a solid hit. The younger director jerked his head back, then smiled for a moment as if in appreciation. He shoved Harry back several feet, slamming him into a wall with such force that the vibrations caused framed pictures to fall.

Stegman glared deep in Harry's eyes and hissed, "You're history, Harry." His teeth had turned crimson from the blood in his mouth. He stuffed a fist into Harry's gut. Then he punched him hard in the jaw, and Harry saw stars.

"Stop it, you bastard!" Rachel rushed Stegman again. She slammed a light stand across his back. Stegman roared and almost dropped from the blow. He turned and seized the light stand, ripping it from her grasp, throwing it back at her and striking her head with a loud crack. Rachel fell backward to the carpet. She lay stunned, curled, and semi-conscious. She could not get back on her feet.

Harry saw Rachel go down and charged Stegman, slamming into him and wrapping an arm around Stegman's neck. Stegman took advantage of Harry's off-balance momentum to flip him to the ground. Harry crashed to the carpet hard, feeling the pain reverberate in his bones.

Stegman pounced on top of Harry, keeping him grounded with several hard hits to the face. Harry struggled to push Stegman off of him, but after receiving a hard slam to the temple, his vision erupted into a swarm of spots.

When the vision cleared, Harry saw the black cable.

Stegman looped a length of electrical cable around Harry's neck and began tightening.

Harry felt his air choked off. He struggled violently, squirming, head turning from side to side.

Stegman stared down at him, a cartoon devil, face red, veins pulsing in his forehead and around his eyes, grinning with red teeth. He exerted every ounce of his strength into strangling the life out of Harry.

Harry's tongue protruded out of his mouth. He felt the blood pounding in his head. He struggled in vain; Stegman had him pinned down securely. Then Harry saw something out of the corner of his eye...

The knife. Lying nearby on the floor. Possibly within reach.

Oh God if I could only...

Harry strained with everything he had to get a grasp on the knife handle. His arm shook as he stretched, but the knife remained just barely out of reach.

Stegman pulled the black cable tighter around Harry's neck.

Harry felt his fingertips brush the knife handle. He struggled not to blackout.

Just a little more... Almost...

Got it.

Harry moved the knife toward him. He secured a grip on the handle. He squeezed it. He lifted the blade and positioned the point to plunge into Stegman's side. All he needed was one final, powerful burst of strength to sink it deep...

But in an instant, Stegman caught the movement. He turned and spotted the knife in Harry's hand.

Stegman let go of the cable and snatched Harry's wrist. He forced Harry's arm down, slamming the hand repeatedly against the floor until the knife came loose and fell from Harry's grasp. He picked it up.

Stegman now held the knife.

He grinned. He raised the blade above Harry's chest. He centered the tip over Harry's heart. He tightened his fist around the handle.

Harry struggled, helpless, looking on in horror.

"Fade to black, Harry Tuttle," said Stegman. "This is The End."

Stegman plunged the blade downward.

Harry shut his eyes tightly and screamed as the blade hit.

Several seconds passed.

Then several more.

Harry realized he was not dead. And he felt no pain.

Harry opened his eyes...confused. He lifted his head and looked.

The knife had a retractable blade. The blade had disappeared up the handle, a harmless prop pressed against his chest.

Harry looked up at Stegman.

Stegman's face froze with a look of complete surprise.

Then Stegman sputtered.

He sputtered a second time, spitting up blood. His eyes turned glassy.

Stegman pitched forward, toppling off Harry, dead. The real knife protruded from his back, sunk deep.

Rachel stood behind Stegman.

She looked down at his crumpled body. "There's your knife, you son of a bitch."

51

Paul raced his Mercedes through a zigzag of Los Angeles streets, trying to shake the persistent white van off his tail.

With one hand on the wheel, he worked furiously to call 911 on his cell phone, fumbling with the tiny buttons, managing to hit every possible three numeral sequence except for 911. When he finally got ahold of a 911 operator, he screamed, "Somebody's trying to kill me!" which felt silly but at least it was accurate. The operator calmly asked for his whereabouts, and Paul provided an intersection, then updated it with another intersection, then had to update it again and again, and eventually dropped the cell phone to the floor during a last minute, high-speed swerve around a stopped bus.

When the van got close, the driver took another shot; and Paul heard a bullet ping off the trunk. Paul promptly increased his speed to Extra Reckless.

Paul was tearing down Fairfax Avenue when the roadway narrowed, crowded from a glut of parked trucks, long trailers, and humming generators: the telltale signs of a movie shooting on location. Only this was no ordinary movie. Today was the day that *Army of Steel* was shooting its multimillion dollar action sequence to end all action sequences in front of the Los Angeles Farmers Market. Paul saw the Farmers Market's white clock tower up ahead. Then he saw a big roadblock swiftly fill his view, and the very long crash began.

The Mercedes smashed through the barricade and entered the film set of *Army of Steel*, closely followed by the white van. Paul Jacobs said "Shit" and managed to drag the one syllable word across forty-five seconds of skidding tires, scattering crew members, screaming extras, exploding craft services tables, pulverized filmmaking equipment, collapsing ladders, bouncing bounce boards, and falling lighting rigs.

The Mercedes came to a final stop when it slammed into the body of an elevated camera crane, causing director Nigel Howard to plummet to the ground, breaking his legs.

The white van spun across the set for another 40 feet, running over two 35mm cameras before bouncing off a 3-ton grip truck and striking a mounted light. A 6000 watt, 54-pound HMI Par light wobbled, then fell, crashing through the van windshield, killing Garon instantly.

Paul remained in his car, face pressed in the airbag, preferring to keep it there, where no one could see him. When he finally gathered the courage to look outside, he was startled to see a young man standing a few feet away, filming him with a video camera.

"Who are you?" said Paul. He felt faint. The eye of the camera lens stared back at him. "Why are you filming me?"

The young man introduced himself. He said his name was Philip. He explained he was making a behind-the-scenes featurette for the *Army of Steel* DVD.

"I think I got some good stuff," he said. "Even better than the actual movie."

52

She approached in a simple but graceful white sundress, smiling at him, stepping down the walk, eyes bluer than the skies, hair lifted by the breeze. He grinned back, felt his heartbeat accelerate, his hands sweat, and marveled that his reaction today was no different than the time he first met her at Richard Metherell's birthday party at the mansion in the Hollywood Hills more than two years ago. He still adored her. She sent the world around them into a softer focus. She thrilled his heart.

Rachel climbed into the car and greeted Harry with a kiss.

"OK, Mr. Suspense," she said. "Where are we going for our date night surprise?"

"If I told you, it wouldn't be a surprise," he told her.

"No sneak preview?"

Harry pretended to mull over the request for a long moment, then said, "No."

He pulled away from the curb, entering the traffic on Sunset Boulevard. They drove into Westwood.

In Westwood, the car approached a huge crowd lined up for movie tickets, stretching around the block. The letters on the theater marquee, bordered in flashing white bulbs, announced the film: Rough Cut.

"You're taking me to your movie?" she asked.

"No," said Harry, and the car continued past the theater.

"Looks like a sell out," she said.

"We're adding new screens every week," said Harry. Although he had not studied the grosses as closely as Paul, he knew that *Rough Cut* was one of the year's biggest smash hits.

Most importantly, it was Harry's biggest success; and he was the film's true auteur.

In the months that followed Harry and Rachel's escape from Marcus Stegman, the *Deadly Desires* story became the most lurid, most sensational, most talked about Hollywood scandal since the last one. Broadcast live, *The State of California vs. Harry Tuttle* earned Harry the biggest audience of his career and tripled his fan base. The D.A.'s office worked feverishly to implicate Harry in the deaths caused by Stegman, but the star-struck jury didn't see it the same way. The high-profile case attracted a "dream team" lineup of attorneys to Harry's side, each posturing for maximum exposure in the spectacle.

Fortunately, Stegman's tapes told the real story. Public sympathy hugged Harry from coast to coast. He soon joined the long list of celebrity acquittals—although he didn't appreciate seeing his name alongside the likes of O.J. Simpson, Robert Blake, Michael Jackson, and Fatty Arbuckle.

Once Harry's soap opera left the TV airwaves, the movie offers rolled in. A bidding war ensued for the rights to Harry's ordeal. The money was astronomical, but Harry insisted on one very important stipulation: he would not sell the rights to his story unless *he* got to direct.

Harry got his wish. Paul brokered a deal between PJ Productions and one of the major studios. Harry received the largest budget of his career, and his pick of the crop of major film stars. A number of Hollywood legends phoned Harry, begging to be in the film. Everyone wanted to be Harry. In the end, Harry went with an unknown, someone with untested commercial appeal, but a lot of talent.

Rough Cut was completed on time, on budget, and previewed to great acclaim. Harry the director was hot—this time on his own merits.

The film's release collided with another highly anticipated movie, the long-awaited sci-fi epic *Army of Steel.* Delayed for 18 months by ongoing production trouble, artistic differences, a prima donna cast, and a budget that mushroomed out of control, *Army of Steel* limped into theaters the weekend before *Rough Cut,* and didn't last long. In many cities, the film was yanked to allow for additional screenings of *Rough Cut.* Around the same time, *People* magazine announced the divorce of Nigel and Julie Howard, and reported that the director had retreated to the English countryside, moved in with his mother, and become a recluse.

In recent weeks, Harry had received phone messages from his ex-wife, now Nigel's ex-wife, asking if he was interested in perhaps getting together for dinner, or a drink or two, just for old time's sake.

Harry never called her back.

He didn't need to. With Rachel at his side, his life was complete. As they drove through West L.A., windows and sunroof open, air rushing in, he felt heaven. Up ahead, he caught a glimpse of his destination, a touch of glow and color. "We're almost there," he said. Rachel straightened up and examined the surroundings. Then the bright, old-fashioned theater marquee came into full view.

The Palace.

Harry pulled up to the curb in front of the historic cinema, restored to its original 1920s glory. The three-sided marquee announced the evening's showing on a bright white grid with bold black lettering,

Super Pickle.

"Super Pickle?" said Rachel.

Harry parked and climbed out of the car. He circled to Rachel, opening her door and offering his arm. She took it and joined him on the sidewalk.

"Good evening, sir. Madam." A spiffy young man with slicked-back hair, a red suit jacket, and white gloves appeared before them. Harry handed him the car keys.

"What in the world..." said Rachel.

Harry guided her to the old-style ticket booth in front of the theatre.

"Two please," he told the well-dressed, senior woman behind the counter.

"With pleasure," she responded, tearing two tickets from an old-fashioned roll. "Enjoy tonight's program."

Rachel started to giggle.

Harry guided her inside the theater.

Rachel's giggle became a gasp. She stepped into the spacious lobby, struck by its elegance. She marveled at the Victorian flourishes. Gold leaf decorated the ceiling. Vintage movie posters brightened the walls. A classic candy counter ran the length of the floor between two broad staircases. The steps wound gracefully to a grand balcony above.

Harry walked up to the candy counter and bought two large buckets of popcorn and two drinks.

"Harry, I'm speechless," said Rachel. "I didn't even know this theater existed."

"It's been newly renovated," said Harry. "It just barely escaped the wrecking ball."

He took her through the double doors into the darkened auditorium, and she gasped again.

Wide rows of plush seats advanced down red-carpeted aisles, three times the size of the average multiplex theater. Purple velvet drapes framed a giant movie screen. Near the foot of the stage, off to one side, a silver-haired man in a tuxedo played a sweeping romantic melody on a Wurlitzer pipe organ.

Harry pointed upward to the dark blue ceiling, where clouds had been painted amid small, twinkling lights to emulate a night sky.

Rachel took in the surroundings for a long moment, and then asked, "But, Harry, where is everyone?"

"This is our own private screening. Sit anywhere you'd like."

She chose the center of the center row, eyes still roaming the wall murals and garland-draped columns. "What are we going to see?"

"*Super Pickle*," said Harry.

"Really?"

"Of course."

"I've never heard of it. Who's in it?"

"Someone you know."

"Who?"

Harry didn't answer.

The organist finished playing, stood up and took a bow. Harry and Rachel applauded. He departed offstage.

The theater lights dimmed. The purple curtains parted.

A jittery silent film came to life on the big screen. The colors were faded. The picture was blemished with scratches and dirt. But the images lit up the auditorium with joyous, youthful energy.

Two teenage boys ran around a suburban backyard, acting out a goofy adventure, occasionally interrupted by hand-drawn dialogue titles that exclaimed worn clichés like "We'll track him to his lair!" One of the boys wore green tights, green 1970s go-go boots, and a green cape created out of a beach towel. The other boy dressed in brown.

"That's Super Pickle," said Harry. "He fights crime. And that's his sidekick, Pretzel Boy."

The scene shifted to a patio deck. Super Pickle and Pretzel Boy battled a third teenager, a chubby kid in a white T-shirt with a red lightning bolt drawn on it in magic marker. He wore a football helmet decorated with glitter and silver streamers.

"That's Super Pickle's arch enemy, Shock Master. Electricity shoots out of his fingertips, see?"

Shock Master pointed his arms at Pretzel Boy and wiggled his hands. Pretzel Boy clutched his chest and jumped off the patio into a bush.

Rachel started laughing. "Harry...is that you?"

"Yes," admitted Harry. "I am Super Pickle. Those other guys, they were my best friends from high school, Kevin and Tim. We had such a blast making those movies."

As the silent reel of film continued, he told her about his earliest moviemaking adventures. He described his cherished Super 8 camera, a gift from his father. He recalled the weekends devoted to plotting, creating costumes, inventing special effects, choreographing battle scenes.

"We'd hold the world premieres in my basement and show

the films on a bed sheet," said Harry. "All the kids in the neighborhood would come. We charged twenty-five cents admission. Ten cents for a matinee."

Super Pickle took a jolt from Shock Master and fell backwards into a screen door. Rachel broke up laughing.

Harry's eyes remained glued on the images of his youth. "These films bring it all back," he said. "For so many years, I forgot why I wanted to make movies in the first place. I got lost, caught up in the business. I did it for all the wrong reasons. I forgot to have fun. Back then, do you think I cared what people thought about *Super Pickle*? Was I looking for respect and admiration in those green tights? Great press clippings? Lots of quarters? No, I just wanted to triumph over evil and have a happy ending."

Super Pickle and Pretzel Boy defeated Shock Master by turning his own hands against him so that he zapped himself. Shock Master rolled on the ground, convulsing for about 30 seconds, before a title card announced "The End!" The screen flickered and turned white, then dark.

Rachel applauded. "Bravo!" She turned to Harry and said, "That was great. Is there more?"

"Are you kidding?" responded Harry. "We're having a double feature tonight, just like the good old days."

"I can't wait," said Rachel.

The next movie began, but it wasn't a Super 8 short from Harry's childhood archives. The screen filled with a crisp, full frame of Harry, recently shot, looking into the camera.

"Hello, Rachel," he said.

Rachel glanced at the real Harry, and he motioned for her to look back at the screen.

On the screen, Harry said, "Rachel, I want to start off by

apologizing for doing this on film. But you know how we artists are—we want everything to be perfect. I think this is Take 42. So I'm going to try real hard not to stutter or garble my sentences, but I'm nervous; so I hope you'll cut me some slack. If it gets real bad, I can always fix it in post, right? OK, lame joke. Rachel...I hope it's no mystery how I feel about you. You are the most exciting thing that's ever happened to me. Even more exciting than almost getting killed. You are the reason I wake up in the morning and I don't have to meditate anymore, or read good reviews about myself to feel happy. The fact that you still love me, even after I lied to you, even after you found out I'm not the great filmmaker you thought I was...that's the best review I ever got. You're my Emmy, my Oscar, my Lifetime Achievement Award. I wanted to bring you to this theater today because it's the most beautiful theater in the world. I wanted to use this setting because it's special, so filled with history; and I thought maybe I would...OK, I'll cut to the chase. Enough babbling, Harry. Save it for the director's cut. Here's the big moment, the payoff, the music swells...Rachel, will you marry me?"

Stunned, Rachel turned from the screen and faced the Harry beside her. He held a small, opened jewelry box. A diamond ring glittered inside.

The movie clip ended; the screen dimmed.

"Rachel," said Harry, echoing his filmed counterpart. "Will you marry me?"

"Yes," she said.

"Through sickness and health?"

"Yes."

"Through blockbusters and bombs?"

"*Yes.*"

She threw her arms around Harry and hugged him.

The organist returned to the Wurlitzer. He played the triumphant theme to the movie *Rocky*.

Harry held Rachel close. He felt like he was emerging from a long and difficult fog—no, an L.A. smog—and had discovered gold on the other side. He had finally achieved what mattered, and that was a wrap.

About the Author

Brian Pinkerton is the author of *Killer's Diary*, *Abducted*, *Vengeance* and other literary disturbances. He lives in the suburbs of Chicago with his wife and two children. His cyberhome is www.brianpinkerton.com.